NOTHING TO SAY

SCARLETT FINN

Also by Scarlett Finn

GO NOVELS
GO WITH IT
GO IT ALONE
GO ALL OUT
GO ALL IN
GO FULL CIRCLE

EXILE
HIDE & SEEK
KISS CHASE

WRECK & RUIN
RUIN ME
RUIN HIM

THE BRANDED SERIES
BRANDED
SCARRED
MARKED

FORBIDDEN PREQUEL DUET
ALL. ONLY.
ONLY YOURS

THE FORBIDDEN NOVELS
FORBIDDEN DESIRE
FORBIDDEN WANT
FORBIDDEN WISH
FORBIDDEN NEED
FORBIDDEN BOND

BOMBSHELLS & BILLIONAIRES (ROXIVERSE)
NOTHING TO HIDE
NOTHING TO LOSE
NOTHING IN BETWEEN: ONE
NOTHING TO DECLARE
NOTHING TO US
NOTHING IN BETWEEN: TWO
NOTHING TO SAY
NOTHING TO GAIN
NOTHING IN BETWEEN: THREE
NOTHING TO YOU
NOTHING TO THIS PREQUEL: ONE WILD NIGHT
NOTHING TO THIS
NOTHING IN BETWEEN: FOUR
NOTHING TO DO
NOTHING TO NO ONE
NOTHING TO FEAR
NOTHING TO DENY
NOTHING TO BEAT
NOTHING TO THE WEDDING
NOTHING TO TELL
NOTHING TO IT
NOTHING TO SEE
NOTHING TO WIN
NOTHING TO OFFER
NOTHING TO PROVE

LOVE AGAINST THE ODDS STANDALONE COLLECTION
SWEET SEAS
HEIR'S AFFAIR
RESCUED
MAESTRO'S MUSE
GETTING TRICKY
THIRTEEN
REMEMBER WHEN…
RELUCTANT SUSPICION
XY FACTOR

KINDRED SERIES
RAVEN
SWALLOW
CUCKOO
SWIFT
FALCON
FINCH

MISTAKE DUET
MISTAKE ME NOT
SLEIGHT MISTAKE

LOST & FOUND
LOST
FOUND

THE EXPLICIT SERIES
EXPLICIT INSTRUCTION
EXPLICIT DETAIL
EXPLICIT MEMORY

TO DIE FOR…
TO DIE FOR TRUTH
TO DIE FOR HONOR
TO DIE FOR VIRTUE
TO DIE FOR DUTY
TO DIE FOR LOVE

RISQUÉ & HARROW INTERTWINED
TAKE A RISK
FIGHTING FATE
RISK IT ALL
FIGHTING BACK
GAME OF RISK

ONE

"WORK. WORK. WORK," Lilya Kearns said to herself, reading and typing, reading and typing, as she'd been doing all night.

Minutiae was important in her role. Details. Specifics.

Making headway was vital. Not only to keep Chester, the boss, on course, but for morale in the team. If she fell behind, catching up could cause delays and lead to a lot of backtracking. So she continued to work, long after everyone else had gone home.

The office wasn't hers. Not exclusively. It just happened to contain one of the computers Eclipse had assigned her employer for the duration of their contract. In total, she and her nineteen colleagues had access to three company terminals. Three between twenty didn't equal much screen time. Being there alone, she was taking advantage of every second.

Keeping them out from underfoot of the professional day-to-day Eclipse machine, they'd been designated the adjacent boardroom as their main workspace. That was her base, though she wasn't often found there. Running around the building was part of her job too.

Offices and boardrooms lined the perimeter of the sub-level around an open-plan bullpen. The true executive floor overlooked the minions, most of whom weren't allowed to ascend the staircase at the head of the polished corporate cavern. No. Because up there were the special people. Like gods meant to be revered, executive-level management worked in their own private sphere on a mezzanine floor looming over the grunts.

How many companies were exactly the same way? With a clear divide between those at the top and those beneath them. She'd seen it so many times. Her line of work involved vast, if temporary, experience with businesses. Many, many businesses.

"Excuse me."

Oh, great, more interruptions.

"One sec," she said, typing what was on the monitor into her tablet so as not to lose her place.

"This is the only open office on the floor. I realize this is inappropriate… and shocking." What was the guy rambling about? "My office is unexpectedly occupied and…" His office? Who—she looked up. Damn. Unable to believe her eyes, her jaw dropped. "There's a good explanation for this."

That was Zachary Kintyre. Eclipse Incorporated CEO. In the doorway. Naked.

Yes, that warranted repetition.

Naked.

Sure, he was covering the really interesting parts with both hands, but the rest wasn't bad to look at. Wasn't bad at all.

As she absorbed the moment, her mouth closed. She sank back in the chair, still sort of in a daze.

"Go in. In."

Another guy appeared behind Kintyre, nudging him into the office, using an elbow to close the door. The new guy was as naked as the first.

"I appreciate this will make a slam-dunk harassment lawsuit," Kintyre said. "My father-in-law is in my office with a reporter… one who doesn't like me. Yes, they do exist. We'll talk settlement tomorrow, but can you go in there and either get rid of them or grab the suit bag from the closet?"

Her lips curled. Maybe glee was inappropriate… okay, it was. She sucked her lower lip into her mouth, attempting to contain her amusement.

"She's laughing," the other guy said. Narrowing her gaze on him, it felt like he should be familiar. Who was he? The nudity was throwing her off. "She's laughing, dude."

"Wouldn't you?" Kintyre asked over his shoulder as his counterpart shuffled up next to him. "Miss… what's your name?"

Her fingertips touched her upper lip. "This could be the happiest moment of my life."

Damn her lips for contorting again, but she needed this pressure release. If she could stay seated, admiring their misfortune for longer, she would, just for the excuse to relax. Unfortunately, it wasn't in her to be cruel. She got up and went to the metal closet in the corner. Not many people got such an experience, she didn't think anyway. What did she know about what went on at Eclipse?

"Odd, because it's my most mortifying."

"Oh, Mr. Kintyre…" she said, unzipping her gym bag. "I don't believe that's true." Retrieving both towels, she stepped back with one in each hand. "I got a big one and a little one. Who gets what?" She raised one, then the other. "Who's bigger than who?" No response. "Guess I should turn and toss."

Giving them privacy, she turned her back and threw both towels over her head like a bride with her bouquet.

"Who's your manager?"

Figuring the question meant they were decent, more decent… marginally, she returned to the desk. "You don't know my manager."

"I don't?" As she sank into her seat, Kintyre folded his arms. Man, he was ripped. These billionaires were clearly driven in more than just the boardroom. "How long have you worked here?"

"Uh…" Her eyes slunk to their top corners for a moment. "About three weeks."

"Great, she's new staff," guy number two said, throwing up a hand.

"She's not new staff 'cause we haven't taken on new staff at this level for months."

"Obviously, you have," she said, smiling, absorbing the intrigue of the bold man, the owner of everything around them. "You have some balls talking down to me right now."

Guy number two nudged Kintyre. "She has a point, we need her."

"You have some balls talking to me like that at all," Kintyre said, his focus steady on her. "You're from Ranby Kearns."

Her smile stretched. This was fun. How often did anyone get to spar with a towel-clad multibillionaire in the middle of the workplace?

Folding her arms, she pushed her shoulders back. "Your Gramercy bid hangs in the balance," she said. "Wonder what the bosses over there would think of this."

"That wasn't confirmation," he said and opened his hand. "Show me your ID."

"What are you security now?" she asked and arched a brow. "I'll show you mine, if you show me yours."

For some reason, maybe the weird energy, guy number two took a deliberate step away from his buddy.

"You still haven't told me your name."

"And you're still not wearing pants," she said, flattening her hands on the desk to push up. "And... I can't help you."

"For religious reasons?"

That was sarcasm, but did it mean he was circumcised? What a crazy tangent. Where did that come from? Not like she was ever going to find out.

She bit her tongue and went for the truth. "Because I don't have security clearance to get into your office. You're on your own."

Guy number two popped back into the periphery. "Give her clearance, Zach, man."

More people around wouldn't be what Kintyre wanted. "If you call security up here—"

"I don't need security," he said, rounding the desk, barging into her chair. "You're on the network."

The desktop computer came with the office, so, yeah, it was on the Eclipse network. Pretty hard to audit their data if it wasn't.

"Why are you so nervous?" she asked the second guy. "Is the reporter after you too? What time is it?"

"You want answers to those questions or are you just going to keep firing them at him?" Kintyre was typing but still spoke before his friend. "It's after eleven. Put your thumb on the reader."

Fingerprint scanners reinforced all Eclipse security.

She bent over to do as asked. "Does your friend not talk?"

"He's pissed," Kintyre said and stood up, tucking his thumb into his towel. Hmm, was it loose? "Go. Upstairs. Get rid of them. Whatever it takes."

"Only because I'm such a good person," she said, whirling around to sashay out of the office and up the celestial stairway.

Wouldn't be so bad for a billionaire CEO to owe her a favor. Teasing him might be fun, but playing with him could be dangerous.

The only other time she'd been on the upper executive floor was during the quick tour they got on their first day. On that day, Kintyre hadn't been anywhere in sight.

Going over to the tall glass door and pressing her thumb to the reader in the silver handle, she got a buzz when it automatically opened.

"Good evening!" she projected her voice to gain the focus of the two men at the opposite end of the room.

The city lights glittered on the other side of the inky black windows. Illumination was lower than during the day. Had they set it that way? Seemed odd.

"Who are you?" the older of the two gentlemen asked. "Where's my son-in-law?"

"Unfortunately…" she started, clasping her hands. "Mr. Kintyre cannot meet with you this evening." This evening? It was after eleven p.m. Who showed up at almost midnight for a business meeting? "You can make an appointment with—"

"He is my family," the older man said, marching over. "I can see him whenever I want."

"Okay," she said, because who was she to argue with warped logic? "Then I would recommend calling him because he's not here now." In that exact room. That wasn't a lie. "I'm sorry."

Not really. It seemed rude, in her opinion. Maybe that was the way the family worked. What kind of guy hid from his wife's father? The guy owned a multinational, not like he'd owe the guy money.

"Where is he?"

"I'm sorry, sir—"

"Is he with Julietta?" the second guy asked, wandering their way. "I'm Reeve Crosby." The reporter, she assumed. Why did he hate Kintyre? Maybe 'cause he gallivanted around semi-nude with his buddies late at night. "Julietta hasn't been in contact with her parents for a couple of days. Henri here, Mr. Ines, is very worried about his daughter's safety."

Ines. Julietta. Damnit. Right. Julietta Ines-Kintyre. The actress. Gorgeous… Weren't the media always talking about her divorce? Maybe the couple were reconciling.

"I understand that. My suggestion would be calling the police," she said, because that was the advice she'd give anyone missing a relative. "They have the resources—"

"No," Henri Ines stated. "We don't need that kind of publicity. The divorce has caused enough disruption."

If the man wasn't willing to call the cops because he wanted to save face, he wasn't really that worried about his daughter. So either it was about power or control… maybe both.

"As I said, all I can suggest is giving Mr. Kintyre a call."

"He should be here."

"If he's with Julietta…" Reeve said, "there's more to the story."

Could be. What did she know? That Kintyre wasn't with Julietta, she knew that… At least he hadn't been while in her office. Maybe the beautiful actress was the reason both men ended up in their naked predicament.

"We will wait here all night. He'll show up eventually," Henri said, whipping around to pace away.

Intrigue on the reporter's face followed him. "Do you believe they're together?"

"Please…" Lilya said before Henri could respond. "You can continue your conversation elsewhere."

Henri spun to face her. "You can't… How dare you… You can't dismiss me."

"No, but security can." This was whatever it took territory. "You can't remain here alone. I'm sorry. I will not take responsibility for leaving you here."

If she was some assistant, maybe new staff, would she be so bold? Maybe not… Actually, yeah, she would. These men were strangers to her. Kintyre wasn't expecting them. If she left them alone and something got broken or stolen, or they died in a horrible building fire, that would be on her.

"No one asked you to be here," Henri snapped.

"I could say the same to you, sir," she said and backed up to open the door.

The men made eye contact, obviously considering their options. What could they do?

Nothing. Getting thrown out of the building would be the kind of scandal Henri was apparently trying to avoid.

So with a huff and a tug on each of his cuffs, Henri marched out of the office. The reporter went too, his curious eye remaining on her until he passed.

Just to make sure they were really leaving, she followed them all the way to the elevator. She waited until they were inside with the doors closed before exhaling.

Job done.

Strolling back to the office, Ranby Kearns

temporary office, she went in, ignoring the men still loitering there.

"What did you say to them?" Kintyre's friend asked.

Either they'd heard the elevator or peeked, so knew the intruders were gone.

"That," she said, retrieving her jacket, purse, and gym bag from the corner closet. "Is between me and those I evicted." She started for the door again. "Any more screwing around tonight, you're on your own. I'm leaving. Goodnight!"

She didn't turn, just waved out to the side and sauntered off. Some people said working too much wasn't good for a person. Could be true... or maybe sticking around long enough could put a person in exactly the right place at the right time.

TWO

KNEELING ON THE boardroom floor, matching files to the codes on her tablet, movement interrupted her concentration.

Someone moving actually.

The big Eclipse boss man, clothed big boss man, strode past the glass fronted boardroom, drawing the attention of many in the bullpen.

He didn't often go anywhere alone, especially anywhere on that level. Curious, she tracked his purpose. Was he heading for the office next door? Yes. Where they'd met last night. Her boss's office.

The cry of joy confirmed someone was home.

"Mr. Kintyre!"

Oh, she had never loved Chester's open-door policy more.

"I was… looking for someone." Kintyre. "Whose office is this?"

"Chester Stevenson," her boss introduced himself.

She couldn't see the pair but could hear her boss's enthusiasm.

"Excuse me," Kintyre said, and came into view again, his back to the open boardroom door.

Hmm, what was bothering the billionaire?

She read the next file number. "Lose something, Kintyre?" she called loud enough to be heard over the susurration of the bullpen.

He whirled around just in time to see a smile tug at her lips.

"I was…" he started before striding in and closing the door. "I thought that was your office."

"We're a small team," she said, retrieving the next file from the box. "Chester runs the show. He gets the office. The rest of us work where we can."

"You were in there last night."

"When no one else was around," she said and teased him with another smile. "Did you come looking for me?"

"I came to thank you for last night. And for your discretion today."

"Yeah, well," she said, shrugging as she turned the file around. "Figure it's never bad for a billionaire to owe me one… If things get tight, I can blackmail you into paying my rent." His lips shifted, just a little, but that was definitely a glimmer of a smile. "Huh…" Sinking back, her shoulders loosened in curiosity. "You're cute when you smile." His brows rose like the compliment was unexpected, though his amusement grew. "Don't look so surprised. Bet you hear that all the time. Your wife must tell you every day."

"Ex-wife," he said, coming a couple of steps closer, twisting his head to inspect her files. "What are you doing?"

"You came down here to find out what I was doing?" she asked, doubting his purpose. "Did your father-in-law get in touch?"

"He's called and I haven't returned."

"Not a very good son-in-law, are you?" she asked, moving a file from one pile to the next. "He's worried about his daughter."

"His various voicemails clued me in on that."

Sitting back on her heels, she couldn't contain her interest. "And you're not worried about her? Your wife—"

"Ex-wife," he said, his eyes leaving her work to meet

hers. "We're divorced."

And for some reason, that seemed important to him. Yet, that wasn't the only thing his expression gave away.

"You know where she is." He said nothing but didn't need to. She laughed. "Maybe I'll have you pay my cellphone bill too… I love being right."

"What were you right about?"

She took another file from the box and sought its identifier. "I don't know your wife, but I like her already. She's got a great sense of humor."

"I'm sorry, I don't follow."

"You're divorced but not done, right?" she asked, checking the file from her list before opening it to cross-reference the log. "Somehow, she got you and your buddy stripped down to your birthday suits… I bet a woman that beautiful can get a guy to do anything any time."

"You think we were sharing her?" he asked. "That I divorced her, still sleep with her, and take my friend along for the ride?"

"What you get up to in the privacy of your marital bed…" she said, going through the motion of her checks. "Must be great, not a worry in the world, fulfilling your every fantasy… It's almost enough to make us regular Josephines sick."

"We're divorced," he said again and surprised her by crouching in front of her. "I don't sleep with her… and I would never invite another man into bed with my wife."

Divorced? Was that his choice or hers?

"Sorry," she said, regretting being glib. "Divorce can't be easy."

"No," he said, standing up. "How long have you been with Ranby Kearns?"

As he slipped his hands into his pockets and glanced around, she stopped reading. "Is this a job interview?" His attention came back. "You have better things to do in the middle of the day than hang around with me. Are you building up to something? Worried I'll tell someone about last night? I won't. You don't have to worry. Your business is your business."

"No," he said and cleared his throat. "I came down

to thank you for your discretion… and to find out if I could return the favor."

"What favor?"

"Is there anything you need? Anything I can do for you?"

Like quid pro quo or was he still thinking about that settlement?

"No, I'm good."

"Really?" he asked. "There's nothing you want?"

"No," she said and exhaled a laugh. "Is it really so unbelievable?"

"Yeah," he said, pulling out a chair from the long table to sit down. "Usually when someone's given carte blanche, they embrace it." Leaning forward, elbows on knees, he clapped before curling his fist into his other hand. "Let me have it."

"What?"

"Your wish list, your fantasy, come on, there must be something you want. Helicopter ride, tropical vacation… trip into space, what?"

"Nope," she said, her butt sliding off her feet onto the floor. "I'm good."

"You've got me cornered… Whatever you want, you'll get. Personal assistant. One million in small bills."

"A million? Is that all my silence is worth?"

"That's the opening offer… now you counter."

Her head dropped to the side as he sank back in the seat, his smile broad. "Are you educating me?"

"Negotiation is what I do, babe."

"You do realize you're negotiating with yourself. I already said I don't want anything."

"Everybody wants something."

"And you think because you have money, you can make all my dreams come true?" His smile dropped. She laughed. "Relax, Mr. Money Bags, there's nothing I want that you can pay for."

"That's an intriguing way to put it."

"Thanks," she said, returning to her work.

"That means there's something you want, something money can't buy."

"Most things worth having can't be bought," she said.

"Enlighten me."

Drawing in a breath, she tipped her head back, shaking wisps of hair from her face. "You haven't got where you are by being dumb. Are you so shallow?"

"Sizing you up."

"Because you think I'm driven by money?" She opened her arms. "Look at me on the floor, up to my elbows in paperwork. Do I look like money's my priority? Compared to what really matters, money's easy to amass."

"Now I really am intrigued."

And he looked it. Wasn't it hilarious that she had the rapt attention of a man with twenty more important places to be?

"Does your wife like it when you interrogate other women?"

"Ex-wife," he said on a light laugh. "You enjoy bringing her up."

"Because you enjoy correcting me. You really want me to know you're divorced, don't you?"

"Maybe I do."

And if they didn't stop smiling at each other, someone was bound to walk by and notice. Yes, he was in the chair with his back to the internal glass wall, but if someone got close enough…

"Only one thing you can do to prove it."

"And what's that?" he asked.

"Take me to dinner."

His smile dropped. "What?"

"Tomorrow night," she said. "Wherever you want."

He gripped the arms of the chair, pushing himself back then swaying forward, his humor gone in the face of new tension. "Oh, uh, that's a tempting offer, but I… it wouldn't be a good idea."

"Okay," she said, picking up her stack of files to drop them back into the box. "No worries."

She put her tablet on top and picked up the box as she stood.

He leaped to his feet too. "It's not that I… I'm

flattered you would ask."

"It's okay," she said, laying a hand on his arm. "Was just an idea." She offered a comforting smile because the poor guy was beyond uncomfortable. "I have to get back to work."

Leaving him in the office, she headed for the executive file room. Kintyre was an interesting character, fun, if sort of a contradiction. He sure made the day more interesting.

THREE

SORTING THROUGH BOXES, organizing schedules, delegating workload. These things were all part of her everyday life. She didn't need Chester sending frantic emails insisting everyone get to the conference room immediately. Delays were frustrating, especially when she got herself in a groove.

Chester was a levelheaded guy. Most of the time. Unfortunately, he was prone to spells of manic panic. That was why he relied on her. In those moments, it was her responsibility to snap him out of it. He didn't usually call all their colleagues to come watch.

Everyone else was there and seated when she arrived. All except Chester, who was standing at the head of the room.

"What's going on?" she asked.

"Sit down. Sit down."

Walking down the room, she aimed for the closest empty chair. "Why do I need to—"

"Mr. Kintyre!" Chester exclaimed.

Whipping around, she saw her boss shaking Kintyre's hand. Behind the latter was another man in a suit. The one from two nights ago.

"Thank you," Kintyre said, stepping aside to present his friend. His colleague? Obviously both. Maybe more since their hobby was getting naked together. "Javier Perez, VP, and senior advisor."

"Yes," Chester said, shaking his hand. "It's a pleasure."

"Hello," Kintyre said, coming to stand behind the chair at the head of the table. The chair he'd sat in the previous day when they'd talked alone. "Ranby Kearns." He scanned the faces around the room. "I apologize we haven't given you a better welcome." His gaze stopped on her. "Would you like to sit down?"

"Maybe," she said. "You're not sitting."

"Manners dictate I shouldn't until all the ladies do."

Somehow, she doubted etiquette was his concern. Still, she pulled out the chair and swerved around the arm to sit.

Even when she was down, he stayed on his feet. Ergo point proven.

"My friend and I are here to remedy our error. While you're here, you're a valuable part of the Eclipse team."

Actually, they weren't. Their role involved remaining neutral. Impartial. They couldn't make assumptions and had to keep an open mind without being swayed by anything... or anyone.

Javier approached his friend's side, his gait loose. "We have a welcome dinner planned for tomorrow night. Cars will come to your hotel to pick you up."

"Limos?" Isha asked.

"Sure," Javier said, raising an arm. "Champagne, caviar, private dining, the works."

Excitement shimmered around the table. For some reason, her eyes drifted to Kintyre's. His were on her.

What was that smile? What was he thinking? Her focus narrowed. Why was it like he knew something she didn't? That thought reminded her of what they both knew that the rest of the room didn't. Those at the table anyway. And that was how they met. More accurately, what he was wearing when they met. She didn't even mean to smile, but somehow a grin spread across her face. Almost like he read her mind, it looked like a subtle laugh left his lips. Yeah, her colleagues didn't get it, but they did. It was a good sign that he had a sense of humor about it.

"We appreciate this effort," Chester said, walking to Kintyre's side, stealing his focus. "We enjoy working here. Everyone has been polite."

"Good," Kintyre said. "Keep a list of everyone who is rude. We'll run them out of here, stat."

Chester's brow strengthened. Yeah, that was concern. Nice to know her boss wasn't totally into the Kool-Aid.

While their business involved slipping into these billion-dollar corporations, they didn't often get personal attention from the CEO. Did Kintyre have an ulterior motive?

"And if anyone's open to bribes…" Javier said, slapping a hand between Chester's shoulder blades.

"He's kidding, Stevenson. We only violate contractual agreements in private. After which, we have plausible deniability."

Everyone else laughed, everyone except her and Chester. Her boss's cogs were definitely turning.

"If there's anything we at Eclipse can do for you at Ranby Kearns, we will deliver. Just reach out."

Javier switched to put a hand on Kintyre's shoulder. "And now we have to go upstairs and make the big decisions."

Her eyes met Kintyre's again. His friend gave him a tug that didn't do much to move him. Next time he tried harder, forcing Kintyre to go. Still, his eyes lingered. For a guy who'd refused a date with her, he sure was interested. What was up with that?

FOUR

DECIDING WHAT TO wear to dinner had never been more difficult. It was a work event. She didn't have to go sexy. Smart casual. Evening smart casual. Evening sexy, smart casual? No. They were in LA. Sexy had a different meaning there. Women went for morning coffee in bikini tops and hot pants... Lycra hot pants, so, yeah, different definition.

She went with smart, sophisticated. Nothing too revealing. Square neck, knee length, respectable.

Taking so long to choose meant putting her earrings in and shoes on at the same time.

The phone was ringing and that meant it was time to go.

The cars were a nice touch lapped up by her colleagues. Some people were easily dazzled. She wasn't one of them. Beauty was in the eye of the beholder... and she'd beheld too many big buck gestures.

Getting to the restaurant took longer than expected. Or it would except she had no idea where they were going.

Everyone got out into the bustling LA air to be greeted by a host in a slick suit. She was at the back of the pack, so couldn't hear much of what he was saying as he guided their disorganized group inside.

As they passed the empty maître d' stand and her colleagues rounded the wall of plants concealing the dining room, someone caught her arm. A quiet gasp passed her lips as she turned to see a young man holding onto her.

"Miss, would you come with me?"

Both odd and rude, his gesture was perplexing. "No," she said, tugging her arm back. "I don't think I will."

"Mr. Kintyre would like a moment alone."

Was that what he did to get a woman's attention? Sent college kids to grab and divert them?

"Where is he?" she asked. "Isn't he coming to this dinner?"

"Alone," the kid said again. "Please."

Her colleagues disappeared around the plant wall without looking back. The fancy restaurant, the VIP treatment, they wouldn't be searching for anyone while the circus kept them busy.

"Okay," she said.

If for no other reason than curiosity, she wanted to know what drove Kintyre. The young man took her through a side door, down a corridor and out a discreet exit to an alley. Hmm, the car parked there was an upgrade from the one she'd got out of on the street a moment ago.

Her guide went over to open the back door and gestured her inside. If the plan was to whisk her away somewhere, her colleagues may notice her prolonged disappearance. Still, intrigue compelled her on.

Kintyre sat inside. Alone. Pouring champagne. Smooth. Probably practiced. She slid in and the door closed behind her.

"Thank you for joining me," he said, offering her a flute.

"What am I doing here?" she asked, taking the glass with no intention of drinking. "I thought we were having dinner."

"We will have dinner."

"There are twenty people waiting inside for you."

His smile warmed. "More than that. Javi's keeping them busy."

"Why?"

"So I can explain… and ask you to dinner."

Shifting closer and to the edge of her seat, she didn't like being confused. "I'm here," she said, putting the flute down on the bar beyond him. "We're having dinner."

"This is a smokescreen dinner," he said, which didn't enlighten her any. "I want us to have dinner. Together. Alone." Her female intuition tingled. "At my place. Tomorrow night."

"That's it?" she asked, folding her arms.

He frowned. "You're not interested? You asked me to dinner. You asked me first."

"I asked you to ask me," she said. "And I meant actual dinner. In a safe, public place. It wasn't code for a booty call. Guess it's true, you can't buy class."

On its way to the door handle, his hand intercepted hers. "This isn't that," he said with enough sincerity to intrigue her.

A couple of silent seconds went by.

"Okay, well, enjoy your sleaze-fest—"

"Please…" He paused until she raised a brow. "It's been a long time since I did this… Jules is the only woman I've dated in half a decade."

She softened, just a little. "You and your wife separated two years ago, didn't you? You must have dipped your toe in since then?"

"Not once."

A guy like him had to get offers all the time. He had to be around a bunch of hot, successful women too. Being single again, why wouldn't he play the field?

"Are you still in love with her?"

"In love with…?"

"Your wife," she said. "I'll admit I didn't follow your relationship in the media. Did she end it?"

"Jules and I are done. Completely. I have no doubts or regrets about that, and I am not in love with her."

"Then I don't get it… You must still sleep with her."

Her certainty bred his half smirk. "Not since before I filed two years ago."

She blinked. "But that would mean…"

He laughed. "Yeah, I'm rusty. I'd appreciate it if

you'd cut me some slack."

"I can do that," she said. "Is that why you said no in the boardroom? When I brought up dinner? It's your reflex to reject women?"

"There hasn't been a woman I've… Yes, when you're married, you get used to being with one person. The divorce was… difficult. Coming out the other side of it hasn't been easy either."

No, it never was. Just because he'd been the filer didn't mean he'd done it lightly or that he wasn't sad to see the end of his marriage.

"You shouldn't rush into anything," she said, withdrawing her hand from his. "I'm sorry I brought it up. Like I said, it was just a thought."

"One that took me a second to catch up with," he said, taking her hand again. "I'd love to have dinner with you… It would be an honor. We just have to be discreet."

"Discreet?" Why was that tingle bugging her again? His request didn't seem to be code for something else. To be sure, she chose to be clear. "I'm not interested in coming over to your place to get naked with you. You're hot, but I'm not that type. Sorry."

A snicker joined his smile. "Don't apologize. That's not what I'm asking."

"What are you asking?"

"That you be ready tomorrow night, at eight, for me to send a car for you. Get in it. It will bring you to my place… Actually, my friend's place. I'm staying with him, but we'll get into that another time. We'll have dinner. Talk. You can leave any time you choose. Fully clothed."

Damn straight. "This dinner tonight is a smokescreen." That was what he'd said. "You're using it to get to me."

"Yes."

Flattering. It shouldn't be, but it was. "My colleagues—"

"Are not being abused. They will get everything they desire. We'll have a meal, socialize, I will greet those from Ranby Kearns as I should have when you first arrived."

Her head tilted. "I know you and your buddy joked

about bribes, but you know we can't—"

"Relax," he said, threading his fingers deeper between hers. "There's nothing sinister going on here. I'm just a guy asking you out on a date."

"But you didn't do it at work. You didn't do it in public. You said discreet, but you meant secret."

"Yes."

Honest, but intriguing. "I can't tell anyone about this."

"No."

"Because?"

He waited a beat. "Because if the world finds out, I lose half my business."

Now that was a reason. Losing half a multibillion-dollar multinational would be damn careless of him.

"Why take that risk?" she asked, processing the shock.

He leaned closer. "I have a feeling you'll be worth it."

"How can you be so su—"

His mouth caught hers, silencing their words. She hadn't expected the advance but welcomed it… maybe a little too much. Warm, slick, certain, this was a confident man. A determined and confident man. He kissed her like he'd known exactly what it would feel like, as though he'd done it a dozen times before. Was the gentle dive of his tongue trying to tell her something? Trying to clue her in on the secret only it knew?

Lost in her attempts to decipher the meaning behind the growing glow in her belly, she was still caught up when he drew back.

"If you're not as sure, say no," he murmured, touching the hair by her cheek. "I'll take it like a man."

"Eight o'clock," she said, licking her lips. "I'll be ready."

As to how she'd get through a meal with him and her colleagues, that was going to be its own kind of torment. Kintyre had come into her life unexpectedly, but it was for a reason. To feel the way it did, there had to be a reason… right?

FIVE

ON FRIDAY NIGHT, everything went according to plan.

The car picked her up around the back of the hotel. Different to the main entrance pick up for their known-about meal the previous night. Clandestine was the theme of the evening and she hadn't even gotten anywhere yet.

"What am I doing?" she murmured to herself as the car drove through broad wooden gates.

The house was impeccable. Glass and concrete, the gleaming white driveway reflected the shining headlights back on themselves.

His friend's house. He'd said they would eat at his friend's place. Did that mean his friend would be there? How could the date be a secret if they were dining with his friend? Was that friend Javier? At least they had history too.

The car stopped. Rather than wait for the driver to come around and open the door, she slid out and went to the front door. Glass, shadowy beyond, the house looked dark. Were they in the right place?

Just at that, light flickered on within, startling her.

Kintyre appeared from behind floating stairs to cross the warm wood floor, a smile on his face.

He opened the door. "Thought you got lost."

"Am I late?"

The moment she got the call that the car had arrived at the hotel, she'd gone downstairs to get in it. How could he think she was late?

He extended an arm to gesture inside, sort of herding her in without touching her. "No," he said. "I was just eager to see you."

As he moved in behind her, she shed her bolero jacket, more interested in what lay ahead than where he put her attire.

"Is your friend here?" she asked when he started across the foyer past the stairs.

"Knox?" he asked, passing a partition wall to enter an immaculate living room. "No, he's in the Bahamas, I think."

"But we're in his house?"

They carried on out the open pocket doors to a covered lanai area with couches, a central, real flame fire, and a bar. The vast pool beyond was lit, giving their intimacy a luxe touch.

"I've been staying with Knox since I left Jules in my place. He's never here and doesn't care."

"Does he know you bring women back here?"

"Woman," he said, opening a hand to the couch. "Would you like to sit down? What can I get you to drink?"

She sat on the edge of the couch closest to the house. "Peach schnapps and cranberry juice," she said, pleased to surprise him. "And if it's a special occasion, I like Sex on the Beach."

That made not only his brows rise, but his lips curl too. "I'll remember that."

She laughed. "It's schnapps, cranberry juice, and orange juice."

Behind the bar, he spread his hands to rest his weight on them as he leaned in her direction. "You drink weaker alcohol on special occasions?"

"I have more drinks on special occasions, so, yes… Seems smart to me."

"When you put it like that…"

Music drifted out from somewhere inside. Low volume, she couldn't figure out what it was. Something wasn't sitting right. Gorgeous guy mixing drinks behind the bar. Mood lighting. Beautiful setting. What was she missing?

Maybe it was his semi-confession in the back of the car. "What you said last night… about losing half your business… that was a joke, right?"

"No," he said, concentrating on what he was doing. "Unfortunately, not."

She didn't get it. "If someone found out about this meeting, you would lose half of Eclipse? How does that work?"

"It's in the terms of my divorce," he said, picking up two glasses to come around and join her on the couch. After putting her glass in her hand, he raised his. "To new friends."

Instead of reciprocating, she put her glass on the low table that surrounded the fireplace and looked him in the eye. "Please explain it to me."

"You don't want to ease in?"

"I don't want to be an accessory to anything illegal."

He laughed and sipped what appeared to be bourbon or Scotch or some kind of hard liquor. "It's not illegal."

He sank into the corner of the couch, raising his ankle to the opposite knee. His feet were bare, his blue jeans loose. The casual get-up was no less striking than Zachary Kintyre in the boardroom. If anything, this gray tee-shirt clad guy was more enticing. Bearing witness to laid-back Zach was intimate, special, privileged almost.

"So what is it?"

"Jules is an actress," he said. Something she knew. "Image is everything in her game. It's something she thinks a lot about… has entire teams working to maintain." Still clueless, she just shook her head. "Reaching a settlement was a pain in the ass. Even with the prenup. It dragged on and on. She's not interested in Eclipse, and it was mostly protected in the prenup." He exhaled. "You sure you want to talk about this?"

"I do if you expect this to go anywhere," she said. "I don't want to be responsible for you losing anything. Especially a company you've spent so long building."

"It comes down to this. Eclipse is mine. Wholly and

completely. Providing I maintain a transition period of… discretion."

Was she just being stupid? "What does that mean?"

As he licked his lips, he snickered. "It means I stay single. Grieve the relationship. Show respect for the wife who puts so much into tailoring what others think of her."

"You're not allowed to be with anyone else?"

"Publicly."

"For how long?"

"A year. Twelve calendar months." Her mouth opened in shock. "I'm eight months in."

The irony wasn't lost on her. "You have four months left?"

"Yes. Sixteen weeks, four days. Ends September first."

She breathed out a laugh. "Ranby Kearns are on a five-month contract." That ended August twenty-ninth, almost exactly when his chains came off. "Talk about a missed opportunity." She slid forward on the couch. "I guess there's no point—"

"It doesn't prohibit me from seeing anyone," he said, putting his glass down next to hers. "We're doing nothing wrong."

"You think it's okay to keep this a secret?"

"I know it is," he said. "I pay my lawyer a lot of money to protect my rights. It's my right to live my life how I want to live it. So long as no one learns of our relationship in the next four months, we can do whatever we like together."

"And then what?" she asked. "I live in New York."

He frowned. "I thought Ranby Kearns was based in Boston."

"It is," she said. "But I don't work there." Anymore. "To be honest, it doesn't matter where I live. My job entails traveling all over the country… Sometimes the world."

"Right," he said. "So even if you were seeing a guy in New York, he'd still have to understand what you do… you wouldn't always be in Manhattan. Is that where you live?"

"Yes," she said, acknowledging his point. "Keeping it secret makes it feel like we're doing something wrong."

"We can talk to Javi about it. He's listed as a confidante."

"And a man I barely know," she said without missing the pun in that. "My work involves me examining yours."

"Yes," he said. His head tilted. "Do you need to declare your relationship within a client organization to your superior?"

"No. Others do, but I'm trusted."

"Do you have a personal relationship with Chester Stevenson?"

A frown lowered her brow. "With Chester?" she asked, struck by something else. Oh… "You don't know who I am, do you?"

Innocence colored his widened eyes. "Should I?" As if the situation wasn't already complicated enough, her ties were only going to tangle their web further. "Javi said they call you 'Lil.'"

"Yes, they do," she said, unable to keep the smile from her lips. "My name's Lilya."

"Okay, so—"

"Lilya Kearns," she said.

In his own surprise, he sank against the back of the couch. "You're Frank's daughter."

"His niece," she said and was about to continue when he sat upright.

"Wait, there's a story about that, isn't there? A story about his niece…" His eyes moved in their sockets. "I can't remember what…"

"There's a story about me and Nathan Ranby, Victor's son."

"Right, yes," he said, pointing at her. "You were supposed to get married."

She smiled. "That's how the story goes."

"Is that what caused the split? Frank bought Victor out."

"Victor got sick," she said and sighed. "Another complicated story…"

His eyes narrowed. "There's something else… Rigley and Klein."

"I used to work with them."

"Yes, but—"

"I really don't want to talk about Richard Rigley." Because she might be inclined to spit. "Doing what I do, I've traveled in a lot of circles. Know a lot of people you do, probably."

"Yet you work under Stevenson."

"My role is integrity and quality," she said. "I basically check everyone else's work."

"You're not under Stevenson?"

"I'm on his team but can't hold a position of authority. I can't direct those I'm assessing and be impartial. There has to be a separation of…" Though he was listening, the light in his gaze felt anything but professional. He was gorgeous, too gorgeous and enticing for her to be sitting there talking about her family and past woes. "I shouldn't be here."

Like he could read her mind, his brow relaxed. "I don't care about complicated," he said, curling his fingers around hers. "Compared to my previous relationship, this will be a cakewalk."

Was this just attraction? He'd said no to her so easily that first time she mentioned dinner… Maybe he thought winning his favor would get him something extra.

"I'm not responsible for the audit," she said. "I audit the auditors. I don't direct their work or their findings. My job is to confirm their work is accurate and based in evidence. That's it."

"I understand," he said, softening to a warm smile. "I have no interest in influencing Ranby Kearns results. Eclipse has nothing to hide."

"Except this."

"For four months," he said, his fingers sliding onto her face.

His touch was so warm, so tender… so intoxicating.

Drawn closer, her breathing slowed. "A lot can happen in four months."

"That's what I'm hoping."

Complicated didn't cover it and their relationship hadn't even got going. Starting anything would be dumb. His choices weren't his own for the next four months at least.

And her next contract took her to New York. She'd have to walk away. She didn't want him to lose his company or to ruin Julietta's career. He'd survived eight months so far without getting himself involved with anyone.

"We should both turn and walk the opposite way," she whispered, edging closer.

"Maybe," he said, mirroring her move. "I'm not that smart when it comes to women."

"No?" she asked, inching in.

His lips came closer. "Instinct always overrules my head."

"You want me to be the sensible one?" she asked, tipping up her chin.

His breath merged with hers. "God, no," he said, his hand sinking into her hair to pull their mouths together.

More than an attraction, need pounded in her chest. She couldn't breathe or think straight when he was so close. Their tongues sank together, touching, withdrawing, pushing further, retreating for the chase.

Oh, God, this was a mistake.

But as her hand slid up his torso. His hot, ripped, solid torso, her nails dug into the fabric covering it. She wanted it gone. Out of the way. All barriers to fade to nothing. He pulled her closer, forcing their bodies together as he bowed her back, their balance anchored by the grip he had of her hair.

One of them should think this through to the end. In a few months, he'd be free to screw around as publicly as he liked. At the same time, she'd be jetting across the continent to her next job in New York. The only outcome of this association would be farewell. There was no future. So why bother?

Damn, if only he wasn't such an incredible kisser.

SIX

THEIR KISS ON the couch became an impromptu make-out session. If he hadn't pulled away and declared it time to put on the grill, God only knew how far they'd have gone.

The eating part of the meal was over, but they were still at the glass patio table, perpendicular to each other.

"Wait!" she exclaimed on a laugh. "You were skinny dipping in your own pool?"

"The company pool, but yeah," he said, enjoying her laughing at his expense.

"Why would you be skinny dipping? And what happened to your clothes?"

"Our new security system was initializing overnight. I forgot about it before it kicked in. By that time, we were in the pool, our clothes in the locker rooms. Initialization locked down all nonessential areas. That meant no getting into the locker or supply rooms."

"So how did you get out?"

"Climbed through the window to the gym and came up in the freight elevator."

The story was so ludicrous, it had to be true. Her stomach ached. From laughter. Nothing else. Had she ever met a successful man who was also funny? The food had been amazing, the drink sublime, the man perfect. The company made the moment. She'd never thought about it before. Just how much an experience relied on who was there with her.

"But wait…" She shook her head and picked up her wineglass. "Why were you skinny-dipping in the first place? You have a pool here. If you were so eager to get naked in the water…"

He tilted his glass to inspect the liquid inside. "It's not as simple as that."

"Tell me, I want to know." Registering his solemnity, her smile slowly faded. "It's not a happy story, is it?"

"No," he said, tipping the rest of his wine into his mouth then showing her a smile. "You want anything else to eat?"

"Tell me," she said, sliding closer, slipping her hand into his. "Why the skinny-dipping?"

He picked up her hand to kiss her knuckles. "Just something that happened a long time ago."

"It's private?"

Their eyes met. "It's not my intention to keep secrets from you," he said and groaned as his head went back. "Damn the fucking clause. Makes me seem evasive from the get-go."

"Do you want me to leave?" she asked, trying to withdraw her hand.

His fingers tightened around hers. "No. That's not what I… My brother made us promise before he died." Startled, she could only blink. "We were dumb teenagers. He'd been sick when we were younger and when the cancer came back… All the money in the world couldn't save him…" His focus drifted. "We think we have security, think that we can overcome any obstacle…"

When their eyes met again, guilt tensed her. "I'm sorry. I didn't mean to—"

"It's okay," he said, smiling as he kissed her knuckles again. "Like I said, it was a long time ago. Talking about him isn't difficult, it's just… Not the happiest dinner conversation."

"I don't mind."

The more she learned, the more she wanted to know.

For a man living so many secrets, he was surprisingly open. She didn't want to pull him down. Pull the mood down.

"So you could say you ended up naked in your own building on a dare?"

"Not a dare…"

"What else would you call it?"

He considered the question for just a second. "Okay, I guess you could call it a dare." Her laughter overlapped his words. "I've been accused of always toeing the line. Always doing the right thing. The honorable thing," he said, leaving her at the dining table to go back to the lanai bar to mix her another drink. "My brother was the spontaneous one. Skinny-dipping was on his bucket list. We all promised to cover as much of it with him as we could… That was one we never got to. In the hospital, he made us promise it would be our way of remembering him, of celebrating his life. Every year on the anniversary of his death… wherever we are we… I thought I was going to make it back here, but we had work and midnight was approaching… It's my brother's way of reminding me it can pay to be reckless, even if it's only one day a year."

She took her wineglass from the table to return to the couch they'd started on. "And did it? Pay to be reckless?"

"Yeah, I guess it did. It brought us together, didn't it?"

"Oh, smooth," she said, settling on the couch, curling her legs up beside her.

He paused to take her in. "I assumed you'd like another cocktail. Would you prefer to stick with wine…? Or I can call your driver if you're ready to leave?"

What time was it? After another mouthful of wine, she reached over to put it on the fireplace.

"I don't want to leave yet," she said and stroked the couch in front of her. "Come sit with me."

He left the half-made drink on the bar to come over and sit with her.

"You okay?" he asked, the lilt of his voice suggesting he knew what was on her mind. "It's getting late."

"Yeah," she said, laying a hand on his chest. "Do you want me to leave?"

His hand covered hers as it began to stroke. "No."

"You filed for divorce two years ago."

"I did."

A man like him without a lover? It was almost impossible to believe he'd gone without intimacy for so long.

Her eyelids grew heavy. "It's been two years... since you were..."

"With a woman?" he asked, the back of his fingers drifting up her cheek.

She angled into the caress. "There's been no one?"

"Since Jules? No."

Her lips curled when his brushed them. "I have a responsibility here."

"You do?"

His feigned surprise tempted her even closer. The game could have only one conclusion. Yeah, it was an excuse to surrender, but she meant it too. Already she was sure of his good heart. The guy had been through the mill on the relationship score. Would it be so bad to show him how easy and indulgent recklessness could be?

"I do."

Guiding his hand from her face to the zipper beneath her arm, he didn't take the hint and tightened his grip on her instead. "I'm in no rush, baby. What you have is worth waiting for."

How could he know that? A shiver went through her, parting her eyelids just a little. Being magnanimous couldn't be easy. Even if she couldn't read most men, the want burning from his gaze consumed her.

"I don't want to wait."

"And I want you for more than one night."

Shit. This guy was either the biggest player she'd ever met, or he was the real deal. What were the chances of that?

"Zachary Kintyre," she whispered, her leg gliding across his lap to straddle him. "Be reckless."

With a hand on each of his cheeks, she eased into the kiss. It hadn't been two years for her, but she wanted to take her time, to savor the joining of their mouths. He didn't touch her, but she wasn't dissuaded. Pushing her hips against his, he stopped kissing her to groan as she rocked over the ridge in his jeans.

"Dive in the pool," she whispered, her hands roaming over him, pulling, squeezing, caressing. "Please, Zach."

"How much wine did you drink?"

"Not enough for you to be worried," she said, placing brief kisses on his lips. "Switch that honor off."

"Yeah?"

"Oh, yeah," she said, biting her lip as she pushed off his lap, claiming his hand as she stood. "Which room is yours?" He got to his feet with a tortured laugh that came out almost pained. "I won't force you. If you're not ready—"

"I want you for more than the night…" His devouring gaze touched her everywhere. "I want you in every damn way imaginable."

"Good," she said, leaning against him. "Let's be naughty… very naughty."

He laughed. "Thought you weren't the type."

"Two years, Zach," she said. "I can't leave you wanting another night." But she didn't want to do anything that may make him uncomfortable. "If you don't want—"

"I want." He scooped her up before she could turn away. "I really want."

Carrying her through the house and up the stairs, he was more than determined, more than eager.

She brought their mouths together, concentrating on maintaining the inferno of their desire while he laid her down in the center of a huge white bed.

Rather than join her, he boosted himself back to his feet. "I don't have rubbers in here, I'll raid Knox's."

Before she could ask if his friend would mind, he'd disappeared from the room. She kicked off her shoes as she shimmied out of her dress.

Two years.

How could a guy like him go two years without intimacy? Not just that he was hot, that was a given. Women would line up for him on looks alone. Her bra joined the dress and shoes. It was the determination of such a driven man, a man always on the go, ambitious, focused, flourishing… If he wanted something, he'd find a way to get it. Had his marriage screwed him up? Was there something she didn't get?

Lying down, she pushed up the bed while shedding her panties, so her head landed on the pillows around the same time the satin hit the floor.

"Doubt he and Jane will—" He stopped just inside the room. Dead. Right there. Mouth open. "Wow."

"I started without you," she said, letting her fingertips trail across her thigh.

She hadn't really, but there was no harm in implying otherwise. Unless there was. He just stood there. Saying nothing. Just… there. Oh, God, was this the moment he realized he wasn't over his wife? The moment he realized he wasn't ready. The man had taken vows. Yeah, many years ago, but still. Someone didn't undertake that lightly, did they?

"I'm sorry," she said, grabbing a pillow to cover herself. "This was too much too soon I—"

"No, no, no," he said, striding across to the bed. "Not too much, not too soon." He sat to take the pillow from her body. "You're beautiful…" That settled some of her regret. "The most beautiful woman I think I've ever seen."

Okay, so that was a line, but she smiled and let him get away with it. "Yeah?"

"Without a doubt."

He leaned in to kiss her again. That was what they needed. That connection, the heat that reminded them to feel, not think.

The pillow lost, he yanked off his tee-shirt as he lay down, tormenting her by taking his time settling over her.

Infuriation came with impatience. "Zach," she panted.

But she wasn't saved. No, God, no, the man's attentive mouth bordered on cruel. He teased her throat, her neck, her jaw, her ear, and down. Mmm, he wasn't shy about exploring. His kiss crossed her shoulder and returned along her collarbone to descend to her cleavage.

Damnit, she didn't have his patience. He was apparently the one who'd gone without for years. Maybe it was an endurance exercise. If it was, she was at her limit.

Tasting one breast and then the other, he sucked her nipple into his mouth, tormenting it with the tip of his tongue.

"I…" Moving against his mouth, her body rose and wriggled, begging more. Pressing herself against him, she wanted more of him, more of his body on hers… in hers. "Zach, I… I can't…"

As he rose above her to find her drowsy gaze, his skilled hand skimmed up to squeeze her breast. "Want me to stop?"

"No," she gasped. "No. No! I want you to start." His slow smile didn't hide its wickedness. "You win. You definitely win."

He laughed. "Are we competing for something?"

"Fuck me, Zach."

"We're a ways away from that," he said, rising higher to admire her body. "No way I'm rushing this."

"Will you rush for me?"

The heat of his laugh warmed the air again. He dropped fast to kiss her mouth, dazing her enough that he could flip her onto her chest.

"I can promise you'll get there first," he said, scooping her hair away to the side. "You're too delicious."

When his tongue met the back of her neck, she squeezed her eyes closed. He was taking his time. More time than existed. More time than she had in her. He kissed the breadth of her shoulders and returned to spoil the back of her neck, then he was gone. Where? Where did he—his lips met her lower back.

"Mm…" The surge of sensation compelled her ass to rise, and it was only his body that kept it down as he trailed the point of his tongue up her spine. "Oh, Zach…"

Shit. Had she ever come with a guy without him touching her pussy? No, that was a clear and categoric no. Already she was fucking close and urged even closer when his body vanished, and the very tips of his fingers trailed up her sides from hips to waist. They kept on going up her arms, straightening them over her head, wrapping her fingers around one of the padded bars of the headboard.

Her legs parted as her ass rose, her knees coming higher.

"Don't do that," he said, stroking her ass. "Don't tease me."

Her mouth and eyes opened. Had he really just accused her of teasing him? "Zachary Kintyre—"

"Don't worry, baby. I forgive you."

The bed moved, then his arms were curling their way around her thighs and hips, drawing her down. His mouth met her clit. Shit. He was lying under her, kissing, licking, pleasuring her pussy with such slow, deliberate deftness that it was impossible to resist responding. Writhing against his tongue, she let him push in deep, moved and circled against him as he sucked her clit, torturing her with his talented tongue.

"Oh, God, Zach," she yelped, gripping the bars in her hand so tight it was possible her nails burst through the leather. "Zach!"

Climax slammed into her. Everything ceased to exist. She forgot him. Her pussy. Even her own name. All that existed was the tension seizing every muscle. Need held it there; waves of pleasure came in a torrent one after the other. She couldn't even breathe, couldn't—

He slammed into her.

Where the hell had he come from?

It didn't matter. The ebb of her climax didn't last long. When he shoved his cock into her all the way to the hilt, another orgasm squeezed him in deep.

"Shit, baby. Fuck!"

Now he had an idea what it was like. She couldn't help her body's reaction to him. Did he have to—

He pulled out, like all the way out. "No, no, no," she said, quickly turning over. "Don't take it away."

As he came down over her, he smiled. "You grabbed on pretty tight."

Looping her arms around him, she pulled him closer. "Thought tight was good."

"Is good. Too good," he said, kissing her slow. "Technically, we've broken the drought."

"Don't even think about it. This isn't done until

you're done. I want you to finish inside me."

He brushed his nose across hers. "And if I don't?"

Trailing a hand down his body, she wrapped her fingers tight around him. "I'll make it impossible to resist. Want me on top?"

"No, definitely not. Hard no." Her frown wrung another laugh from him. "I want you to come back for seconds. Would you come back to a guy who finished in seconds?"

"Oh, you've passed the interview already," she said, working her hand until his eyes closed in ecstasy. "You got the job."

"So sure?"

"Very sure."

"Good," he said. "Grab the headboard."

"Mm mm," she said in refusal shaking her head each way with each sound. "I want to feel you…"

He descended to kiss her. "Oh, you'll feel me. Every fucking inch." Her fingers loosened when he advanced until she guided him into her. Arching into the delicious slither of him filling her slow, she purred in delight. "Feel that?"

"Mm," she said, nodding, her body writhing in response to his rocking.

"Open your eyes and look at me." She did, bringing him such feral satisfaction that it bled from his every pore. "This was it…"

"It?" she asked on an exhale. "You feel so amazing."

"This was what I was waiting for."

The gravity of his words lingered for just a second before his hips increased their pace. Pumping in and out of her, he was the sweet caress she needed to push her up to that apex again. Hitting it hard, her body bucked and his surged forward.

Shit. Fuck. Shitting. Fuck.

He collapsed beside her.

Whatever just happened was not what she'd expected. Whatever that was, and it had no name, he'd surpassed all expectation… And every guy who'd come before him.

"Let's get married," she panted, blinking through the

stars in her eyes.

"What?" he asked on a laugh.

"Yeah." Despite her trembling body, she flipped over, propping herself on her elbows and clasped hands. "We should get married."

"Vegas?"

"Doesn't have to be fast," she said like she was pondering it. "Though I wouldn't want you to change your mind, so… Yeah. Vegas." He laughed again, gathering her up to roll her onto her back. "You can have affairs. I don't care about fidelity so long as you bring it back to our bed every night."

"The sex that good?"

"I'm not so sure I wasn't the one waiting," she said, wearing a grin as she looped her arms around his neck. "Oh, the afterglow."

"If it does this to you, we're doing it twenty-four, seven."

"You have money," she said, boosting herself up to urge him further down. "We don't need jobs."

"Guess we can cash out the stocks and sell the company."

"Sell?"

"Yeah, if we're doing it all day and all night, who would be at the helm?"

"You're right," she said, running her tongue along his lower lip. "Just sell it."

"Okay," he murmured, kissing her slow. Losing herself in the sensation of him taking her over, it was heat and comfort all in sync. His lips retreated a couple of millimeters. "You need anything?"

Nothing more than she had in that second, which was a sure sign sanity had fled. "Is that driver just waiting in the driveway?"

"He gets paid whether or not he works," he said, tasting her again. "The meter isn't running."

"Do we need to call him to get him here?" Which was her point, not the money. "How far is he?"

He put more space between their mouths. "What does it matter?"

"I guess it doesn't, I can call a cab." If she could remember where her purse was. "I'll need the address."

"Oh," he said, sitting up, running his hands through his hair. "She thinks she's leaving." He flashed her a smile. "It's Friday night."

"Which means?"

"Unless you've got a second job in the area, you don't have anywhere to be until Monday morning." Vaulting back over to her, he stole a kiss as he jumped from the bed. "Settle in, babe. We're just getting started."

As he strode from the room in his full naked incredibleness, she sank back against the pillows. She'd just screwed the boss. Not her boss, but a boss nonetheless. And he was inviting her to stay. She shouldn't… but she would.

SEVEN

"IT'S GETTING LATE."

"So you keep saying," he said, a smile on his face as his fingertips trailed up and down her spine. "I can send someone to the hotel for your things."

Lying in the comfort of his magnificent bed, the practical was a distant thought on the horizon. Did they really need clothes… ever again?

"Oh, yeah?" All weekend, his smile bred hers. "I'm so happy you're not the type of guy to rush into things."

"I'm a real steady guy."

When he rolled onto his back, she bounced over to fold her hands under her chin on his chest. "And how long will this stay secret if you move me in?"

"Thought you and your colleagues didn't socialize at the hotel."

"We don't set mealtimes, but we'd notice someone checking out."

"So we don't check you out. I'll pay for your room."

Flights of fancy could be dangerous, but she had started it. "Ranby Kearns pay my expenses."

"Right," he said, running his fingers through her hair, spreading it across his chest. "Then what does it matter where you sleep?"

"Two days and two nights, you're already talking commitment," she said. "I was kidding about the marriage thing. You know you don't have to marry every woman you sleep with, right?" Shifting, her head sank into the deep, sumptuous pillow. Oh, the idea of staying forever was sure tempting. "I should get up."

Zach laughed, coming closer. "It's after midnight, Amour." Her lips curled when he swept her hair away to kiss her shoulder. "You're safer here."

Raising her hand, she flattened the pillow enough to peek at him through one eye. "I'm not so sure about that," she said, her mouth still lost in the pillow. "You've been ravishing me all weekend."

"It'll be difficult to keep doing it if you leave," he said, sliding an arm around her waist to pull her against him. "Stay with me, please."

"I have to be at work at eight," she said, widening her smile. "Our bubble has to burst sometime. I wonder how many news outlets are reporting you missing or dead… I'm a bad influence."

They'd put on movies, though ended up making out or making love and missing most of them. As for news? He banned it. He'd also turned off his phone after the third time it rang, refusing to let it interrupt them. No man had ever turned his phone off for her.

"To a man like me, privacy is a myth," he said, running his fingers through her hair. "Finding a woman who'd rather stay locked up with me than parade around the city, you're rarer than a unicorn… I say we make a habit of this."

He pushed the sheet away from her lower back to run his fingertip slowly from her ass up her spine with a feather-light touch.

Shivering, she groaned and rolled away. "That's cheating."

"I know all your soft spots now, Amour. I'll exploit them every chance I get."

Swaying to her, he scooped her hair aside and tickled his lips against the groove behind her ear.

This time, it was a whimper that escaped her lips.

"Oh, you're a player," she said, resting a hand on his pec. Every time she touched his chest, she couldn't resist the urge to stroke him. "I can feel my heart breaking already."

"Good," he said, ducking down to kiss her cleavage. "That means I can worm my way in."

As he eased her onto her back, she extended her arms to flop them around his neck. "Don't make me fall for you if you're going to break my heart," she murmured, parting her lips to welcome his kiss.

She heard it before he did, or before he reacted anyway. That was saying something because she wasn't always the most aware person, especially in the cozy cocoon of bed.

It could be that the man kissing her enlivened her too much to really switch off.

A door beyond the bedroom opened and closed. Grabbing Zach's shoulders to push him back, his mouth never reached her throat.

"Zach, there's someone in the house," she said. "If that's your friend—"

"I got it," he said, vaulting from the bed and snagging his trunks from the floor.

He'd just stepped into them when a female voice beckoned from downstairs.

"Honeybun!"

He froze with the underwear halfway up his legs. His chin rose until his wide eyes fixed on the double doors of the bedroom.

"Shit," he exhaled.

"Who is that?" Lilya asked, sitting up, grabbing the sheet to her chest.

"Wait here," he said, pulling up his underwear and marching out, leaving the door open a crack.

Vague light warmed the space between the double doors. It had to be emanating from downstairs.

"Jules?"

"Honeybun," the female voice was so much brighter and happier than Zach's.

Lilya had never met Julietta Ines-Kintyre, yet she recognized her voice. It was like having a movie playing in the next room. At first, it took her a few seconds to process being near someone so famous, which was odd because she hadn't felt that way about Zach. Sure, he wasn't a movie star, but he was well known.

"What are you doing here, Jules?"

"Can't I just come and visit my gorgeous husband?"

"Ex-husband," he said. "Go into the living room."

The floating stairs hung over the foyer that led into the open plan living space. Slinking out of bed, she tiptoed to the door, snagging her dress on the way.

"The only time you come to visit me is when you need something." Zach's voice was quieter, probably in the living room. "I know it's not money because I just gave you a bundle on top of your alimony and I'm still paying your credit cards. Use those if you need something."

There was a pause. Lilya held her breath while putting on her dress, waiting to see what the known beauty would say.

Julietta groaned, though it wasn't any normal groan. The star made even exasperation sound dreamy. "Okay, it's just a stupid little thing. No big deal. I have to give you a heads up about something."

"A heads up," he said, wary. "You know, you shouldn't be coming around my place unannounced. Didn't we talk about this?"

"Knox loves me, Zee-Bee. He doesn't mind me coming around… Any time I show up where you are, people are dying to get us together. It's like destiny."

While they'd been a couple, the media flashed their gorgeous picture everywhere. No one in the Western Hemisphere would mistake either of their identities or that they matched in beauty and charisma.

"Whatever, you're here now. Just, next time, call first."

"I've been trying to call you for two days," Julietta said. "I was worried. Arnett was worried. Huey was worried… Javier…"

"Probably didn't return your call," Zach said.

"Actually, I didn't talk to him. Elsie offered to connect me. I said no."

"Because you know he wouldn't have told you

anything," he said. "What's going on, Jules?"

"Can we maybe sit down? Get a drink?"

"It's late," he said. "If you want to get some rest, I'll get you a car and—"

"Or I can stay here," Julietta said. "Do you remember what—"

"Jules," Zach said, cutting off the woman as she became more flirtatious. "Heads up about what?"

"I've got good news… Amazing news."

"Great," he said. "Next time, send an email."

Julietta laughed, though it hadn't sounded much like a joke. "This is in-person news."

In the following pause, she edged the door open a little more to squeeze out. If they went outside or into the kitchen, she might miss what the heads up was about.

"Spit it out, Jules."

"You're going to be a daddy!"

The world screeched to a halt.

A daddy?

Weren't they divorced? That's what Zach said, and the press too. The media got copies of official papers from somewhere… didn't they? Zach told her Jules was the only person he'd dated for years.

"I'm waiting for you to explain what the hell you're talking about," Zach said.

"I'm pregnant!" Julietta exclaimed like she was delivering joyous news. "You always wanted kids."

"Yeah, and you were always against it," he said. "Something to do with your figure and your career, if I remember right."

"Oh, that's forgotten. I'm not against it now. Come here. Come touch my belly… You want to meet your daddy, little one?"

In shock, closing her mouth was impossible. A daddy. They were going to be parents. So they'd slept together… recently. More recently than two years ago anyway.

As soon as it clicked, she returned to the bedroom to grab her shoes and purse. A clandestine extra-marital affair wouldn't help whatever was going on in their marriage.

Her weekend with Zach had been amazing. But, clearly, the guy still had something going on with his wife. Wouldn't be the first time a man had lied for sex. Lesson learned… in theory. Creeping down the stairs, she didn't want to interrupt the couple's reunion or whatever it was.

Without putting on her shoes, she slipped out and ran across the driveway to walk in the cool grass down to the gate. She'd get a cab back to her life. Why did she let her hormones take over with him? Never again.

Just went to show that no matter how old she got, some things refused to sink in. He'd wanted a secret relationship. Not because of the divorce but because he and his wife were… something.

Complicated was right. Too complicated.

EIGHT

CONCENTRATING WAS TOUGH. Had she really given him a line about it being her responsibility to break his sexual drought? Eurgh, it was embarrassing.

Go away unhelpful questions. Read the report. Forget him and read the damn report. Read. Concentrate. Read. Forget about him. Read. Forget about the weekend. Read. And sneaking back into the hotel like some debauched, immoral whore.

Though wasn't she exactly that? A homewrecker. If anyone found out she'd spent her weekend underneath Eclipse's CEO, that's what she'd be called.

The Kintyres were having a baby together for crissakes. A child. The little one deserved better than a father who lied to women for sex, yes. Beyond that, it wasn't her place to wedge herself between the couple. Parenting together meant something. A woman carrying a man's child, it was a sacred bond. A connection that had to be treated with respect and reverence.

Although having never been there, how could she know for sure? Funny how the concept hadn't occurred to her until she was the woman between father and child. He should get back with his wife. If they were intimate enough to make a baby, there had to be enduring feelings there.

Didn't there?

No, see, that wasn't concentrating. Her mind just wanted to circle and taunt. Everything came back to her stupidity. She'd fallen for it. Denying it was impossible. Sure, she tried to justify it, to excuse her actions, but there was no excuse. She'd believed him. Been falling for him. Really thought they were starting something special.

Shit.

What an idiot.

The executive file room contained filing cabinets, shelves, tables, objects, stability that usually comforted her.

But seriously?

She'd thought the sex was her idea. Maybe she shouldn't make decisions in the company of desirable men when she'd been without one for so long.

When had she started missing sex? It was a non-feature in her psyche, not something she needed with any urgency… until Zach.

The door opened. On reflex, she looked up expecting to see a colleague.

Instead, Javier Perez entered.

He paused, registered her presence, then lifted a phone to his ear.

"She's in the executive file room," he said, causing her frown. "Yes, I'm looking at her right now."

"Guess I don't need to ask who you're talking to," she said, rising.

He lowered the phone. "You have to hear him out."

"No, I don't," she said, closing the file.

"Okay, right, you don't," he said. "But you should."

"You shouldn't get in the middle of this. You're a confidante, I get it." Though maybe even the contract was a lie. Why would they need a confidante for a secret relationship when the couple were still together? "I won't cause any trouble. Unfortunately, I'm related to the CEO of my company, so if you call him to ask I be reassigned, he'll want to know why. I won't tell him, but he's no idiot."

"We don't want you reassigned."

"Okay," she said, picking up the file. "Then there's no problem. You stay in your lane. I stay in mine. We don't ever have to be anywhere near each other again."

"You don't understand."

"I'm sure I don't and it's not my place. Really. I hate drama. I'd rather just get on with my work."

"You can do that."

Relief. "Thank you."

"After you hear him out."

Her lower jaw shifted forward. This guy wasn't there to cool tensions. If he kept talking, and saying things like that, she'd be inclined to ratchet up some tension of her own.

"Are you really going to—"

The door opened again and Javi stepped aside.

Damnit, she was cornered. They were both in front of the only exit, blocking her way out.

"Amour—"

"You don't have to do this," she said, keeping her eyes trained to where the wall met the ceiling. Gritting her teeth for a second, she gathered herself. Why did she feel so... vulnerable? "I'd rather be left alone."

Men had screwed her over before. No, she was no humiliation virgin. Why was this time any different?

"I know you heard Jules last night—"

"I will not go to the press," she said. The moment she'd turned her phone on after leaving his place, the news alert about the baby flashed up. She hadn't even opened a news app or looked at a TV fearing what she'd see trumpeted there. "I won't say anything. No one has to know about—"

"This is complicated."

"No," she said, taking a step back when he took one forward. "I don't want you to come over here."

There was a whole damn room between them, twenty feet at least. Shelving and filing cabinets flanked him. Still, it felt too close.

"It's not mine," he said, calmly, like he feared spooking her.

Trust her, if she could've got away with fleeing, she'd have done it already. "You don't have to explain."

"I do because everything I said to you was true. Everything, Amour. I didn't lie to you. I haven't been with

Jules since before filing the papers."

"That was two years ago."

"Yeah."

"Pregnancy doesn't last two years, unless she's secretly an elephant," she said, sneering at him. Did he think she was that stupid? "Look, it's no big deal. We had sex, it was good and now it's finished. Let's just chalk this one up to experience and move on."

"You had sex?" Javier asked.

She could only shake her head. "Yeah, okay, big surprise. Can I leave now?"

"No," Zach said, his attention pinned on her. "But Javi can."

It took his buddy a second. "Right. Shit. Excuse me."

After his friend departed, the door clicked shut. In the silence, the air seemed oppressive. She couldn't help but flinch against it.

"You don't have to do this," she murmured, shaking her head again. "Please, Zach, you got what you wanted. Won't you please just leave me alone?"

"Jules is pregnant. My ex-wife is pregnant. But the baby isn't mine. You're right, it's physically impossible for it to be mine because we haven't had sex in two years."

"Is it some IVF thing? Is that what you're going to tell me? That you donated for her?"

"No," he said, raising a hand as he came a few steps closer. "It wasn't my sperm. The child is not biologically mine. If it takes a paternity test to prove it to you, I'll take one."

"It's all over the news," she said. "And it doesn't matter. By the time the baby is born, I'll be long gone."

And that future couldn't come quick enough.

"I don't want that. Jules screwed this up. I didn't want you to leave last night. I put her in a car and went back upstairs… you were gone."

"There wasn't much to hang around for. Though sleeping with your wife in our sex sheets isn't exactly classy, I didn't think her finding the bed occupied would do you any favors."

"She didn't stay over. Damnit, Lil, I get that you're

pissed, why you're pissed, but will you just let me explain?"

"What is there to explain? You think after one weekend together we should plan our future? You can't be with a woman for another four months without losing your company."

"Publicly. I can't be with a woman publicly—"

"And now the world believes your wife is pregnant with your child. Having a secret boyfriend is one thing, having a secret boyfriend who's also reconciling with his wife… What would that involve exactly?"

"We knew this would be complicated. I told you… The baby isn't mine."

Hearing that tone, seeing the sorrow in his gaze, she wanted to believe him. "If it's not yours, why would she tell the world it is?"

"Because she's…"

He sealed his lips.

"You can't tell me," she said, exhaling an ironic laugh. That line was becoming his catchphrase. "Is this something else in your divorce contract?" She dumped the file on the desk. "You know this contract seems damn convenient. You want to sleep with me? Oh, but we can't tell anyone. Your wife is pregnant. Oh, but it's not mine. Why is your wife saying otherwise? Oops, I can't tell you."

"I know it seems that way. This doesn't look good." He pointed at the laptop on the table. "Google it. Google me. You'll see I'm no asshole. This is not my doing. I'm not one of those guys who strings women along or jumps from one bed to the next." He took another step. "You know me, Amour. Nothing was a lie… Can't you trust me?"

He seemed so alone. A man surrounded by people. A man coveted all over the world. Yet, he seemed so alone. Maybe she wasn't the only one feeling vulnerable.

"Did you tell her?"

"Tell who what?"

"Your wife."

"Ex-wife," he said. "I told her I was seeing someone."

That was a surprise. "You did?" He nodded. "That's allowed?"

"Everyone involved in the contract knows about the clause. There are people listed, others who know about it too and are bound by its NDA."

"People who? You and Javi?"

"Yes. The lawyers, Jules and her… confidante." That was… intriguing. "A few of my friends are listed."

"Knox?" He nodded. "You live together. I suppose that makes it difficult to hide a relationship from him."

"I don't need to hide anything from Knox. Me and my group have violated more than a few NDAs between ourselves. I trust them."

"What about me?"

"I trust you."

"No, your divorce contract, if you can tell every woman you're attracted to—"

"One." She frowned, but he smiled. "The contract allows me to tell one woman. I can tell as many as I like that we have to keep the relationship a secret. I can only tell one why."

"And you told me," she said. "I was your one."

"Yeah," he muttered, strolling around the end of the table. "You're the only woman I've wanted to tell. The only one I've been close to."

"I don't like lies."

"I haven't lied," he said, his fingertips skimming the tabletop as he came around, getting closer every second. "The baby isn't mine. I don't want Jules." He stopped up close. "There's only one woman I want."

"I don't want to…" She sank around slowly, putting her back to the table as he came even closer. Right up close until their bodies touched. "I don't want to fall for a line. I'm old enough to know better."

"If it was a line, and I only wanted you for sex, why would I be here?"

Good point. He'd had her. Chasing her now wouldn't be worth the aggravation.

"Zach…"

He stooped closer. "Mm?"

Her hands slid onto his body beneath his jacket.

"I won't ever call you Zee-Bee."

His laugh was almost silent. "And here I thought you couldn't get any more perfect."

Scooping his hands around her jaw, he tipped her head back and joined their mouths.

NINE

"ZACH," SHE WHISPERED, breaking their kiss. "We can't... Someone will come in."

"Javi's at the door," he said, boosting her up onto the desk, brushing his lips across hers again. "Trust me."

"How do you know he's there?"

Running his hands up her thighs, he pushed her skirt over the elastic of her hold-ups. "Trust me, Amour."

That soft voice, the way he leaned in, the sensation of his breath on her cheek before he stooped to kiss her neck... oh, God, she lost her sense, and herself.

"This is not fair," she murmured, her head sinking back, her fingers combing into his hair.

"I want you."

The growl shook her from within. She could trust him or push him away. Somehow, even knowing the latter would be better for them both, she straightened her toes to drop her shoes and let her legs coil around him.

"We won't stay secret long if I can't stay quiet."

"Your pleasure would be worth losing half the company for."

Shit, that was hot. He'd give it up for her? Take the risk, just to be inside her? She pushed his jacket from his shoulders and loosened his tie. She wanted to touch him, needed to put her hands on his body. Her own hurried fingers were eager to undo his buttons. She didn't even think about what he was doing until his mouth closed around her nipple.

Her jacket was gone, her shirt open, her breast scooped from its cup.

"Don't take your time," she said, knowing his default was tormenting her for a long time before uniting them.

Lifting her hips from the table, she started to wriggle out of her panties, but he took over, sliding them down her legs and off.

Then his mouth was back on her, his hands squeezing her ass, pulling her to the edge of the desk. Her muscles clenched tight, holding her at an angle to stay as close to his kiss as possible. How she missed his bed. If she'd stayed…

Opening his pants, he was already hard, so hard, so hot, so in need.

"Fuck me," she panted, her head pushed back by his as he tasted her throat. "Please, baby… Shit, Zach… Kintyre."

His mouth rose to her lips for another quick kiss. "You only use my last name when you're pissed," he said, kissing her on a laugh.

"Get your cock in me and I'll stop being pissed."

"Yes, ma'am," he said, planting a hand on the table by her hip as he slid himself home.

Oh, it felt good, too good. This was why she made excuses for him, why she thought the best, why she trusted his word, even if it was naïve.

"Better?" he asked.

Bliss radiated through her. "Much."

He pulled back and slid in again. Their smiles rose in unison.

"You like that?"

"I like that," she said, raising her legs around him, locking them at his back. "Think Javi will watch the door all day?"

"I think he'll watch it all month," he said, rocking his hips. "I pay him enough."

Her laugh became a moan as she sank down onto her back. The slow, languorous pace matched the mood in her heart. The connection needed to be appreciated while she had it. After being spoiled by him all weekend, adjusting to being without him had been tough. Tougher than it should be.

"Amour?"

Her eyes opened… just. "Don't tell me you have to get back to work."

Bowing over her, he swept her hair from her forehead. "Nothing could take me away from this moment," he murmured, kissing her brow. "Thought I lost you for a second."

"For a second, you did."

Inhaling, her body arched into their union, moving with him, holding and releasing him, savoring every tantalizing second.

Forever wasn't supposed to be on the table. But reorganizing her life appealed as the build up accelerated through her. She could live in LA. In his bed. She'd travel for work, but could come home to him, couldn't she?

"Zach," she gasped, forcing her hips closer to his. "More… Shit…"

Oh, she should be quiet. Grabbing the semi-open edge of his shirt, she pulled him down, tightening the embrace of her fingers on the fabric.

"Like it?"

"I like it…" And as he got faster, her volume got louder. "Oh, fuck, yes! I like it!" He may have snickered; she didn't care. Didn't care about yelling or the desperation in her pleading. "Zach. Zach!" Climax ripped through her, grabbing every cell of her body, driving it to its limit. "Zach!"

"I'm with you, Amour… I'm…"

His words heralded a hissing roar of surging hormones and pounding endorphins. He'd needed her. Somehow, when she blinked open her eyes, panting in unison with the man still looming over her, he seemed less alone.

"Was I too loud?"

Her question was sincere but ended with a laugh

that was joined by his.

"You were incredible."

When he slid out, she had to physically stall her lower lip from pushing out in petulance. "You know what I thought when we were together on Friday night?"

"What did you think?"

Her drowsy focus stayed on the ceiling, even as she heard him getting dressed. "That you were either the biggest player I'd ever met, or the real deal."

In time with him straightening, she rose onto her elbows.

"I'm no player."

"Then that only leaves one option."

He came back to kiss her again. "I guess it does. Come over for dinner tonight and we'll find out."

She groaned. "Ah, oh, no, see…" She eased him aside to slide off the table. "I don't have a great track record at coming to your place for dinner."

"Because you tend to stay for days?" he asked. Shimmying down her skirt, she bent over to right her shoes. He caught her hips to pull her ass against him. "I want you to stay."

Straightening up, she put her feet in her shoes. "It's complicated."

"We knew that," he said and turned her around to cup her face. "We knew it would be complicated, Amour. Come over for dinner and I'll try to explain."

"You can't explain here?"

"It will take too long and… I don't enjoy talking about it around people."

Like there was a possibility of a bug in the room or colleagues listening in? If that were true, they were in all kinds of trouble already. That said, she could understand him not wanting to wade into his personal business at work in the middle of the day.

"Okay, I'll—"

"Text me when you're done for the day," he said, going to grab her phone from further down the table. "We'll be waiting on the curb."

"We?"

"Me and a car," he said, handing over her phone. "I'll give you my number."

"I don't think that's a good idea."

"What? Texting me? Having my number?"

"Me in the back of a car with you," she said. His hungry focus was already drifting over her body. "The first time we were in a car together, you kissed me."

"And I may do that again," he said, walking her backwards to the table edge. "And again. And again…"

She laughed as he stooped to nuzzle the sensitive spot behind her ear. "Exactly the problem."

Though she was hardly immune, her arms were already snaking their way around him, signaling her surrender.

The sound of the door opening shattered the moment. Rather than turn away, he put an arm around her to hold her against him. Maybe she should've buttoned her shirt.

"Jav—"

"Yeah, I know," he said. "But you're late."

"I don't give a damn about—"

"It's okay," she said, unlocking her phone to put it in his hand. "I'll text you."

As he put his number in her phone, she finished buttoning her shirt and threaded his tie under his collar.

"I called my phone," he said, leaning over to put hers on the table as she tied his tie. "That means I have your number, so if you don't text—"

"I'll text," she said, wiping the remnants of her gloss from his lips. "I kind of made a mess." Her fingers tried their best to comb his hair back into order. "Sorry."

"We'll make a bigger mess later," he said, ducking to kiss her.

His steps away were decisive, until she noticed his jacket on the floor. "Zach," she said, swiping it up to hand it over when he turned. She didn't expect him to come back and kiss her again. "Go… Get out of here."

Her smile had to be as broad as his. Would be difficult to play the stoic CEO in whatever meeting he was late for if he was still thinking about her.

She ran her hands through her hair as he strode on

out. He went past Javier who swung the door over behind them, though he ducked back in, wearing a smirk of his own.

"Smells like sex in here."

"I'll open a window," she said, folding her arms.

He disappeared snickering. If it smelled of sex in the room, she didn't want to think about what she and Zach smelled like. She'd go to the gym at lunch. Have a shower. A long shower… If she was going to Zach's after work, they'd probably… No, they had to talk. Be serious. Be honest. She wouldn't be distracted by his hands, his mouth, his incredible tongue.

Stalking to the window, she opened one and another then went to turn the air conditioning to max. She needed to calm down. To cool her hormones. Shit. What was she getting herself into?

TEN

"ZACH," SHE SAID, laughing, pushing his hand from her shirt buttons as they tripped up the stairs to his house that evening. "We're here to talk."

"We'll talk," he said, using his fingerprint to open the door then sweeping her around into his arms to take her inside.

"Oh, why do I even try?"

Fighting it was pointless. They had to quench their need. Had to find a way over the apex of their desire to get to the talking. She couldn't talk with him fizzing up her endorphins.

His mouth found hers as her shoe caught on the stairs and she fell. Or she would've fallen if he wasn't braced to catch her. Not that he stopped them going down. No, he lowered her onto the stairs, keeping their mouths linked while she went to work opening his shirt.

"Folks around here sure are friendly," a woman said.

She gasped, pushing away from the kiss.

Zach gave her no space. "Shit," he hissed.

"What the hell?" she said, socking his shoulder. "How many more hot women are going to show on your doorstep? Is she pregnant too?"

"No," the stranger said, popping something from

her cupped palm into her mouth. "I think my fiancé should know before this guy, don't you? I'll let him down gentle, Zach, honey."

Muttering to himself, Zach boosted himself up and offered a hand to pull her onto her feet. "I'm going to guess you're not alone."

"Good guess," the stranger said.

As Zach straightened himself up, she scrutinized the woman. "Wait, I know you…" The stranger's brows bobbed. "How do I—"

"Lilya Kearns meet Roxanna Kyst," he said, fed up.

"Oh my God!"

"Yep," Roxie said, but was quick to look at Zach. "Zachary Kintyre."

He left her side to go kiss Roxie's cheek. "Nice to see you."

Roxie nudged him. "I don't believe you mean that."

"Where is he?"

"Out back."

"Alone?"

Roxie smiled. "Think that's likely?"

"Hmm." He glanced at her. "I'll just—"

"Want me to get rid of her?" Roxie asked.

"No!" he exclaimed, offended. "Shit, Rox—"

"We're fine," Roxie said, waving him away. "You go. We girls have things to talk about." Zach disappeared into the living room, buttoning his shirt. "I met your dad."

"My dad's been dead for twenty-five years."

"Then I didn't meet your dad," Roxie said, tossing another thing into her mouth before extending her hand. "Nut?"

"No, thank you."

Roxie nodded in a turn to head deeper into the house. "If Frank isn't your—"

"He's my uncle."

The huddle of men outside in the backyard was an intriguing sight. But Roxie didn't go to them. She took a right and went into the kitchen. Another woman was already in there, wearing an apron, dicing something.

"Jane, this is Lilya. Lilya, Jane."

"Nice to meet you," she said, suddenly conscious of how many people were present. "Who are all—"

"This is her house," Roxie said, pointing a nut at Jane before hopping onto a stool.

"This is not my house," Jane whispered toward her friend then smiled at her. "Roxie and I have lived together for years."

"Right," she said, recognizing her too. "You were in the news last week for—" She gasped. "You married Knox Collier!" Another gasp as she recoiled in understanding. "Shit, he said Knox, I didn't know he…" Her eyes met Roxie's. "This is Knox Collier's house."

"Uh huh."

"Oh my God." CollCom was a media empire. Run by the Collier family, they had more money and influence than… anyone. "Oh my God!"

"That's pretty much how she reacts every day," Roxie said, gesturing at Jane again. "And she's fucking him."

"Rox," Jane chastised again and went to open cabinets. "And we didn't get married."

"You don't have to be married for half of everything to be yours," Roxie said and leaned to the side. "She's still twitchy about the money."

"Are you a friend of Zach's?" Jane asked, bringing a bottle of something over to pour it in the wok on the stove. "His girlfriend?"

"Girl—no," she said, trying to shrug it off. "Nothing. Oh, no, I'm nothing. Nothing like that. I'm just a friend."

"Wow," Roxie said, sinking back, finishing her nuts. "Thanks for the heads up. I'm engaged to one of his friends. I had no idea they were that close."

"I didn't mean that we—I—"

"You're cruel," Jane whispered.

Roxie was smiling again. "She's his sex-on-the-stairs friend." Oh, God, could this be going worse? "Have you had sex on the stairs, Jane?"

"In this house? No."

"Oh," Roxie said, spinning her stool to plant her elbows on the kitchen island. "So you have had sex on other stairs? This I have to hear. With Knox?"

"Why—I…" Jane sighed and dropped her shoulders. "You enjoy flummoxing people."

"I have to keep my skills polished," Roxie said, exhaling on her fingernails to buff them on her chest.

"For your boyfriend?" Jane asked. "Fiancé, excuse me."

"How long have you been Zach's sex-on-the-stairs friend?" Roxie asked. "Have you moved in?"

"We've known each other a week," she murmured, intrigued by what was happening in the yard.

The men outside were standing on the other side of the pool. How many were there? Plenty and the conversation wasn't at all animated. They were serious. Somber. Stern. Mad at each other or the situation? If they were giving Zach a hard time—

"It's best to let them get it out of the way," Roxie said, leaning back into her line of vision. "This is what they do."

"They?"

"They went to school together," Roxie said. "When things happen, they appear in each other's lives. Sometimes they stick around. Sometimes there's a video call in the middle of the night. They keep in touch."

"They care about each other."

"As Jane puts it, they care about each other."

"Who are they?"

"Okay, I'll tell you, but you'll never remember," Roxie said, hopping off her stool to come put an arm around her while pointing at those outside. "Next to Zach is Matteo Reid. On his other side is Xavien Rourke, then it's Zane Dyce, Knox Collier, and my guy, Zairn Lomond. Rourke and Dyce are single… Though sometimes when he pisses me off, I threaten to rent mine out, so don't hesitate to give me an offer." Roxie returned to her stool. "Believe it or not, that's not even all of them. Gauge is having his own crisis in Chicago… lucky guy. And Kinloch's lost in Montana somewhere."

"Kinloch," she murmured then snapped to. "Kinloch Gramercy-Peake?"

Wearing another smile, Roxie peeked at her friend.

"Merci was right."

"Merci?"

"Reid's fiancée. Seeing Kinloch with them surprised her too. He owns Gramercy and is selling Gramercy."

"Yeah, and there are only three realistic bids," she said, going to the stool next to Roxie's as the brunette lunged over the counter to snag the bag of nuts. "Two of which are out in that yard."

"All's fair in love and business... That's their motto."

"They came because of... the pregnancy. The baby."

"Yep."

"Because Julietta is pregnant and they think it's his."

"Think?"

Shit. Oops.

"They're good friends," she said. "To care about their friend."

"We've had a raft of it recently," Roxie said.

"It?"

"Get togethers," she said, sliding off her stool. "There's a bar outside?"

"Oh, uh, yes."

"Come with me," Roxie said, already crossing to the patio to descend into the sunken lanai area.

Hurrying to follow the confident woman to the bar in the corner, she expected the men to move or acknowledge them, but they didn't.

"What do you drink?" Roxie asked. "Cocktails?"

"I... whatever is fine."

"I've been practicing," Roxie said, scooping some ice into a cocktail shaker. "My guy knows every cocktail and mixed drink like ever invented. It's an interesting party trick."

The women carried on working. Roxie was mixing drinks. Jane was cooking. The men were conversing. She was... nothing. Superfluous.

"You know, I don't have to stay," she said and took a step backwards. "There's a lot going on here tonight. I should leave you all to..."

"No, stay."

"No," she said, retreating further. "I'll call later."

Going into the house, she couldn't believe it had taken so long to excuse herself. What the hell kind of secret relationship could they have if she loitered at his house during his personal time with his friends?

"Lilya!" Roxie called after her, but she kept going.

At least until she rounded into the foyer and saw the profile of someone on the doorstep. "Shit," she hissed and leaped back into the living room.

"Good," Roxie said. "You decided to stay—"

"Reeve Crosby is at the door."

"Who?" Roxie asked, peeking around the partition wall that doubled as her visual shield. "Who's Reeve Crosby?"

"A reporter," she whispered, closing her eyes. "This is insane."

"Don't worry, honey, I got this." Roxie strutted into the foyer before she could get hold of her. A few seconds went by and then Roxie declared, "Mr. Crosby!"

She fell back against the wall, closing her eyes.

"You're… You're Roxanne Kyst," Crosby's voice carried from the threshold.

"Indeed I am. Meaning I'm supposed to be here. Are you supposed to be here?"

"I'm looking for a comment on my story—"

"Really?" Roxie asked with exaggerated excitement. At least, she hoped it was exaggerated. "Cool. What's your story about?" Her tone changed. "Wait, it's not… Are you writing something negative about my friends?"

"Why are you here, Ms. Kyst? Isn't it right that Zachary Kintyre lives here?"

"Yep," Roxie said. "We're having a torrid affair."

Her mouth fell open. Had she really just…?

"This is Knox Collier's house," Crosby said.

"Yeah, they take turns."

"You okay?"

Her eyes opened to a gang of frowning men by the patio doors.

She focused on Zach, the one she knew. "Roxie's talking to a reporter," she whispered, gesturing toward the foyer.

"Shit," one guy said, rolling his eyes.

Wait, that was… That was Zairn Lomond.

"Piece of cake," Roxie said, suddenly striding past her.

"Lola… What did you tell them this time?"

"Nothing," Roxie said, all feigned innocence, slowly sashaying her way to him. "There may or may not be a story later about your friends tag-teaming me… You should text Salad."

"Mm hmm," Zairn said. "My crisis event, ladies and gentlemen."

"Hey, Skippy, you put a ring on it. No buyer's remorse allowed. No returns, refunds, or exchanges."

"Why was he here?" Zach asked. "Why was Crosby here?"

"Yeah, Knox," Roxie said, taking Zairn's hand to coil his arm around her as she nestled against him. "Why are reporters showing up at your house?"

"You know, at this point, it's potluck which of us they're writing about," Knox said. Shit, that really was Knox Collier. "Where's Jane?"

"Kitchen," Roxie said. "She's cooking dinner."

"She doesn't have to do that."

"She wants to do that," Roxie said. "Don't make her feel bad about it. It's how she makes sense of the world. Oh, and by the way, we were talking, and Jane wants you to put this house in her name. Solely and completely her name."

"Consider it done," he said, distracted.

Roxie's broad smile was joined by a brow bob aimed

at her. "See."

The guy hadn't paused or questioned, just agreed. It didn't seem to bother him anyway, but he was already striding into the kitchen. Maybe they'd talk more about it in there.

"Is he gone?" she asked. "The reporter?"

"From the doorstep? Yeah," Roxie said. "Just give him a minute to clear the driveway. He'll probably hang around outside for a while though. They do that. Lurk and linger. If there's a back way out, that would be a better escape route."

The men drifted outside. Zairn took Roxie with him until Zach was the only one left.

"Escape route?"

"It was Crosby," she said, staying against the wall as he approached. "Is he writing about Julietta?"

"I don't know. Maybe."

"Her father was in your office—"

"I know, it's complicated," he said, sighing at the words as he laid a hand on the wall above her head. "I say that a lot, don't I?"

"You do," she said, touching his torso. "Your friends care about you."

"Yeah, they do. And Jules sent out a homing beacon with that press release."

"Like the bat signal."

He laughed. "I guess. They won't stay long… unless we need them to stay."

"This is Knox Collier's house. Knox Collier lives here."

"Yeah, him and Jane will probably stick around. Don't think they've settled on whether to make LA or New York their base."

"Oh, the conundrums first-world billionaires face. You can just pluck a city from the sky."

"Knox can. He's a Collier."

"You know, when you said your friend's name was Knox, it didn't occur to me he'd be that Knox."

"His friendship gives us a little wiggle room. It was

no mistake Jules chose a Collier competitor to release the story."

"Because if it was CollCom, he might've intercepted it?"

"Maybe," he said, his hand sliding higher so he came in closer. "But we did have our phones off all weekend."

"Your choice," she said, enjoying his smile. "Is there a back way out?"

His smile disappeared. "You were trying to leave."

"Your friends are here and Roxie already saw… This is supposed to be a secret."

"These are my friends," he said, his loose hand finding hers. "They're an extension of me. Trusting me is trusting them."

"This isn't about me. I'm not bound by any clause. It's not my company at risk."

"It's not at risk in this house. Not while it's just us."

"But if Reeve Crosby got in—"

"The only way he gets in is if he breaks in. Then he has bigger problems to worry about. And actually, in a way, my friends give us cover."

She lowered her voice. "Yeah. You failed to mention that you're best friends with another Gramercy bidder… And that you're best friends with Kinloch Gramercy-Peake."

His head bobbed. "Yeah, okay, maybe I failed to mention that." His fingers tightened on hers. "When would I have slipped it into conversation?" Okay, maybe that was valid. "I don't usually talk business in bed with a woman." Her chin rose. "Jules, I didn't discuss it with her. If you want to talk business in bed, we'll talk business in bed." He tried to restrain his smile but failed. "If that's the hot talk that gets you off…"

He laughed and she shoved him, he rocked back.

"Will you call me later?"

"No," he said, backing up to pull her from the wall. "Because you're going to stay and have dinner with us."

"That's not a good idea."

"Crosby is outside, and there's no back door. You're a prisoner until the coast is clear."

Which could be in five minutes or five hours.

"I could get in trouble for being here."

"How?" he asked, walking backward, guiding her toward the patio.

"I'm supposed to be impartial. After your audit is done, we're going to RCI."

Matteo Reid's company.

"I think if I can be here with him and remain professional when it's required, you can too."

"Professional?"

He stopped just at the threshold of the patio. "It's possible there may be a development on the horizon."

"A development?"

"In the Gramercy sale."

"Someone's dropping out?"

"You want to know?" he asked and tucked her hair behind her ear. "Start the business talk at the table and you ladies won't get a word in edgeways."

She smiled. "I don't think anyone could stop Roxie being heard."

"Uh, who's talking about me?" Roxie hollered from the patio.

Zairn was the one behind the bar when they went out.

"You just proved her point, Rox," Zach said, putting an arm around her. "Who votes Lilya stays for dinner?"

Various yays and nods went around the group.

Roxie raised both arms. "That settles it. You're staying."

ELEVEN

"I THINK IT'S a brilliant idea."

"It would be a public event," Zach said. "A global affair. Maybe they'll make it a national holiday. Rourke, you've got pull there."

"Not *would* be," Roxie said. "*Will* be. It's going to happen."

"Lo—"

"No, I don't see why it shouldn't," she said. "One governor can't hold that much sway."

"Over what happens in his own state, he does," Zairn said, curling his fingers around the back of Roxie's neck.

"Says something when you're too risqué for Vegas. Shit."

Seated around the patio dining table, dinner was done. The eating part anyway. Everyone was full and night had descended around them.

"People have bachelor parties in Vegas every day," Roxie said. "There must be a hundred every night."

"Yeah, but not like Zairn's."

"First thing you have to do is decide on a best man," Rourke said. "Who do you want to plan your last night of freedom?"

"I'll plan it," Roxie said, flashing the table a smile and getting a polite laugh. "I'll dance. I'll strip. And I'll screw the groom."

"How is that different from any other night of the week?" Zairn asked, shaking her a little.

"There's gotta be some kind of tradeoff system," Rourke said. "Reid stood up for Kintyre."

"Yeah, the only one who's followed through so far," Knox said. "Reid asked you…"

Rourke nodded. "Doesn't count if it doesn't happen. I lost all my deposits on his bachelor party."

"Imagine how much he lost on the wedding," Zach said.

A phone buzzed and Rourke was the one to lean back to type into his device.

"You know that thing will give you migraines," Roxie said.

Rourke glanced around the table. Everyone was looking at him. "What?"

"It's this woman," Dyce said as Rourke went back to his typing. "She's got him all tied up."

"Oh, is that what it is?" Roxie asked. "Maybe we should spend some time on that. Who is she? Will it be a quadruple wedding?"

"We should get back to the best man talk," Rourke said, putting the phone down. "We've never had three guys engaged at the same time."

"Uh, Knox is not engaged," Jane said, reaching for her almost empty wineglass.

Knox caught her hand to divert it to his lips. "Yet."

"Okay, well, yet," Jane said, literally sinking into a swoon when her eyes met those of the man kissing her knuckles.

That was sweet. Love that was so undeniable. She smiled at them. It gave everyone hope. Gave her hope anyway.

"I think we should talk about the baby first," Roxie declared, pushing her shoulders back.

Now all eyes turned to Zach. Even those of the enraptured couple. She squirmed. This was private. She didn't want to be there while he was discussing it with his close friends. Would he tell them the truth?

"Is Jules still living in your place?" Rourke asked. "Or is it her place now?"

"Kesley's living there with her," Zairn said. "When she's not in our hotel suites."

"You haven't been intimate with Julianna for over two years," Roxie said. "The baby's not yours."

"No," he said without hesitation, turning the base of his glass on the table.

"Why cover for her?"

"Maybe because they were married," Jane said. "She has her reasons for telling the press the baby is his. If she's hurt or in trouble, they were married, there has to be some love still there." A bunch of snorts and snickers went around the table. "What?"

"Kintyre's the most stand-up guy there is," Rourke said. "Jules walked all over him while they were married. Nothing's changed since."

"That's not true."

"So tell the world the truth," Rourke said, pointing toward the house. "Go see if Crosby's still out there. Hell, send out an all-points bulletin from Collier's phone. He's got AP on speed dial. Get the truth out there now."

"He can't do that," Zairn said.

"Why? Why not?"

"Contract runs another four months," Reid muttered.

The guy didn't say much. She wasn't sure he was actually listening most of the time.

"Fuck the contract."

"Yeah, that's a great idea," Dyce said. "You can't be anywhere near Diva, Rourke. How would you feel about sharing Mosaic with her? Huh?"

"We dated; we weren't married."

"Which only makes it worse," Knox said. "If Jules can get her claws into Eclipse, she will just to make a point. Just to be the noose around his neck. Can any of us say we'd like our exes dipping in and out of our business decisions whenever they chose?"

A few eyes dropped, everyone pondered for a few seconds.

"The contract requires you do nothing to disparage, damage, or impugn her reputation. You are under a gag order. She can say anything she wants."

"It's insanity," Reid said. "Why did you sign it?"

Zach raised a hand. "Please, let's not go back there. It's done. This is where we are."

"Make it clear to her there will be payback."

"I'm not getting into that. I don't want revenge."

"Do you?" Roxie asked.

All eyes routed to her.

"Me?"

"Yeah," Roxie said. "You're hiding your relationship. Sneaking around like you're the other woman while this entitled—"

"Lola."

"No," Roxie said, pushing Zairn's hand from her leg. "I wouldn't stand for it. You think I'd let anyone go around making up lies about you?"

"We're getting married," he said. "And you make up lies about us all the time."

"That's different."

"As always with Miss Roxanna Kyst."

"Don't," Roxie said and bounced around in her chair to look him in the eye. "You want to fight about this? Let's fight."

"I don't want anyone to fight," Zach said. "None of us can change this. It's where we are."

"Your girlfriend can."

"You know I can fix this," Knox muttered without lifting his head. "You know it takes one phone call."

"And we all end up in court," Kintyre said. "I told you we're playing this straight."

"Soon as the contract's up, the gloves come off," Knox said. "I won't need your permission then."

"You want to get in a dogfight?"

"It's embarrassing you think anyone could match me," Knox said, picking up Jane's hand to kiss it before rising. "Another drink, Blossom?"

"We didn't buy the wine."

Knox snickered and glanced back at her on route to the bar. "He's living in our house rent free, but if it'll make you happy, I'll give him the two thousand bucks."

Jane's glass stopped halfway to her mouth. For a moment, she just blinked at it, then quickly put it down. "This wine cost two thous—Roxie stop drinking it."

"You suck his cock, honey, he can buy the wine."

There was something refreshing about Roxie. So many of the people in her life were conservative and starched. The men around the table could probably identify with that kind of corporate environment. Someone telling it like it was every once in a while, was a required reality check for everyone.

"I see what you see in her, Mr. Lomond," she said without considering the words.

"Wow," Roxie said, grabbing her fiancé's thigh. "She called you Mr. Lomond and hit on me in the same sentence. Let's take her home."

"No pets. We're not home enough to feed them," Zairn said, pulling Roxie over to kiss her hair. "It's Zairn or just Z in this company, Lilya."

"Outside this company, you have to be all prim about it, because your guy hasn't grown a set."

"Roxie," Jane scolded.

"Your uncle was at Reid's engagement party, Lilya," Zairn said. "He's an interesting man."

"You've met before."

Zairn smiled. "We have. Several times. How's Nathan doing?"

"We broke up."

"A while ago from how I understand it," he said. "He's in the club so often, his contribution pays the power bill."

"He's in a difficult place in his life."

"Ranby Kearns was supposed to be his birthright, then his dad sold to your Uncle Frank."

"He still works for the company."

"Yeah, he's Frank's right-hand man… Bother you?"

She snickered. "If you're looking for palace intrigue,

you'll be disappointed. I left Boston after we broke up. They can eat each other at the top, that's not for me."

"You don't want it?"

"Is Julietta's child going to inherit Eclipse?" Roxie interjected, picking up her wine. "If the child's going to grow up believing you're its daddy, Zach, it's got to get something, right?"

"She has a point," she said. Roxie opened an appreciative hand her way. "Not that the child should inherit Eclipse, but that the truth will have to come out eventually. You can't let this child believe you're its father unless you plan to be its father. And if you are planning to do that, you can't pull the rug out from under the little guy."

"Nothing's the baby's fault," Jane said.

"And who said trusting the women on the inside would change our dynamic?"

"The child has to know, the world has to know, before it's born."

"We don't disagree."

"And who knows, maybe you'll have your own babies one day," Jane said, smiling, her eyes flicking back and forth between them.

"They've known each other a week, honey," Roxie said, patting her friend's hand. "Give them a minute."

"Known each other a week, but she's already on the inside," Rourke said. "You sure you can trust her at our table?"

"He's allowed one," Dyce said.

"Yeah, and he picked her already. You thinking with your head or your cock? 'Cause my cock thinks things around her too."

"Does it matter?" Zach asked as Knox returned to the table with two drinks. "She won't tell anyone, and it's not like I've had dates lining up."

"Because you chose not to pursue anything," Zairn said. "You made a choice to wait the year out."

And then she came along and ruined everything.

"We can trust Lilya," Zach said. "I trust her. We're together. She knows what's going on."

Together? Were they together? Given all he'd trusted

her with, she couldn't exactly call them casual.

"Guess that's why I'm out of rubbers," Knox said. "Saw my bathroom was upside down. Figured you raided it."

"Yeah, sorry."

"It's okay, we don't use 'em anymore."

"Knox!" Jane whined. "Do you have to tell everyone about our sex life?"

"Blossom, I'm a man with the world's biggest megaphone planted in every home, business, vehicle, retail and leisure facility in the world. Be grateful I haven't taken out a full-page ad or a hundred of them." He kissed her shoulder. "And you lived with Roxie, she talks about sex all day and all night."

After a moment of apparent reflection, Jane laughed and leaned against him. "You used to ask me how many rubbers were left in my nightstand."

"Was my way of checking I didn't have other men to ruin."

"If I used that benchmark, you've been a busy guy since the last time I was here."

"Difference is, you were in the Chicago apartment alone."

"Until Roxie came home."

"I was there by then. And with Z in New York, RK didn't have a cock to ride. I doubt they use condoms anyway."

"We don't," Roxie said, offering the addition.

Condoms. They hadn't used a condom at work. Why was she just thinking about that now? It hadn't occurred to her at the time. Not for a second.

She was on the pill, so pregnancy wasn't a problem, but what a sign of trust. Zach hadn't been with a woman for two years. The chances he had some nasty infection were low. But he hadn't even asked about her sexual history, he just trusted her.

Her hand slid off the glass table onto his leg. Anyone who cared to look would see. She wasn't ashamed. Let them look.

"If she's on the inside, she must know about the Baker," Rourke said.

Everyone stilled, except Zach.

His hand came down over hers. "We haven't got to that yet."

TWELVE

"I DON'T KNOW the Baker," Roxie said.

"Busybody," Knox murmured under his breath, his whisper of a smile matching Roxie's.

Private joke? Apparently.

"You don't need to know," Zairn said, pushing his chair back. "It's time for us to go."

"Oh, are you leaving?" Jane asked and turned to Knox. "Are we leaving? We are spending the night together, aren't we? Are we? We don't have to, if you don't want. You're home, you want your space. I can give you space. Rox, I may—"

"Yes, we're spending the night together, Blossom. We're spending every night together from here on out."

Roxie leaned in at her friend's side. "He says that then jets off to Italy."

"Maybe I will jet off to Italy, RK. Unlike your guy, I'll take my girl with me. Your guy needs a break from you, like rehab, every once in a while."

"Yep, this is true." The beauty released a melodramatic sigh, stopping just short of laying the back of her hand on her forehead. "I'm his addiction… But we've done it in Italy," Roxie said on a fake huff. "We don't need to go there together."

"Italy, Blossom?"

Jane just smiled. "I love you already. You don't need to impress me."

When their eyes met, something private passed between them and they leaned in to share a brief kiss. It was sweet. This was a tight-knit group with obvious history. Comfort surrounded them, ease, the aura was warm and cozy, safe.

"Where was the first place you two had sex, Lilya?" Roxie asked. "Was it here?"

She glanced at Zach who just shrugged.

"Yeah," she said, slowly switching her focus. "Upstairs."

"In his bed?" Roxie asked and she nodded. "Jane's first time with Knox was here too. In a bed upstairs." Roxie glared at her fiancé. "How come our first time was on a floor? A closet floor?"

"In Italy."

"I didn't say it wasn't a classy floor."

"A floor is a floor. You can't contain yourself, Lola. Is it my fault I'm your drug?" he teased, turning her claim on its head.

"Reid, where was your first time with Merci?" Jane asked.

"We don't talk about that." Roxie was quick to jump in. "That is not a good story. Not a good story at all. Did you say it was time to go, Casanova?" While stroking Jane's hair, Roxie stood. "Are you coming with us or staying here?"

As Jane stood, she touched Knox. "Can't they stay?"

"There's not enough room for—"

"If we're done, we'll hit the road," Rourke said as he and Dyce stood. "You need us to stick around?"

"No," Zach said, going to shake hands. "I appreciate you coming."

"We're always at the end of the phone and it's a good drive."

"Drop me at the airport?" Reid asked. "I have a jet ready and waiting."

"Aww, he wants to get back to Merci. Give her a hug from us."

Everyone said their goodbyes until only the three couples remained.

"Now can they stay?" Jane asked. "Roxie is my best friend, I don't want—"

"You don't have to sell me, Blossom. Invite anyone you want to stay," Knox said, running his fingers through the ends of her hair. "It's your house… or it will be when the paperwork gets here in the morning."

"What does that mean?" Jane asked and flipped to her friend. "What did you do?"

Roxie put Zairn's hand on her shoulder and held it there, forcing him to follow when she sashayed away. "Come on, baby, let's reenact our first time… in a bed. We'll call it a do over. Gives you a chance to try improving your score."

Knox put an arm around Jane, taking her away from the table. "Goodnight."

And then there were two.

"Should I call a cab?" she asked, stacking their plates. "I'll help you clean up and—"

"No, leave that. A service will come by in the morning." Of course it would. "Stay the night," he said, threading their fingers together. "Stay the night with me."

Any doubt she had about spending the night dwindled in the ecstasy of his kiss. It was a kiss that didn't break on their journey upstairs and into his room. Their need hadn't gone far and quickly consumed them both. Sating their hungers had to come before satisfying her curiosity.

THIRTEEN

LYING IN THE streak of moonlight breaking through the gap in the curtains, carnal sounds from another room echoed along the hall.

"No one will get much sleep tonight," she said, shifting her head on his shoulder.

"Maybe it's time for me to get my own place."

"I don't mind," she said, brushing her knuckles back and forth on his chest. "I like Roxie and Jane seems sweet."

"She is. Not the type any of us thought Knox would end up with."

A scream joined a yelp and then there was silence.

"It's like being back in college… Although back then, the guys wanted to outdo each other." Her lips curled. "You're competitive men, aren't you?"

There was a pause before a snicker. "Yeah, you ready again or…"

Rolling over, she propped her upper arm on his shoulder, resting her head on her hand. "Tell me about the Baker."

"Talk about a gear change," he said. "We don't need to talk about that in bed."

"Maybe not, but when else are we guaranteed time alone?"

Not at work. Not at dinner if they were going to be sharing with Zach's friends for the foreseeable future. In the back of a car? Maybe. But how long was the story? Would they be driving in circles for days?

"Julietta values her career above everything else. She craves the fame. Relies on it. I didn't see it when we got together, I didn't understand how much attention she needed."

"More than you could give?"

"More than any one person could give," he said. "She has to be the center of the world. The center of everything. I did what I could, but…"

"But…?"

"Knox and I have been friends so long, I forget who he is. We all grew up with the Colliers. Those of us who didn't have tables to go to for holidays ended up around the Collier table more often than not. It meant a lot to us. That they were kind people, flamboyant sometimes, sure, Mimi especially but… They were family to us. Their connections didn't matter. They didn't talk about it and we didn't ask. Maybe that's what comes with being such old money, they didn't care about name dropping or showing off."

Listening closer, her head shook a little on her fist. "What does that have to do with your marriage? With Julietta? She wanted you to use your connection to the Colliers for her career?"

"Oh, that was a fight almost every day of the week. Knox was polite, Cam too, though she quickly figured out he'd been gone from the game a long time. Caspian's almost impossible to get on the phone… Thena was patient, when she didn't have to be, and Mimi was… Mimi, Knox's grandmother." His head tilted. "She's a lot like Roxie."

"Tells it like it is?"

"Yeah," he said. "Says what others might be thinking but wouldn't dare say out loud."

"Not a bad way to be."

"No," he said, opening his fingers in her hair. "Unless you're married to a woman as sensitive as Julietta. She's everything you'd expect a high maintenance woman to be. We called Rourke's ex Diva, but Julietta gave her a run for her money. There were tears and tantrums, her feelings were hurt, she needed to be coddled."

"Couldn't be fun."

"Well, she wouldn't act like that in front of the Colliers. She'd be a consummate hostess or party-guest. Behind closed doors though…"

He'd dealt with the fallout by himself. "I suppose, when you're married, you should be allowed to be your true self in front of your partner. Isn't that where you can express your emotions even if they're negative?"

"Yes," he said. "I agree. A marriage is supposed to be a place of safety and sanctuary for each individual."

"But it has to be fair too. It can't be just one person taking and the other receiving. It has to go both ways."

"Space in the marriage was something I gave up early on. I didn't need the same level of attention Jules did. I didn't mind supporting my wife, dealing with her demons. Her ability to be so close to her emotions was one of the things that drew me to her initially. On the flip side of those tantrums, she could be spontaneous, vivacious, expressive."

"All the things you don't get on a day-to-day basis in the office."

"Right."

As she'd thought about the conservative environment earlier. "But something changed, it had to change…" And that brought them back to the original question. "Who is the Baker?"

He took a deep breath. "When she figured out I wasn't going to use my relationship with the Colliers or Zairn or anyone else to further her career, she went looking elsewhere."

She frowned. "Elsewhere?"

"With her insecurities comes a need to be needed, to be pursued, I suppose. She chases that excitement… What I didn't know before I married her was just how far she was willing to go to secure a role." This didn't sound good, and he paused for quite a while before continuing. "There's a guy. Another guy. A guy who was willing to use his connections to secure her roles. In fact, he's the guy bankrolling the movies, so he can get her almost any role she wants."

"Oh my God," she said, sitting up. "She cheated on you?"

He smiled and made eye contact with her for the first time in a while. "It wasn't about cheating. Yes, they had sex. She got what she wanted, and he did too, but…"

Another long pause.

She dipped her head. "But…?"

"Her marriage was the least of their concerns. He's married. Older than her with kids of his own. Remember how I told you Julietta's reputation was everything to her? Well, this guy's got one of his own he protects just as fiercely."

"Oh my God," she murmured, absorbing this truth. "I can't believe it. It's so…"

"Shakespearian," he said on a snicker and sat up to touch her face. "It's okay, baby, it didn't hurt me. My pride maybe, but I knew about it a while before I confronted her. She gave me the tears and all the usual platitudes as she begged forgiveness."

"Did you forgive her?"

"Yeah," he said. "And then I filed for divorce. Irreconcilable differences."

"You could've buried her. Her reputation and his too."

"I could've, yeah. I had to pull more than one of the guys back from the brink a few times."

"You didn't let them help you?"

"It wasn't about helping me. She didn't have anything I wanted, anything I needed. All I wanted to do was protect Eclipse. Every time she asked for something, I gave her it. I just wanted it to be over."

"No wonder, she broke your heart."

"No, see, that's the thing," he said, his touch trailing down her body. "I didn't care. Even when she was a mess, begging forgiveness, I realized, I didn't care. I didn't care that she was with another guy. I wasn't hurt or upset. At some point along the way, I'd just… stopped caring. I didn't feel hurt or hate, I was just done. We should never have gotten married in the first place. It happened fast, we rushed into it. But whatever we felt at the beginning, it wasn't enough to build a marriage on."

"Is that why you chose not to pursue a relationship for the year required in the contract?" As Zairn had said. "You didn't want to rush into anything again?"

"Maybe. Being with Jules was a rollercoaster. I might have been done with the relationship, but that didn't mean I wasn't exhausted. I needed a break."

"Then I came along and wrecked that," she said and winced. "I'm sorry I asked you to dinner."

He caught her face to pull their lips together for a kiss. "I'm sorry I didn't jump on the chance when you first presented it. I've had a break. I've had all the alone time I need. We're not just talking the last eight months; it was two years without a relationship. Two years on my own. I needed it. I did. But I don't need it anymore."

"You told your friends we're together."

"Aren't we?"

"Until my Eclipse contract is up."

"Maybe that's all we need," he said. "I like you and I want to be with you, but we don't have to put more pressure on this than there needs to be. I have a habit of running into things without looking both ways. It's my default to do the responsible, the respectful thing." And he shouldn't feel the need to build a lasting relationship with every woman he slept with. "We should take this a day at a time. Let's just be together."

Actually… "That sounds nice," she said. "In so many areas of our lives, there are expectations, requirements. Someone always needs something from us."

"Maybe this is the one place we don't expect or require anything."

"I like that," she said and kissed him before backing off. "Why do you call him the Baker?"

He smiled. "Because he makes her dough rise."

She laughed. "That's funny." Pushing him onto his back, she climbed onto him again. "Let's find out if something else will rise for us right here."

"Yes, ma'am," he said, scooping her hair out of the way to join their mouths.

FOURTEEN

FOR THE NEXT three weeks, life trundled along. At work by day, they didn't see much of each other. And each evening, she went out the back of Eclipse and into a car that took her to Zach's. They were playing with fire, no doubt about it. Her colleagues were already whispering about her and probably suspected she was fraternizing with someone. They'd never guess who. Never guess it was the CEO of the company they were there to audit... would they? To appease their suspicions, she really should spend a few days in the hotel, like everything was business as usual.

But being with him felt too good.

Their life together, surrounded by his friends, was the happiest she'd ever lived. Maybe it was the man or the perpetual sun, but everything felt right and well in the world.

Roxie had disappeared for a few days the previous week. Something to do with Zander Gauge's crisis in Chicago. They all rejoiced on her return, even Knox, though he was better at hiding it.

"Anyone home?" she called out as she closed the front door behind her.

Jane and Roxie were sometimes there when she got back from work. The guys rarely were. Though there were times she had the place to herself. When no one called back, she assumed this was another of those times.

A glass of wine. Maybe a soak in the tub. Zach wouldn't be long; she'd wait for him before eating. Properly anyway. She went into the kitchen and snagged a few grapes. Not exactly a firm foundation for her stomach, but the wine wouldn't care.

She pulled open one of the pocket doors enough to slip out onto the patio, intending to go to the bar. Only a couple of steps closer, she stopped.

Sitting in the lanai, with her own glass of wine, was Julietta Ines-Kintyre. Right there. In front of her. Alone.

Shit.

"He said there was someone, but I didn't believe him," the sophisticated beauty said, assessing her as she sipped. "Not until I found out he was leaving the office so early every day. He never does that unless he's seeing someone… At the start of the relationship anyway, you'll soon become an office widow, just like I was."

What should she say? Deny it? Defend him? Apologize? Why was her tendency leaning toward the latter? They were divorced. Separated. Julietta had cheated on him and lied to the press about the paternity of her child.

Yep, that was what she needed. A quick rundown of the woman's crimes removed all hint of contrition.

"What do you want?" she asked because the interloper had to be there for a reason.

"You don't understand him."

"Oh, God," she said, deliberately rolling her eyes. "Okay, I don't understand him, and you don't need to be here."

"I'm allowed to be here. We have an understanding," Julietta said, enjoying another drink.

"Is that good for the baby?"

"So he did tell you we're expecting?"

Keeping a straight face was tough. Thank goodness Roxie wasn't there.

"The entire world knows. You announced it in the press."

Though interest had waned since the initial spike. As was always the way with media moods.

"He has to support his child."

"And he will," she said because telling her it was BS might be a step too far before talking to Zach about how they should play it. "Is that why you came here? For money?"

"He gives me plenty of money."

"I'm sure he does."

As did the man who bolstered her career no doubt, especially if he was the father of the baby.

"I came here to talk to you," Julietta said, leaning forward to put her glass on the fireplace. "Would you sit down?"

The house wasn't hers, yet Julietta spoke with utter entitlement. That probably came with being such a coveted actress. Confidence oozed from the beauty, and why shouldn't it? A whole squad of people probably told her how perfect and magnificent she was every day.

"What do you want to talk about?" she asked, folding her arms, showing she had no intention of sitting down. "Are you here to warn me off? To feed me some tale of tragedy?"

"No," Julietta said, her smile wry. "You want to fuck my husband? Fuck my husband. I don't care."

While Zach was always eager to remind her of the "*ex*" part of that title, Julietta neglected it with ease.

"You're divorced."

"Yes. For now."

Okay, that was disconcerting. "You think you'll get back together? That he'll wake up one day and want you again?" She snickered. "He doesn't regret divorcing you."

"Oh, he will... When I get my hands on half of his precious baby."

"Eclipse. That's what you want? His company?"

"I don't care about his company, and he knows I don't care about his company. What I care about is... leverage." Julietta glided to her feet. Like an elegant swan, she coasted toward her and up the lanai stairs. "I wanted to meet you. Now I have."

"Yes, now you have."

"If you don't want to talk, I'll wait until you're feeling more... receptive."

"You do that."

Keeping stoic wasn't easy when Julietta's smile became so amused. "Oh, men are so predictable." She sighed. "You are everything I need."

The beauty touched the end of her nose and continued into the house. Like she owned the place, Julietta strolled past the kitchen and through the living room. Backing up, she kept an eye on the stairs, ensuring the unwelcome guest didn't take more liberties and go up. She couldn't see the front door, but after a minute or more, she relaxed, assured the woman wasn't snooping in the rest of the house.

That meeting was... unsettling. If Julietta had a plan, she was a part of it, and that couldn't mean anything good.

She paced a while then drank some wine.

What would Roxie do?

She didn't have to wonder and rushed to grab her phone from her purse to dial. Please say Roxie's phone was charged. Zairn made it his mission to keep his intended's phone battery full, but Roxie didn't make that job easy.

"Hey, honey," Roxie said, inspiring her relief. "You doing okay?"

"I think I need to talk to Knox."

"You think?" She didn't enjoy talking to the Collier... or even looking directly at him. "What happened? What's going on? Are you with Zach? You can't be 'cause he has Knox's number—" Roxie's voice changed. "No, Knox is fine, honey. It's Lilya. You've got Jane worried. We're at the club. Come meet us."

"The club?"

"Crimson."

"Oh, I can't come to Crimson."

Roxie laughed. "They listen to me around here... These days anyway. Wasn't always that way in LA. Remind me to tell you that story sometime."

"I don't think it would be a good idea for me to—"

"Come on, Zach can meet you here." If the shit hadn't hit the fan by the time he was done at the office. "We serve coffee and fruit drinks if you don't want alcohol," Roxie said, "but it sounds like you could use a cocktail. Your driver will be in the driveway. He can wait downstairs and take you home any time you want."

"But if Knox—"

"I told you Jane is here, right? Jane, Knox's better half. She's like Knox's kryptonite. If something has happened or you've fucked up, there's no one better than Jane to break the news."

The woman had a point.

"Let me get changed."

"Good girl."

FIFTEEN

"YEAH, IT COULD be bad," Roxie said, pondering. "It could be very bad."

The Crimson LA nightclub had private pods in the middle of their VIP area. It was like a living room, right there in the center of an exclusive club. With couches and a coffee table, Roxie had an app on her phone to control the music, its volume, and the temperature too. So she'd been able to recount her run in with Julietta with relative ease. Conversation wasn't something she'd usually anticipate in a typical noisy nightclub. But in a Crimson LA private pod, Roxie Kyst controlled all.

"Something is off."

"Yeah," Roxie said. "Could be she wants to scare you or cause friction between you and Zach."

"Why would she be lying in wait like that?" Jane asked. "It's creepy. Any of us could've been there. How did she get in?"

"Their little posse all have access to each other's security networks," Roxie muttered, still reflective. "Someone probably authorized her at some point during the marriage and no one ever revoked that clearance."

The pod door opened and two men came in: Knox and Zairn.

"That's something I would get on right away," Jane said. "That's really unsettling… I don't think I want to stay there now."

"Stay where?" Knox asked, sitting next to his girlfriend on the long couch.

Jane accepted his kiss but squeezed his thigh as he settled. "Why does Julietta have access to your house?"

"Your house, and does she? Kintyre might've revoked it after her last unwelcome visit."

"Can you check, please?" Jane asked as he fished his phone from his pocket.

While he went about typing and swiping, Zairn sat with Roxie in the armchair just big enough for the two of them.

"Is she a Queen?"

"Julietta? Yeah," Zairn said to his fiancée. "Last I heard."

"Can you undo that, please?"

"You said please, which I know isn't easy for you, Empress, but that's not my call."

"How the hell isn't that your call?" Roxie asked. "You own the building. Every Crimson building. They're called 'Crimson Queens.' Doesn't it follow that the guy who hands out the title—"

"Rouge owns every Crimson building, and I didn't say I was unable to do it, I said it wasn't my call."

"So whose call is it?"

"Kintyre's," both Zairn and Knox said together.

"We don't mess with each other's women. When it comes time to include or exclude, we leave that to the guy who's fucked her."

"Very scientific," Roxie said, laying her hands on the arm her fiancé draped across her lap.

"If she's a Queen, she'll be at the dinner," Jane said.

On an animated inhale, Roxie sat bolt upright. "Oooh, if she's a Queen, she'll be at the dinner." Excited, Roxie tugged Zairn's sleeve. "Stop all this talk of kicking her out the club, Casanova. The dinner's next weekend and I want Lilya to come. Make her a Queen."

"That's Kintyre's call."

"No, you're fucking me," Roxie stated. "That means you take care of me, and I want you to take care of Lilya. Kintyre will say yes anyway, he's nutty about her."

"Then it won't hurt to check, will it?" Zairn asked. "You know, I've been working all day, you could try the, 'how was your day, dear?' opener once in a while."

"We've been working on edits all day and you didn't ask me, did you? Ha, see, two-way street, Skippy. You might make more money than I do, but that doesn't make my contribution any less significant. This uterus over here will bear your children."

"If I choose to put one in it."

"Who is that?" Jane asked, pointing at something on Knox's phone.

"My mom."

"Why doesn't it say that?"

"'Cause that's not how she's saved on my phone," Knox said and shifted to look at her. "You want to know if I've got ex-girlfriends in here?"

"No," Jane said and exhaled as she turned to Roxie. "No sex on the stairs for us."

Roxie laughed. "I'll stand guard."

"You want to have sex on the stairs?" Knox asked, confused.

"Not now I know your mother could walk in without warning."

"She never shows up at the house."

Zairn smiled, caressing his fiancée's outer thigh. "If Thena wants your attention, she summons you. You go to her, not the other way around."

"And the front of the house is glass," Knox said. "Anyone walking up there can see the stairs inside whether they have clearance or not."

"Get it switched out for Dyce glass," Zairn said.

"No point if we're selling, then it will be Kintyre's problem."

The guys enjoyed their amusement.

"Kintyre is buying your house?" she asked.

"We'll have to go back to New York eventually," Roxie said. "Maybe you should ask him to relocate, get the

Julietta problem off your doorstep."

"The Julietta problem?" Zairn asked. "You want to explain that?"

"No," she said, quickly drawing Roxie and Jane's attention. "It's nothing."

"It's nothing," Roxie said and Jane nodded. "Nothing at all."

SIXTEEN

ZACH DIDN'T EVEN ask why she was at Crimson; he just came in and joined the conversation.

They talked, they laughed, they even danced a little, and then it was time to go home.

In the Crimson basement, they approached two black cars, there, ready and waiting.

With her fingers linked between Zach's, she'd follow him into whatever car he chose. She scanned for cameras. Were they allowed to hold hands?

"Girls call shotgun," Roxie said, scampering away from Zairn to snag Jane's arm.

"Girls?" Zairn asked. "You brewing a caper, babe?"

"Never you mind," Roxie said, turning to go backward as the driver opened the door. "Come on, Lilya."

"You don't have—"

"I'm fine," she said, letting go of Zach to join Roxie and Jane in the backseat of the first car.

No one said a word until the vehicle started moving.

"We need to know Julietta's game," Roxie said, carrying on their conversation without missing a beat. "You don't want the guys to know?"

"Not if she's trying to make trouble with me and Zach. I don't want to play that game."

"The first thing we have to do is figure out the game," Roxie said. "She's definitely up to something."

"You think?"

"I think she's pregnant with another man's child, but wants Zach, a guy from our crew, to take responsibility for it."

"You know, you were right," she said, admitting her failing. "The night we were eating when all the guys were here. I have let Zach down."

"You've known him a month. Back then you'd been together a week. You couldn't have known you'd still be together now."

Her frustration was quickly becoming anger. "Julietta has gagged him. But I never signed anything, doesn't that leave me free to say whatever I want?"

"You can't announce to the media he's not the father," Jane said. "If you do that, she'll announce your relationship and then she gets half of Eclipse."

"You and Knox been talking about it?"

Jane squirmed. "I wanted to know why he didn't just fix it like he can."

"He's too close to Zach," Roxie said. "But Julietta only gets half of Eclipse if the relationship is confirmed. How likely do we think that is?"

"If Julietta leaked it to the press, they'd have to stop seeing each other. Completely," Jane said. "At least until the contract is up."

"We wouldn't be able to keep going like we have."

"No," Roxie agreed, "because the press can be relentless. They'd follow you everywhere, him too, until they confirmed it themselves."

"So any time we tried to get together, someone would be lying in wait, ready to expose the affair."

"It's so stupid," Jane said. "It's not even an affair. Reid was right. Why did Zach sign that contract?"

"Something we can work on later," Roxie said, retrieving champagne from the fridge. "First, we need to figure out who the daddy is."

"It feels wrong," Jane said, picking up a couple of flutes as Roxie worked the cork out of the bottle. "To snoop into someone's business like that."

Roxie paused. "Is it right that Julietta put her pregnancy on Zach?" No, it wasn't. And she did have her reasons. "If we find out who the father is, completely by ourselves, without help from Zach or his known group of friends, we're not violating any contract, are we? And who says what we do with that information? We don't have to expose it. Maybe it just helps us understand why Julietta is doing what she's doing."

"And what game she's playing."

"Right." The cork popped from the bottle. They all ducked, though it only fell to the floor. "So we figure it out together as innocent members of the public."

"How do we do that?" Jane asked, raising the flutes for Roxie to fill them.

She handed one off to her and picked up another.

"We start by figuring out what she does all day," Roxie said. "And who she has in her life."

"You want to follow her around?"

"If it comes to it, but I say we start somewhere more static. We need a car."

Not very static and not very explanatory. "We all live in New York," she said. "I don't own a car."

"What's wrong with our regular cars?" Jane asked.

"That the guys provide?" Roxie asked. "That come with a driver who might report back to our men? Our men, who may be subpoenaed to stand up in court if this all goes sideways?"

The smirk Roxie wore was enough to provoke her laugh.

Jane was more cautious. "You think we'll end up in court?"

"No, honey," Roxie said, putting an arm around her friend to give her a squeeze. "You're too pretty to go to prison."

"I've been to jail in LA."

"Hmm," Roxie said, her lips moving to the side for a moment. "And see how quick Zairn got us out? Knox will have you out in half that time now he's crazy in love with you."

"I don't want anyone—"

"No one is going to jail," Roxie said. "The worst they'll do is fine us."

"Or give half of Eclipse to Julietta."

"If you don't want to do this, we won't," Roxie said, making eye contact with them both, one after the other. "But Julietta's playing a game and right now, she holds all the cards. If she confronts you or Zach, if she threatens to out the relationship..." Which some could argue she'd already done by the way she showed up at the house. "We need something in our arsenal, some way to fight back."

By not telling Zach about the visit, she liked to think they were protecting him. If she and her cohorts found out something themselves, without the help of the men, they could use it to protect him further. Protect him from anything Julietta might try to leverage.

"We need a car," she said, nodding once in agreement.

After holding her breath for another second, Jane sighed in resignation. "Knox has cars."

"Great! Where?"

"In his garage," Jane said.

"Where's that?"

"Around the side of the house, there's a tunnel into it on the next plot."

"He has a separate plot of land just for his cars?" she asked, deadpan.

Roxie laughed. "What a life, huh?" She said it. "If anyone asks, we're having a spa day on Friday."

She'd have to sneak away from Chester, but that shouldn't be too difficult. "Okay, and that's relevant to our plan?"

"Yes," Roxie said. "Because we take the morning for all the glam nonsense, freeing up the rest of the day."

"For what?"

"We're going in."

"Where?"

"Kintyre's house."

"We've been staying at..."

As Jane trailed off, she figured it out too. "Julietta's house. You want to go into Julietta's?"

"We take a car, so we can go where we want without anyone keeping track of us. As cover, we claim the beauty treatments take all day, then we drive over to Julietta's and wait for her to go out."

"How do you know she will?"

Jane gasped. "The Queen Dinner is on Friday!"

"Bingo!" Roxie said. "It's not just a dinner, there's a whole protracted drinks reception thing at the start. Then there's food and more alcohol during the speeches and entertainment."

"Julietta is a Queen, but maybe she doesn't want to go to something connected to her ex-husband's best friend."

"Maybe not under regular circumstances," Roxie said, tapping a forefinger on her glass. "But she'll go because her best friend needs her there."

"Her best friend, who—"

"Kesley Walsh."

"The actress?"

"Zairn's ex who is living with Julietta in Kintyre's house," Roxie said. "No way Kesley misses the dinner she planned. Trust me, it's the highlight of her year."

"We know they'll be out."

"Yes, and chances are they have their own beauty regime for an event like the Queen Dinner."

"So they might go out early," she said.

"And if they don't?" Jane asked. "We'd be late to the drinks reception, late to the dinner."

Raising her glass, Roxie exaggerated a mock hair toss. "I'm the Empress, honey. The party waits for me… and I've got to make an entrance."

SEVENTEEN

"FEELS LIKE WE'RE in a movie," Jane said, sliding down in the front passenger seat.

They'd driven around for quite a while. Down this lane and that, into more than one private driveway, trying to find the best vantage point to view the Kintyre marital home.

On a ridge higher than the residence, they were by a construction site about a football field away from Kintyre's. Although their view was of the back corner, they could see that the front gate was open at the end of the long driveway.

"In a good way?" she asked, an arm hooked over the shoulders of the two front seats.

"We should've brought the Cadillac," Roxie said, opening her purse. "That's a movie car."

Except they needed something discreet, not something flashy.

"Will Knox be mad?" she asked, laying a hand on Jane's arm. "That we took his car?"

"He doesn't care about things," Jane said.

Roxie twisted around. "And he doesn't get mad at Jane 'cause he lurves her."

The smile that raised Jane's lips was joined by color in her cheeks. "Can you tease me about that when Zairn loves you the same?"

"Not the same. My guy wants to throttle me more than he wants to jump me." Roxie caught a tendril of Jane's hair to tuck it behind her ear. "You're Knox's delicate blossom."

More color. "He's not always gentle with me."

"Oh," Roxie said, exaggerating her lean in. "Tell us more."

Jane's eyes flicked back and forth between them. Though it looked like she was frightened and timid, when she eventually exhaled, she laughed. "I don't hear you talking about your sex life."

"I talk about my sex life all the time," Roxie said, rummaging in her purse. "Usually to the world's media." Tugging something out, she raised it up. "Ah ha!"

"Oh my God," Jane said as Roxie took the binoculars to her eyes. "Where did you get those?"

"They're Toria's."

"Of course they are."

"Isn't Toria coming to LA?" she asked. "I hear you talk about her all the time." And to her. "Doesn't she want to be here?"

"She's in New York living the life," Roxie said. "If we ever worried about her adjusting, those concerns are gone now. She's living like she's in '*Sex in the City*' full throttle."

Since moving to New York herself, she hadn't exactly embraced all it offered. Not in the dating pool anyway. Was that something she'd do on returning home? Zach got her back into the swing of being with someone again. Somehow, the thought of random sex and date after date with strangers wasn't appealing.

"What do you see?" Jane asked. "Is there anyone in the house?"

"I don't know, I'm waiting," Roxie said, still using the binoculars. "Waiting… Looking…"

They hung there in a silence so protracted that when a cellphone rang, all three of them jumped.

"Did you match your ringtone to—" Jane stopped when Roxie took a cellphone from her purse. "That's not your phone! That's Zairn's phone!"

"Yeah, you really think my phone will still have any

juice this late in the day?" Roxie asked and answered, handing the binoculars back to her. "Zairn Lomond's phone... I'm his assistant." The crazy woman winked at them. "No, absolutely not... Of course we're aware of it— he's aware of it... A quote?"

Jane grabbed her friend's arm, shaking her head. "No," she whispered. "No, Roxie."

"I couldn't possibly give you an official quote," Roxie said. "No, he's otherwise engaged... With Roxie? Yes, absolutely with Roxie." Her laugh was quiet, but Jane wasn't as amused and still shook her head. "Oh, they're always at it... He neglects his professional responsibilities for her all the time... No, Roxie is the one pushing for him to be focused... If he stopped making the big bucks, she'd be out of there like a shot."

"Roxanna," Jane hissed.

"It's not like he's wanting for female attention... No, he has all the assistants on call for when Roxie doesn't satisfy him—"

Jane snatched the phone away and hung it up. "Stop doing that to him!"

"It's funny," Roxie said, taking the phone back. "It helps the business."

"For him to be a love rat?"

"A playboy with a high appetite," Roxie said, doing something on the phone. "Yes. And I always tell the world it was me in my streams. The public like someone to screw around with the media once in a while."

"I can't believe you took his phone."

"I gave mine to Tibbs. I didn't leave him cut off."

"And he didn't question that? Your phone won't be charged."

"Tibbs is a sweetheart; he'll charge it. It's Z's fault, he tells the staff to give me whatever I want. This time it happened to be his phone."

"Can't he track it?"

"I disabled the GPS," Roxie said, holding the phone between them. "Who knows which is Kintyre's?"

"Oh my God," Jane said. "That's the security app. How they access each other's security systems!"

"Why do you think I needed the phone?" Roxie asked. "We have to get into Kintyre's house somehow. You don't think it's easier to have authorized access than bring a SWAT team down on our heads?"

"Oh, God," Jane said, burying her face in her hands.

"Why don't you try users?" she said when Roxie struggled to find the address as they all seemed to be coded. "See if you can authorize a person rather than going through the address."

"Good plan," Roxie said, returning to the menu and selecting users before scrolling down and selecting one without hesitation.

"LB?"

"Lola Bunny," Jane explained, her hands dropping from her face. "You'll regret this, Rox. It's a violation of trust. It's a—"

"Oh, wow," she murmured, watching the screen as Roxie scrolled down.

"Wow what?" Jane asked, grabbing Roxie's wrist to pull the device closer. "You're authorized… everywhere."

Every single listing under Roxie's username was green: authorized.

"He said my clearance was higher than his," Roxie muttered. "What an asshole." But she was smiling and quickly came out of the app to go back into contacts and raised the phone to her ear. "I need him… I don't care what he's doing, Tibbs. I need him now… Yes, pull him… Now, Tibbs." And Roxie wasn't usually so serious. Something it appeared Jane was thinking too when their eyes met. "Nothing… No, Casanova, I…" Closing her eyes, Roxie took a deep breath in. "I love you… That's it—oh, and don't let me forget I owe you a blowjob." She hung up and dropped the phone back into her bag. "Where were we?"

Her pointed look at the binoculars reminded her of their purpose. The house. Right. Looking through the lenses, she adjusted them to bring the image into focus. The white concrete structure had a multi-level yard. Gorgeous. Glass with a terrace all the way around the upper floor. Perfection… that suited Julietta.

"I don't see anyone."

"It's a beautiful house," Jane said.

"And it could've been yours, Lil," Roxie said.

"I'm not surprised he gave it to her," she said, checking out the closest bedroom. Was that the master? Their marital bed. "He's like that."

"Kind? Generous?"

"Both," she said just as a figure walked into the room. "Someone is there. It's not Julietta, it's… It looks like Kesley Walsh." Though she only knew her from the movies. Another person walked in, and another. With equipment. "Oh, God."

"What?" Jane asked, snatching the binoculars to look for herself.

"Looks like the beauty regime came to them."

"Shit," Roxie said, folding her arms. "We should've known."

"Julietta's there too… And a guy with a zillion garment bags."

"Guess we're settling in," she said.

"Yeah," Roxie said, straightening in her seat to put the car into gear. "We'll need supplies… Pink's anyone?"

"We have dinner later."

"Yeah, in like four hours," Roxie said. "I didn't have lunch."

"Okay, but no ketchup on Knox's seats. I don't know if he lets people eat in his car."

"Relax. The point is not to leave evidence," Roxie said. "We're in stealth mode. Don't worry so much."

"Someone has to," Jane said, putting on her seatbelt. "I think you're worse when Toria's not around."

Roxie landed a grin on her friend. "Someone has to make up for the deficit."

"No, they don't. Let's try sane and normal sometime."

"Where's the fun in that?" Roxie asked, speeding down the hill.

EIGHTEEN

WITH THEIR FOOD and drinks, they went back to their vantage point and watched for four and a half hours. Eventually, the beauty crew cleared out, and a limo showed up in the driveway. It still took the two actresses another twenty minutes to finally walk out Kintyre's front door.

"That was exhausting," Jane said as Roxie navigated them down the hill. "Feels like we should be on our way home not just getting started… What are we looking for exactly?"

"Dirt," Roxie said. "And a clue about the father of Julietta's baby."

"It could be anyone," she said. "Maybe a one-night stand."

"Maybe."

Although Zach had told her about the Baker, that didn't mean the Baker was the father. Was the affair still going on? Maybe. Zach hadn't revealed the guy's identity, and she didn't expect him to, she'd certainly never ask. Putting him in that position would be unfair. And until that moment, knowing would just have been nosiness anyway.

But if Julietta was bringing the fight to them, knowing bolstered their position. And who knew? Maybe they could find out something Zach didn't know, something that could protect him from Julietta's game-playing.

With full entitlement, Roxie drove up the driveway but parked at the side of the house. Opposite where they'd been watching. Good thing about all the driving around initially, they knew the best places to hide from prying, or curious, eyes.

"I don't know how I get into these things," Jane muttered as they got out of the car.

"We're not doing anything wrong," Roxie said, coming around the hood. "We're not going to steal anything. We just want to look around."

"Why do they feel like famous last words?"

She had to admit, even her heart was racing as they crept around to the door. Just because the women were gone didn't mean there wouldn't be staff around. They'd done their best to count those they'd seen. Roxie was great at coming up with the nicknames that helped them keep track. But staff could come in at any moment.

As Roxie put her hand on the panel by the door, she held her breath. If it didn't open, did that mean the cops would be called? Security? Someone would be notified of an intruder—

The door clicked and the three of them looked at each other.

It was Roxie who took the plunge and pushed it open.

"See," Roxie said, striding inside. "Piece of cake."

But the danger wasn't done with yet.

"Let's work fast. We still have to change into our dresses for the dinner," Jane said. "We can't be too long." The wide hallway led straight into an open plan living space with a kitchen by the rear. "Where will we find evidence? The trash?"

"We'll have to split up," Roxie said. "I'll go upstairs."

She left them to run up the beautiful staircase and Jane split off to go into the kitchen.

If she'd been married and the relationship ended in divorce, the marital home would be the last thing on her wish list. Standing there, looking out the glass walls to the backyard, she imagined them there. Julietta and Zach. And

Julietta didn't have to imagine; she'd lived it. Sitting outside in the evening, talking under the stars. Entertaining their friends. Barbecue, drinks, music, festivities. How many birthdays had they shared there? How many anniversaries? Had they bought the house together or was it Zach's before the marriage?

"Lilya?"

Jane's voice brought her out of her daze. "Sorry, yes," she said and went to the kitchen. "Find anything?"

"They like wine," Jane said. "There's nothing interesting in the fridge. We should look upstairs in her bathroom cabinet."

"Okay," she said, going up the stairs with Jane. "What for? To find out if she's on medication?"

"She should be taking prenatal vitamins. Supplements for the baby." They got to the top of the stairs. "I don't know that Kesley has drunk all that wine by herself, and you said Julietta was drinking at Zach's. Is she looking after her baby?"

Coming from Jane, the question was completely genuine. Anyone else might think dirt. Might think they could use the neglect or abuse as leverage. Not Jane. Every word from her was laced with concern; she actually cared about the baby. It didn't matter that the infant wasn't connected to them, she was just that caring of a person.

They didn't know which bedroom was Julietta's. A blonde décor marked the glowing white marble of the floor. All pale shades and subtle touches. That might work if there were blasts of contrasting color or bold art pieces. As it was, the pastel just gave the place a kind of sickly feel, in her opinion.

They went into the corner room they'd been spying on not so long before.

Roxie came striding out of the closet. "This is Kesley's room," she said. "I recognize the clothes and accessories."

The three of them traipsed into the bathroom and stopped.

"Okay," Lilya said, cringing at the framed picture on the vanity. "That's kind of creepy."

A photograph of Kesley with Zairn. Obviously taken while they were together because they were embracing each other.

"It's not creepy," Roxie said, slinking over there. She picked up the picture to look closer. "It's… kind of heartbreaking."

"Don't touch things," Jane said, snatching the picture to put it back in its spot. "The more things we touch, the more evidence we leave. Where's Julietta's room?"

"Somewhere else," Roxie said, leading the way out.

Her reaction to the picture was intriguing. "It must be difficult."

"What?" Roxie asked. "Difficult for who?"

"You," she said. "Knowing other women…"

"Fantasize about my fiancé? Not especially."

"Really?"

"Jane and Toria knew him before I did, fantasized about him before I did."

"How can you be okay knowing other women throw themselves at him?"

They went into another bedroom to look around, checking nightstands, dresser drawers, closet space.

"They can throw all they want," Roxie said. "Zairn won't bite."

"Is it really possible to be that secure with a guy?"

Roxie took one of the scatter pillows from the bed to fluff it up. "You think Zach would sleep around?"

"No," she said, shaking her head. "But that's not the same. Even if he did, we're… not as committed."

"It's a fling?" Roxie asked, smiling at Jane. "Sound familiar?"

Jane came to stand at the end of the bed. "Knox and I started as a fling. Here in LA, I kissed him… and slept with him… I thought it was done, he didn't."

"I don't know what will happen with Zach and me. We're taking it a day at a time."

"Best way to do it. Zairn and I are the same, just with… intentions. Isn't everything a day at a time? We never know what's around the corner."

"Yes, but your fiancé spends half his life in

nightclubs. In the dark. Drinking. Women around, wearing not many clothes, it would be easy for him—"

"It's easy for any cheater. If someone is that kind of person, if they need the validation of sexual attention…" Roxie came around the bed, gathering them with her as she swanned on out into the hallway again. "They'll find a way. Whether they're a nightclub-owning playboy or a monk with a vow of chastity."

"True," she said.

"I trust Zairn. I love Zairn. And if he wasn't happy with me, if he wanted out of the relationship, he'd tell me." She paused with a hand on the next door handle. "Plus, you know, the world's press is always trying to trip him up and sniff out a story. If he wants to cheat on me, they'd make it extremely difficult for him to get away with it."

"And he knows Roxie isn't the type to go quietly," Jane said. "She'd take a body part or two with her if he made a fool out of her."

"Fastest thing you have to learn with a guy like Zairn, or Knox, maybe Zach too," Roxie said. "Don't believe everything you read. Take it in, process it, and then look him in the eye. If you love him, if you're in our kind of relationships, you know if your guy's lying to you." Roxie opened the door and in they went. "Ah, this is more promising."

"Knox wants to protect me all the time," Jane said, the three of them gliding into the huge bathroom. "But he'd never lie to me, not about something like that."

"Doesn't mean others wouldn't lie about him," Roxie said. "Some people will try to make a quick buck by selling a false story or trying to extort our guys. They're old pros when it comes to things like that."

Jane opened the bathroom cabinet and smiled. "She's taking the vitamins."

"They're there," Roxie said. "Doesn't mean she's taking them."

From a conversation about the openness of relationships to Roxie assuming the worst of someone else.

She smiled and processed the risk these women were taking for her. "Thank you." Rox and Jane paused to look at her. "For being here, for doing this. You both have better, safer places to be."

"You're one of us. Zach's one of us. We stick together."

Even though she might be temporary in Zach's life, these two women lived in New York too. Maybe they could maintain their friendship, no matter what happened between her and Zach.

"I wonder if she has a diary," Jane said, walking past her to go back into the bedroom.

"Does anyone keep a diary these days?" Roxie asked, following her friend.

She went too. "If they did, wouldn't it be digital?"

Jane already had the top nightstand drawer open and with a flourish and a smile, she picked up a small fabric covered, hardbound book.

"Wow," Roxie said, hurrying over. "You're like Columbo."

"We can't read it," Jane said when Roxie tried to take it.

"Why else are we here?" Roxie snagged the book from her friend to flick through it. "If she's going to write about her secret lover, isn't her diary the place to look?"

"Or if she had a one-night stand," she said. "We might not learn the guy's name, but we could narrow down the timeline."

"Yeah, except..." Roxie tipped the book upside down to show them the pages as she flicked through.

Rather than screeds of text, it appeared to be more of a daybook than a secret thoughts stash.

"So it's useless?" Jane asked, almost hopeful.

"I wouldn't say that," Roxie said, taking a more careful look. "We can see where she's been, where she's going... We should take pictures. Give me your phone."

"No!" Jane objected.

"I only have Zairn's."

"What if Knox sees? I don't hide things from him."

Except in cases of breaking and entering. Roxie looked at her. She slipped her phone from her pocket to hand it over. Roxie put the book on the bed to snap pictures of the pages.

"How far back should we go?"

"Anything could be relevant." And although she hadn't thought about it until that moment, anything they snapped could be evidence at a later date. If needed. "We'll figure it out later. Just take as many as you can."

Because they'd have to get out of there. The Annual Crimson Queen Dinner would already be in full swing. Its most valuable member hadn't yet made an appearance… They had to get out of there fast.

NINETEEN

THE QUEEN DINNER.

They changed in the car. In the club parking lot the previous week, Zairn had asked if they were cooking up a caper. It sure felt that way as they scrambled around in the car and in Kintyre's driveway zipping up silk frocks and satin gowns.

Made up. Hair fluffed. They drove to the dinner with usual Roxie flair.

When they sped up to the front of the hotel, Roxie slammed on the brakes, bringing them to a lurching halt.

"Everybody out," Roxie said as the doors opened. The valet guy waited for the key but faltered when he registered Roxie's identity. A group behind a rope line by the entrance screamed and squealed, calling Roxie's name. "Give my friend the ticket."

The other valet guy held a ticket to Jane though he was still agog staring at Roxie.

Jane tucked it away in her purse. "It's okay," she said, linking their arms to take her inside. "Rox will be there a while."

"How does she handle that attention?"

"Most are nice enough," Jane said, following the elegant signs through to the rear of the sophisticated building. "Roxie doesn't mind people. She'll take pictures and sign autographs if they ask. She doesn't think of herself as famous, famous, but with all the coverage they've had this year, people are eager to be around her. I don't think she gets how popular her streams are. She's a bona fide star. People recognize her before Zairn most of the time these days."

Three suited guards stood at a podium by double doors up ahead.

"Wow."

"Except maybe in this room," Jane said with a laugh as they reached the podium. "Jane Simmons and Lilya Kearns."

The professional smile of the central host descended to the list of names in his binder. He scanned the list once, then again, then his finger slid down the paper as he checked it a third time.

"Miss Simmons," the man said with concern. "Your name is here and I see your ruby." Jane touched it in her hair. "But I'm sorry, I don't see Miss Kearns."

"That's okay," she said and took a step back. "I shouldn't be here anyway."

"No, you should," Jane said, pulling her back to the podium. "Zairn must've updated it. He wouldn't forget."

"He's a busy guy," she said, smiling. "It's not a big deal, I'll see you back at the house."

"If you go back to the house and the guys are there, they'll just march you back down here. Roxie—"

"Roxanna Kyst?" the host asked, a little flustered. "Uh, maybe, Miss Kearns, if you have your ruby—"

"I don't have a ruby."

"Oh, she can have mine."

Before Jane could even get close to touching it, the guy showed her a hand. "Unfortunately, it doesn't work that way."

"Okay, it's really okay," she said, showing her honest smile. "My room is upstairs. I'll go and relax up there."

"No, but—"

"It's okay," she said again, sliding Jane's hand from her arm to retreat.

After a few backwards steps, just as she was about to

turn, the host tensed and grabbed his podium in both white-knuckled hands.

A voice rose from behind. "What's the holdup?"

"Roxie!" Jane said, hurrying to meet her friend. "They won't let Lilya in."

"Why not?" By now, the women were at her side. Roxie looked her up and down. "Is there some dress code I don't know about?"

"She doesn't have a ruby," Jane whispered, though not very discreetly.

"Oh!" Roxie said and widened her smile. "That's okay, I have a bunch of them."

In her ears, on her hand, though the gem in her pendant was a diamond.

"Miss Kyst…" the host said as the three women approached. "I'm sorry. The rules are very strict."

"You know, my fiancé isn't that big on strict rules. Boundaries? Yes. Rules? No."

"I understand you want—"

"Want me to call him? Better yet, want me to get him here?"

The hotel might like that.

"It's not necessary to—"

"If you make him come all the way down here, he'll be pissed. We do a lot of business with Grand hotels all over the world."

"I understand that, but Miss Walsh—"

"These are her rules? I can get her here too. She'd be more likely to call the boss man than me. It's any excuse for her."

"I would love to—"

"Listen, this is the way it is," Roxie said. "You get all three of us or we turn and walk out. Not like we don't have anywhere else in the city to party. You've heard of Crimson, right?"

"I'm sorry, I—"

"No problem," Roxie said, backing away. "We'll just—"

"No!" the host said, leaping out from behind his podium. "Please…" He gestured to the entrance, and the guards stepped aside, opening the doors as they did. "Please enjoy your evening."

"Thank you," Roxie said, nodding once. "Zairn's an incredible tipper."

Weird that she'd add that, but the susurration of conversation distracted her fast. Entering the huge ballroom, the number of people was unexpected.

"How many Queens are there?" she asked.

"I don't know," Roxie said. "This many?"

The three of them stopped under the covered perimeter to take in the room. Circular tables occupied most of the space. People were sitting, milling around, schmoozing. Maybe the partygoers were waiting for Roxie, who knew?

A pianist on the stage provided the music and servers scuttled around offering champagne. It was astounding. There had to be two hundred people present, at least.

After a few seconds, Roxie let out a short laugh. "They're like headstones to the failed relationships of our guys. Here lies this ex and that one, tried, toiled, and failed."

"When you put it like that," Jane said, "I'm not surprised they avoid it."

"Isn't it a recipe for disaster? Don't the women get jealous and catty?"

"It's a sort of rule that the most recent Queen takes the new woman under her wing when they're granted Queen status... which I guess makes you Jane and Toria's responsibility."

"Has Zairn slept with all of them?"

"God, no," Roxie said.

"Good, because that would be weird. Who came before you?"

"Uh, that's not a good story either."

"Why would—"

"Roxie!" someone called out, attracting their attention.

When the woman broke from the crowd to come over, arms open, it was more than a little uncomfortable to recognize her as Kesley Walsh. They'd been in her bathroom.

Snooping. Seen her private picture of her ex on display.

Jane took her hand; it was nice to sense the woman squirming. Maybe she wasn't the only one thinking of their felonious behavior.

Kesley pulled Roxie into a hug, and they did the double air kiss thing. Funny. Roxie so wasn't an air kiss person, it felt like theater rather than a genuine greeting.

"Everything going okay?" Roxie asked.

"Yes," Kesley said, beaming. "Everything's perfect." At least it was until the woman noticed her. "Who's your friend?"

Julietta knew her. Was Kesley that good an actress or was she really surprised?

"Lilya Kearns meet Kesley Walsh. Kesley, Lilya."

"We don't have room for extras," Kesley said. "When did she get her ruby?"

Roxie yanked off her ring and grabbed her hand to thrust it onto her finger. "Perfect! There you go, now she's engaged to him."

"I should call Zairn."

"Uh huh," Roxie said and gestured for Jane's purse. "You can absolutely do that." Jane handed it over and Roxie grabbed out Zairn's phone. "As soon as it rings, I'll answer it and grant her permission to be here. Go ahead. It's like roleplay. Let's workshop."

"You have his phone?"

"I'm sure the kitchen can rustle up enough food. Lilya can take Toria's place, she's still in New York. There. Problem solved!"

Roxie passed Kesley to greet the others baying for her attention. The woman might be full on, but she cared. About her friends. Her guy. Their livelihood. Taking on Zairn had meant taking on Crimson and all that came with it. Somehow, none of it fazed Roxie. Would it be that easy for her if she got deeper into Zach's world?

TWENTY

SHE FELT SICK. Actually sick. Maybe Kesley's unhappiness with her appearance extended into poisoning the food. Maybe it was the champagne. She'd only had two flutes, but it wasn't sitting right in her stomach.

The food had been great. She'd been fine until a few moments ago. God, she didn't want to embarrass herself or cause a scene. Being who she was, Roxie got pride of place at the central table. People stopped to talk to her regularly, even while she was eating. Rude? Yes. But Roxie didn't complain.

For a woman who didn't like to control herself around the press, she was amazingly patient and personable with individuals. Zairn had nothing to worry about with his woman out in the world. Roxie had to be the jewel of the Crimson brand and she didn't disappoint.

The background music stopped. Murmurs continued until a feedback blast from the stage silenced everyone.

"Sorry," Kesley said, tapping the microphone. "Sorry. Hello! I wanted to take the chance to thank everyone for being here." Her smile was a million megawatts. Were all actresses so glamorous? Kesley was old Hollywood gorgeous and just as refined. "It's been a wonderful night. The food was amazing, our thanks to the chef and the whole kitchen." As she clapped, the rest of the room took the cue and applauded. "The music and the décor, everything has been wonderful."

Jane turned to Roxie who sat between them. "Shouldn't you be up there doing that?"

"Why do you think you're planning my wedding?" Roxie asked, stirring her drink with a fingertip. "I couldn't organize my way out of a paper bag. This is Kesley's baby. It's fine. He'll be in my bed tonight. This is sort of her consolation prize."

"She does spend a lot of time with him," Jane said, making eye contact past her. "Kesley hangs around with Zairn a lot, especially when he's traveling."

Zairn's ex liked to take control of the dinner and had organized the whole thing. That was fine. Though maintaining such a link stopped the woman from moving on. Apparently, Kesley was clinging on to the possibility of rekindling their relationship. She had to be. Why else would she do it?

Had the woman seen Roxie and Zairn together? It was clear the pair only had eyes for each other. Unless there was some major flaw in Zairn's character that she was missing, he was besotted with his fiancée. Roxie was sure he wasn't the type to stray. Was he the type to string a woman along?

No. The couple's security was enviable. They were in love. They were forever. Roxie seemed damn sure about that.

So that led to an obvious question. "Why?"

"She likes his connections," Jane said. "And he takes care of problems for her."

Odd, but she didn't want to push. If Roxie was okay with it, she had no reason not to be.

The next round of applause interrupted their conversation. She didn't know who they were thanking or what the clapping was for, but she joined in.

A spotlight swung around as the lights dimmed. It stopped on their table, more specifically, on Roxie.

"Shit," Roxie muttered behind her static smile.

"We should've seen this coming," Jane whispered.

"Mm hmm," Roxie said as the room chanted for a speech. "Okay." She stood up and cleared her throat. "I should—"

"Come up on stage," Kesley called from the dark end of the room. "Everyone wants to see you."

"I don't need a stage!" Roxie said, kicking off her shoes and grabbing the back of her chair to stand up on it. "There, that's better! Hello!" Roxie was good at projecting her voice. "Thank you all for being here. And we owe all thanks for tonight to Kesley. Didn't she do an amazing job?"

She wouldn't have rebounded that quickly. Roxie must be used to switching it on for the masses. The woman had no idea she'd be expected to make a speech or be the focus of the room, but she bounced and went with it with enviable aplomb.

Her stomach lurched so abruptly that she grabbed for the table. The room laughed at something Roxie said and she used the sound as cover to sneak away. She needed to get to the restroom. Fast.

TWENTY-ONE

EMPTYING HER STOMACH didn't make her feel much better.

When was the last time she puked from drinking too much alcohol? It couldn't be the alcohol; they hadn't consumed much with dinner. Maybe it was her day's diet. They'd had hot dogs and soda that afternoon, not exactly the most nutritious meal. Juxtaposed with the delicate haute cuisine of the Queen Dinner, her body didn't know what to make of it all.

She scooped up some water from the faucet to rinse out her mouth and grabbed a mint from her purse. Her cheeks weren't pale, her skin not clammy. Yes, she was feeling better. Whatever the issue, it had passed.

Staying in the restroom all night wasn't an option, and if she snuck off, Roxie and Jane may worry. She got herself together and returned to the ballroom. Walking down the covered perimeter, she passed the closed double doors, surprised to see someone, a man in the shadows, his shoulder propped on a pillar, admiring the woman still standing on a chair addressing the room.

Zairn. That was Zairn.

Good. If it had been anyone else, his scrutiny would be all kinds of creepy.

She stopped beside him. He glanced her way, but only smiled.

"What are you doing over here?" she whispered. On the chair stage, Roxie regaled the enraptured room. "You waiting 'til she's done?" He nodded. The pride on his face was so filled with love it humbled her. It actually warmed her on the inside. "You really love her."

"I really do," he murmured. "She's crazy most of the time, but I love her crazy too."

"She talks about you the same way, you know. She loves you the same."

"I know," he said, transfixed even as he boosted his shoulder away from the pillar. "If you're going to tell the story, Lola, tell it right!" The room, including Roxie, turned toward his voice. "You ate all the shrimp, I got none, and that boy you blamed almost got fired."

"I told the truth in the end."

"Moral of the story?" he asked, winding through the people and tables, focused completely on his fiancée in the center of the room. "The truth will set you free?"

"Oh no," Roxie said, shaking her head and frowning. "The moral of the story is, take the time to cover your tracks. Don't get caught."

"Work smarter, not harder?"

Roxie's smile returned when he stopped by her. "Exactly, Casanova." His hand ran up the back of his fiancée's leg to disappear beneath her skirt. "You checking up on me?"

"Couldn't keep away."

"Time for bed?"

"Yeah," he said, innuendo thick in his voice, though she couldn't see his face. "Say goodnight, Lola."

Roxie dropped her hands to his shoulders. "Goodnight, Lola."

Zairn took her waist, and she hopped down from the chair. The room erupted in more applause. Maybe not as contrived as the other praise, the guests actually cheered when Zairn tipped up Roxie's chin to kiss her.

Sometimes the fairytale came true. It sure appeared that way when looking at the enamored couple. If love was an expression, it was written across both of their faces.

While the room quieted and the lights rose, she returned to the table.

"I'm going home with Zairn," Roxie said, holding onto him as she bent to put on her shoes again. "We don't want to drag Jane home though. Will you hang with her a while?"

"Yeah," she said, nodding, ignoring the roil in her belly. God, not again. What else was there to throw up? Thank goodness she had a room upstairs. An early night was in order. All the excitement screwed her system. But saying no to Roxie wasn't an option. Not after what the women had done for her that day. She forced herself to smile. Smile through it. Fake it. Aim for enthusiasm. "Absolutely."

"Toria said she was going to call," Jane said, all bright and bubbly. The innocence of her, the beautiful woman's naïveté, it could get her in a lot of trouble. Roxie would be used to supporting her friend. She didn't mind stepping into that role for the night. "I don't want her to miss everything. I've heard there will be fire eaters!"

Was that wise in a room full of perfume and taffeta?

"Wow, that will be fun."

Did that come off as genuine? It sounded better in her head.

"Okay, goodnight," Roxie said and kissed her cheek, Jane's was next.

"You need this," she said, slipping the ruby from her finger.

"Oh, yeah." Roxie slid the ring back onto her finger again. "For a minute there, Casanova, you were engaged to Lilya."

"And she needed your ring because…"

"Someone didn't put her on the list," Roxie said, swatting his chest. "And someone didn't give her a ruby. I was this close to staging a walkout."

"I'm sorry, Lilya. We have a new person on staff, some things are taking a little longer than usual."

"That's okay. It all worked out in the end."

"I thought Astrid was coming to join us this week," Roxie said, threading her fingers through Zairn's. "What happened to that?"

"Figured you knew more than I did. Toria's got her tied up in some project."

"Guess it's catching," Roxie said, smiling at the women while Zairn remained confused. "You two be safe. Z has an account with the Grand. You need anything, charge it to him."

That wasn't encouragement or even a tease. Roxie's concern was sincere; their friend didn't want them left in the lurch. The woman was always looking out for others. And Zairn? He didn't blink. His fiancée offered them the store and he just kept on admiring her without concern.

"We'll be okay," Jane said.

"Yeah, but seriously…" Roxie said, "booze, beds, the building, whatever you want."

Okay, so there was the tease. She laughed. Roxie had great timing.

They hugged and then the couple disappeared.

"Are you okay?" Jane asked.

"Am I okay? Yes, why would—"

"You disappeared during Roxie's speech."

"Yeah, something didn't agree with me." She smiled. "I'm better now."

The lights dimmed again and a circus medley rose. "Oh! I better call Toria!"

Jane rushed to the front of the table, phone already aloft. Others seemed as excited by it. She scanned around to the back of the room. The bar. Perfect.

TWENTY-TWO

MORE ALCOHOL WOULD be a bad idea. Jane flitted around with her phone on a video call to New York, sharing the fun with Toria. The bar was a nice perch to keep an eye on festivities, even if her drink was virgin.

At least it was nice until someone sidled up next to her.

"I thought it was you," Julietta said, smiling at the bartender.

Would it be rude to hiss like a cat scaring off a rival? "It's me."

"Cristal, please," Julietta said, sliding on to an adjacent stool. "Are you ready to talk?"

"What do you want to talk about? The dinner was excellent."

"Exquisite. Company was agreeable."

"For the most part," she said,

The bartender came over with Julietta's drink and disappeared just as quickly. "You work for Ranby Kearns."

"Guilty."

"Frank Kearns is your uncle."

"Also true."

"You and Nathan Ranby broke up over ownership of the company."

Slowly, her attention rounded to the beauty. "Why do you think that?"

"Am I wrong?"

"It's none of your business."

"Your children would've inherited the business. Your uncle owns the controlling share. What Frank Kearns says goes. He wanted you more involved in what was happening at the top. He tried to promote you. Has tried several times."

"What difference does any of this make to you?"

With every new statement, Julietta was erasing any guilt she may have had over their snooping earlier in the day.

"Kesley has been my friend for a long time. Things were much easier when she was with Zairn."

She smiled. "And you were with Zach? Quite the little foursome."

"I suppose you think you're a cute little sixsome. By all accounts, I hear Knox Collier is sunk. Never thought I'd see the day."

Her perfect nose pointed up in the air as she drank her champagne, oozing superiority.

"Your marriage to Zach is over."

"Yes," Julietta said, lowering the glass, a wry smile twisting her lips. "Reassure you of that often, does he?"

If this woman wanted to start with the snark, she'd be more than happy to respond in kind. Someone touched her shoulder before the words came.

Jane swept around to her side. "What are you ladies talking about?" her friend asked, perfectly polite.

"We haven't been formally introduced," Julietta said, offering Jane a hand. "Julietta Ines-Kintyre."

"Jane Simmons."

The women shared a short, slight shake, both appearing eager to be free of the physical contact.

"You know Knox Collier," Julietta said, somehow sneering at Jane though her expression didn't change.

"Yes," Jane said, glancing at her. "I know Zairn, Roxie, and Zachary Kintyre too."

"So you think."

"I'm sorry," she said. "If you have something to tell

us, please do. Otherwise, you're just being rude inviting yourself into our evening."

"You think you know Zairn… Knox, and Zachary. We all think we know them until something brings their true selves to the fore." The actress slid off her stool. "Tell Knox if he wants to start a war, Teagan will be more than happy to fight back." Another smile. "Enjoy your evening."

They watched her glide into the crowd, then made eye contact. "What does that mean?"

"I don't know."

"Who's Teagan?"

"I don't know," Jane said and raised her purse when it glowed. "My phone." She quickly retrieved it and answered. "Hey, babe… I'm still at the dinner." She gasped, her gaze darting this way and that. "Your mother is here? Oh my God! Knox, why didn't you tell me?" Jane's panic was cute, or it would be if Julietta hadn't just laid down a gauntlet. "No, I can't run away because—actually…" Jane sat on a barstool, her fingers curling around her throat. "Can you come get me…? No, because Roxie wanted to drive and…" She braced in a wince. "I'm sorry. We brought one of your cars." Her contrite guilt vanished as her mouth opened in affront and her whole body loosened. "Stop laughing at me!" The couple was adorable in such a different way to Roxie and Zairn. "I don't want to… It's LA, I don't know it, it's nighttime. Driving stresses me out. I haven't driven for years. I've been drinking too. Alcohol. I can't get a DUI with your mom in the room." Though the DUI wouldn't happen in the building, so what did that matter? "Roxie left in Zairn's car. I can get a cab, but I don't know what they'll do with your car if it's here overnight."

"I have a room upstairs," she said, laying a hand on Jane's knee to get her attention. "You can stay here with me."

"You're not coming back to Zach's?"

She shook her head. "I'm tired."

Jane returned to the phone. "Okay, well, Lilya has a room, so we'll just stay here… Roxie will come get me tomorrow… No, Kno—you don't—I will—" She lowered the phone. "He's on his way."

She laughed. "He doesn't want to spend the night

without you."

"He might do that anyway," Jane murmured, curling in closer. "Apparently, his mother is in the room."

"You've been in LA a month. You haven't met his family yet?"

"I met his brothers. Caspian at CollCom, though I don't know if he was actually paying attention or not. Cam, his younger brother, I met on Crimson Isle in the Bahamas before we came here. His parents have been away on some cruise somewhere. They just got back today. His mom skipped the dinner but is here for drinks." She exhaled, closing her eyes. "I'll make such a fool of myself. The things I've heard about her... I make a fool of myself around Knox enough, but he loves me, he has to accept I'm anxious."

"And the sex," she said and smiled. "You can distract him with sex."

"And there's that."

"If you want to go upstairs and wait for him there, we can."

"I don't want to ruin your night."

"My night was over a while ago," she said, finishing her drink and hopping off her stool. "Come on."

Jane went with her, clinging to her arm as they exited the ballroom. "Is it really lame that I'm running and hiding from my boyfriend's mother?"

"God, no. If he wants you to meet his parents, the least he could do is be present."

"Good point. Maybe we can go down together... when Knox gets here."

TWENTY-THREE

GETTING INTO THE room to free her feet from her shoes was a relief.

"Do you want a drink?" she asked, opening the minibar.

Jane shed her shoes too. "Oh no, those things cost a fortune."

"I know. But Ranby Kearns pay so…"

Jane laughed, taking the pins out of her hair, including the ruby. "Thanks, but I'm okay. I don't want to drink anymore… not if I might come across his mother. After maybe, before, not a good plan."

She grabbed some sweats and a tank from the dresser. "I don't envy you. I'm going to get changed. Be back in a minute." She nodded at the TV. "See if there's a movie on or something."

Getting out of her dress felt good. The shower tempted her, but she avoided it, electing to wash her makeup off in the sink and get changed.

She'd just pulled the tank down over her waistband when Jane shouted. "Lilya!"

Whatever the panic, it was enough to get her rushing out of the bathroom. "What? What's…?"

Jane, kneeling in the middle of the bed, nodded

blindly at the TV.

An image came up on the screen, a wedding photo. Zach and Julietta's wedding.

"…recent news about the couple expecting their first child, this new development is unexpected," a female voice said. "Reports remain unconfirmed, though we have heard from more than one source that Zach is in a new relationship… a relationship with a colleague, if our sources are accurate."

No, they so were not, but her knees buckled, and she sank onto the bottom of the bed. "Oh my God."

"No one is sure exactly how long this relationship has been going on or if it is serious or not. What is clear is he's between two women. Will he continue to lead them both on, or will he make a choice?"

Her phone rang. Jane's wasn't far behind, but neither of them moved.

"Oh, Lilya…"

Her friend's sympathy was almost pity. It settled deep in her stomach. Eclipse. He couldn't lose Eclipse.

"Surely the baby alters things," said a male voice from the TV. Images of Zach and Julietta were interspersed with muted video of them at premieres and award parties. God, they look so good together. So beautiful. Matched to a tee. "If he was seeing someone else, that woman surely has to appreciate fatherhood is going to change things for him."

"Maybe, Ted, though the couple are divorced. That can't be a path they chose lightly. If they couldn't hack being together before a child, will they manage it after? A child puts a lot of pressure on couples… on marriages. Would they get re-married?"

"The couple have been seen together in recent days," Ted said. A picture of Zach sitting with Julietta on the outer deck of a restaurant flashed up. "This was taken just two days ago. A sign of reconciliation?" More pictures of the same scene appeared. "This meeting didn't mean much when we assumed the couple were preparing to raise a child together."

"Now it seems that may not be true, or that it could be hindered by a third party in the relationship."

"Julietta remains in their marital home. It's no secret Kesley Walsh has been staying there too. But sources confirm Zachary Kintyre is indeed still living with Knox Collier."

"So maybe the reports are accurate? Do we know if anyone is staying there with him?"

"It's safe to say closer attention will be paid to the couple's movements, especially when we want to identify this mysterious other woman… Zairn Lomond's car was seen entering the property more than an hour ago." Night shots of the car driving through Knox's gates took over the images of Zach and Julietta. "Of course the famous Queen Dinner took place tonight. It's unclear if Roxie is with Zairn or if she remains at the event."

"And Knox Collier is in town, isn't he?"

"Yes, his wife has been seen around the city talking to various companies, arranging some kind of reception. Perhaps the family didn't take news of their haste well."

"They asserted the couple were not married when the first reports leaked. Whether that's true or if they've done it since is another mystery."

Both male and female laughed. "The lives of the rich and famous, huh?"

The TV muted and the remote landed on the end of the bed not far from her.

"I'm sorry, honey," Jane said.

Shock consumed her. "I can't go back there, at all."

Jane came down to hook an arm over her shoulder, leaning on her from behind in a hug. "Zach will figure it out."

"There are three months left. We can't take the risk. I won't let him risk his company."

"Maybe he thinks you're worth it. Maybe he wants you, no matter the cost."

"If he does, I have to be smarter," she said, standing up out of Jane's embrace. "I can't let him do it. He'll want to do the responsible thing. He has to realize that's defending the people in his company, the fiber of it. He can't let Julietta get her hands on it."

"Maybe if we knew who the father was…"

"This was exactly what we feared happening," she

said. "That she would find a way to leak it and then she'd get her hands on Eclipse. She's been waiting for this. Lying in wait like some sick, twisted…"

"Why?" Jane asked. "Because she still loves him?"

Her head moved in a loose shake. "I don't know, I…" Zach had said she'd pleaded after he confronted her about the affair. Julietta wanted forgiveness. Except in the yard, during her surprise visit, she hadn't cared about them sleeping together. "She told me to fuck her husband, she didn't care."

"Okay, if she doesn't want him back—"

Someone knocked on the door. Not just a polite, gentle knock either, a pounding. Urgent. Threatening.

"Blossom!"

"Oh my God," Jane said, leaping off the bed to run across the room to throw open the door.

Before it even ricocheted off the wall, Jane was already up in Knox's embrace, clinging tightly, her arms locked around his neck.

Knox came in, carrying Jane with him, and closed the door again. "You okay?" he asked her. She just nodded. "Blossom…" He soothed his girlfriend, combing his fingers into her hair. "Baby, you're okay. I got you."

"But it's so sad," Jane wailed.

She was crying? Why was she…? Oh, God, that just made her guilt worse.

"We'll fix it," Knox said, gathering her hair into his fist as he sat on the edge of the bed, arranging Jane on his lap. "I'm here now, we'll fix it."

"They can't be together; they can't see each other."

"No, they can't," Knox said, making pointed eye contact with her. "You get that, right?" Again, she nodded. "No matter what he says, no sneaking around—"

"Don't do that," Jane said, pulling back to swipe at the tears on her face. "Lilya is not the bad guy."

"I know, Blossom."

"But you're intimidating her, and she's done nothing wrong."

Knox exhaled, stroking the hair from Jane's face, his whole demeanor became softer. "You know what I get like when people I love are threatened." Jane's hand rose to his jaw. "Zach has a lot at stake here."

"Lilya doesn't want to ruin him," Jane said, caressing him. "How was she supposed to know this would happen? She knows she can't go back, her heart is breaking, and then you come in and be scary and unsupportive?"

"I'm sorry, Blossom."

"Don't say sorry to me. Say sorry to Lilya."

"He doesn't have to," she said. "I know Zach has a lot at stake. I don't want him to lose anything."

"Lose his number."

"I will."

"We'll have to pull your clearance at the house."

She nodded. "Yes, I understand."

"Why do we have to pull her clearance?"

"Because there's always a chance a third party will get into the system," she said.

"Will you fix it so they can be together, my love?" Jane asked, her hands trailing to his chest. "Please?"

"In three months, they can be."

"Not in three months. So they can be together now! Lilya will be back in New York by the time his contract is up."

"Maybe this is for the best. Get a clean break now. They can go their separate ways. No one loses anything."

"That's not what you thought about us."

"I was in love with you," Knox said. "A herd of stampeding bison couldn't have kept me from your bed."

"Maybe Zach feels the same way about Lilya."

"Maybe he does, but until—"

"So you can fix it," Jane said. "Fix it so they can be together now."

Knox exhaled.

"He can't," she said, fearing Knox might be considering something drastic. The couple looked at her, but her focus stayed on Jane. "He can't do anything because what she said downstairs—"

"Was a threat," Jane said. "Oh my God." She flew from Knox's lap. "She knew this was going to happen!"

"Wait," Knox said, standing up. "Someone threatened you?"

"No," Jane said, shaking her head as she returned to her lover's embrace. "She threatened you. Oh my God…" Almost as soon as they were around her, Jane pushed out of his arms and came to her by the TV, driving her fingers through her hair. "She was threatening my guy and I just stood there."

"Hey!" Knox barked. "Someone want to take a breath and tell me what the fuck I'm missing before I go nuclear on the whole damn town?"

Her eyes met Jane's. Telling him was risky given they didn't know how he'd react.

"If you want to talk…" she said, "I can go down to the bar and leave you alone."

"No, you can't," Knox said. "Out in public is the last place you should be right now, Lilya. Especially by yourself. Why would you want to leave?"

"Because you might be unhappy," Jane said, turning to him. "I suppose she figures it's better not to be here if you're in a rage."

"I'd never hurt you."

"I don't want to hurt you either," Jane said. "Can you maybe just accept that Julietta is trying to get you to play her game? You, Zairn, Zach, she's trying to provoke you into making a move."

"Why?"

"I don't know. For Eclipse, I guess."

"She doesn't give a shit about the company."

"Leverage," she said, suddenly struck by the memory of the word from the lanai deck at Zach's. "She wants leverage."

"Julietta?"

"Yes," she said, overcome by clarity. "Oh, I'm an idiot. She wants to use Eclipse as leverage against Zach."

"Because she knows in three months he's free and clear," Knox said. She pointed at him in agreement. "If she doesn't get her claws into something she can manipulate him with—"

"He's free to tell the truth about the baby, the Baker, everything."

Knox was startled. "He told you about the Baker?"

"You didn't tell us about the Baker," Jane said.

"He didn't tell me who he was, just broad strokes. But in three months, Zach has no reason to keep his mouth shut."

"If she exposes your relationship, that shows Zach has breached the contract," Jane said, "she gets half of Eclipse."

"And uses every ounce of that control pulling for or against him, manipulating him every day, and keeping his gag on tight. Shit."

"Sounds right."

After a tense moment of reflection, Jane went to her purse on the bed to retrieve something she then took to Knox.

"What is this?" he asked.

"The valet ticket," Jane said and put her hands on his shoulders to try boosting up. "Kiss?"

"No," he said, shaking his head. "No kiss."

"You won't miss me tonight?"

"No, because you'll be sleeping next to me."

"I can't leave Lilya here on her own."

"I'll be fine."

Knox raised an open palm. "She says she'll be fine." Jane tilted her head, curling just the tips of her fingers against him. Less than three seconds later, he groaned. "Fine. Nobody move. I'll call Marty."

"Who's Marty?" she asked as he walked away.

Jane came over. "His Tibbs."

"We need a suite at the Grand," Knox said into his phone and turned to eye his girlfriend. "Yes, I am aware." He spouted off a few more instructions, then hung up. "Marty's taking care of it."

Already he was dialing again.

"Who are you calling now?" Jane asked, going to his side to peek at his phone.

His arm curled around her shoulders automatically but gently.

"My friend," he said, his eyes locking to hers as he extended the phone to her. "A perfectly natural and normal thing to do given he's just been mauled by the media."

A call from friend to friend would be expected. Only it wouldn't be Knox on this end of the line.

"Thank you," she gasped, rushing over to snag the phone as someone answered.

"Knox?" Zach snapped.

"It's me."

And his exhale of relief put tears in her eyes. "Amour."

TWENTY-FOUR

"I'M SORRY ABOUT this," she said, dipping her head down.

"It's not your fault," Zach said. "I should've seen it coming. Where are you? I'll come—"

"At the Grand, with Jane and Knox."

"The dinner," he said on a sigh. "You're at the dinner?"

"We were. Jane and I had just come upstairs when… Roxie's already at yours with Zairn."

Jane's waving caught her attention. "We're going downstairs for a minute," she whispered.

Her smile was instant. "Meeting the in-laws?"

On a shrug, Jane sighed. "Apparently, unless I want to elope, I'll have to meet them sometime."

"Stay here, Lilya," Knox said, firm, no screwing around. "Do not leave this room."

"Okay," she said as the couple threaded their fingers together and slipped out.

"What's going on?" Zach asked on the phone.

Privacy was nice. Better than doing this with an audience. "Knox's mom is at the dinner. He's taking Jane to meet her."

"Thena can be a hard woman to please, especially

when it comes to her boys. That said, I think Mimi was worrying there would never be an heir. Jane's her ticket to security. Does she want kids?"

"Zach," she said on an exhale, sitting on the bed.

"I know. I know what you're going to say."

And he was trying to divert her from it?

"There's nothing else we can do," she said. "We have to finish this. There's no other way out that doesn't involve you losing Eclipse."

"Part of it."

"Even that part is too much. Julietta has manipulated this whole situation. Your instinct was right. You should've seen the year out. We've given her an in and she's going to use it."

"You think it's her?" he asked.

"You don't?"

"I do," he said, his tone tight. "Trouble is, I'm biased. If someone else had another explanation, I'd be happy for them to be right."

"I already have my room here at the hotel. Jane has asked Knox to stay. He's getting a suite."

"Good," he said. "That's good. I can come over and—"

"No," she said, certainty was vital. "You feel responsible for this. You're not. You did nothing wrong. We did nothing wrong." She moistened her drying lips. "But it's done now. It has to be done. We said we'd take this a day at a time—"

"If this is about my lunch with Julietta on Thursday—"

"No," she said of the pictures they'd shared on the TV. "You're entitled to lunch with whoever you want. We didn't ever say this was... I'll be back in New York in a few weeks."

"You're happy to say goodbye now?"

Her eyes closed to the heaviness inside her. "I think you're an amazing guy." Never had forever seemed so long. "One who maybe I'd want to see more of... if circumstances were different."

Maybe she was playing the martyr a little. Someone

had to. Their relationship hadn't exactly been casual, but there had always been a big question mark over whether they could have a future. Julietta had just pulled that pin for them.

"After the contract's up—"

"If you want to call me, I'll answer," she said, containing her smile. "I'll be in New York then. At RCI."

Back in her life. Her apartment. Her existence before Zach Kintyre strolled into her office.

"You travel for work, that's always been the case."

Being with him, living in his house, sleeping with him every night, it had been the happiest she'd been in a long time.

"One day at a time," she said like she had before. "For now, we have to stop seeing each other. We can't sneak around. We can't take the risk. We just can't. It would be insane to sacrifice half of your multibillion-dollar company for a few weeks of sex. You might not regret it now, but you would in the long run, when Julietta's calling every play for the rest of your life. You said at the end of the marriage that every time Julietta asked for something you surrendered it because you wanted it to be over. If you give her half of Eclipse, it will never be over. You'll never be free of her."

He cursed under his breath. "How the fuck can she screw around in our marriage and still manage to screw me after I cut ties?"

"It's not fair. You're right. You're a good man. An amazing man. I hate what she's doing to you. And to your friends."

"What is she doing to my friends?" he asked, his concern renewed.

"Nothing, I… that's something between her, Jane, and Knox. It's not my place to say anything." Although she kind of already had. "I don't want to play her game and I don't want you to play it either."

"The only solace is that she hasn't outed you," Zach said. "I can take the heat. That's nothing. Getting with her, knowing how high profile she was, I'm used to the ridiculous attention."

Though he didn't deserve to be living under siege. That was only made worse by knowing how Julietta would enjoy pulling the strings in secret.

"I had an amazing time with you," she said. "I don't regret it."

"Neither do I."

She aimed for bright and cheerful, though her smile was half-assed. "At least now you've had your rebound, you're ready to move on to the real thing. Only thing I'd suggest is waiting until the contract is up before starting anything potentially serious. Julietta's playing dirty."

"I don't think she knows any other way."

Maybe not.

Her smile faded. "Goodbye, Zach."

This really was goodbye. The lump in her chest came with the tear that trickled from her lashes.

"Goodbye, Amour."

Over as fast as it started. He'd been honest on their first date. They'd shared trust. He meant too much to her. She wanted him to have his freedom. His company. His life back. If the price for that was walking away, it wasn't too high, and she wouldn't make him feel bad for how things worked out.

TWENTY-FIVE

KNOCKING ON HER door the next morning brought her out of the shower. No one had visited since Knox and Jane said goodnight, but she checked the peephole anyway. Just in case Julietta had sent reporters.

Jane and Roxie. Shit.

She opened the door fast. "What are you doing here?" she asked, tucking in her towel as they came into the room.

"It won't do," Roxie said, propping herself by the TV on the dresser. "It won't do at all."

"What won't do?" she asked, glancing at Jane.

"Zairn's upstairs with Knox. They're hatching some plan of their own."

Wary, her neck prickled. "That could be a bad idea—"

"Teagan was a girlfriend of Cam, Knox's brother," Roxie said.

Surprised, she stumbled a couple of steps closer. "How do you know that?"

"She asked Zairn," Jane said, passing to go sit on the end of the bed.

"You just asked him?"

"Yeah," Roxie said, unapologetic. "How else would

we find out who she is? And he's smart enough to keep a lid on it around Knox."

"I was surprised too," Jane said. "But Rox has a point. Knowing that Julietta brought it up means Zairn knows what to look for. Knox would go crazy if anyone went after his baby brother. Even I wouldn't be able to keep the reins on him and he listens to me about most things… even if he then goes and does the opposite."

Roxie boosted herself up to sit on the dresser. "You underestimate your power. You'd be able to talk him down, honey; he's wild about you. But we don't need to be irritating any sore spots. Zairn will keep an eye out."

"Did you tell Zach?"

She didn't anticipate Jane's question. "No, we… I only talked to him on Knox's phone last night. I didn't tell him anything."

"Good. Zairn will keep the bulls in their chutes," Roxie said. "Leaving us to deal with the bigger issue."

"The bigger issue?"

Roxie opened her arms. "Who's the daddy?"

"Oh, God," she said, going to sink down by Jane on the bed. "Are we really going to keep doing this? Zach and I ended our relationship last night." Jane put an arm around her. "It was more difficult than I thought."

"It always is." Roxie's sympathy was appreciated. "I know it's tough, but Julietta has forced our hand on this. It would just be too risky to—"

"I know," she said, nodding. "Oh, I know. We don't plan to sneak around behind Julietta's back. There's too much at stake."

Everyone seemed eager to remind her that the relationship had to be over. Was love the difference? Her friends were with their forever people, did that skew their perspectives toward everyone being in the same position?

"What would you do if Zairn's ex was holding something like this over him?"

"Roxie's not an accurate barometer of sense."

"Do as I say," Roxie joked, "not as I do."

"Actually…" Jane said, dipping closer. "'*What would Roxie do?*' is a sort of motto for saying to hell with everything."

"Not everything," Roxie said as they laughed. "In moments of doubt, it nudges you to live wild and crazy. To care less about what people think and more about seizing the moment… It doesn't really apply here."

The laughter faded. "No, Zach's worked too hard to give up his life's work to his ex-wife. And it's more than that. I don't want her looking over his shoulder from now until forever. Eventually he'll meet someone else, probably get married and have kids. It wouldn't be right if Julietta lingered in the background of everything. He deserves to be happy… to be free."

"Yes, he does," Roxie said. "And so do you. So when we get back to New York—"

"Oh, here we go," Jane said on a sigh.

"Here we go, what?"

"You're about to tell Lilya that you'll fix her up." Jane leaned in. "Roxie's determined to pair up all her single girlfriends."

"Worked for you and Knox, didn't it?"

"That was less matchmaking and more…"

"Hot, animal attraction?" Roxie said before Jane could find the word. "Not a thing in the world wrong with that."

"Unless it loses your guy his company."

Roxie bounced off the dresser to come sit at her other side and take her hand. "You and Zach are done, it sucks, but it's where we are."

"Doesn't have to mean you're done with us," Jane said. "We will not abandon you."

"I appreciate that, but I can't be going over to Zach's. I can't be the unknown woman seen sneaking into his house."

"In Chicago, we've got the sneaking thing down." Roxie shifted their hands to her lap. "Want to come to Chicago?"

She laughed. "How would Zairn feel about you running away?"

"Oh, I do it all the time. We're only here because I ran away with Jane. He knew getting with me that the chase would never be over… keeps the passion alive."

These women were more valuable than she could express. "Thank you for the offer, but I have to finish out the contract at Eclipse."

"Yeah, if she didn't, that might raise questions."

"Just like if we stop searching for the daddy, it might raise questions. It won't answer them anyway. Zach can't go creeping around, the press will watch him like a hawk, for a few days at least. Until the next scandal distracts them."

"Knox is working on that," Jane said. "Don't break up with Zairn again."

"You broke up?"

"Only to sell papers," Roxie said on a shrug. "You weren't only with Zach for publicity, were you?"

"No!" The whole point was not to attract attention. "Why would you think—"

"It shouldn't matter if you're with Zach or not, you care about him, don't you?"

"Yes."

"Our mission isn't over. We have to figure it out."

"Who the daddy is?" she asked.

"You don't want to know?"

More than she really should. Was that natural curiosity? Something she'd feel about any mystery... or was it Zach?

"What did Zach tell you about the Baker?" Roxie asked.

Shooting to her feet, she took a step and spun around to face them. "I'm in a weird gray area right now. I don't want to betray Zach's confidence."

Roxie made a face. "She has a point."

"It might look vindictive," her other friend said. "But you ended on good terms, didn't you? You and Zach didn't fight, the end was amicable."

"Yeah," she said, drawing the word out.

"We need to do this for him."

"Rox, she might not want—"

"How many times have we protected each other? Zach means something to our guys, that makes him family," Roxie said and looked at her again. "Will you help us?"

How could she say no? Zach did mean something to

her. And he meant something to these women who'd become her friends. Was she going to walk away just because they weren't sleeping together anymore?

"Let me get dressed."

As she stood, Roxie leaped to her feet. "While you do that, I need your phone."

"Pictures," Jane explained, "of the diary."

"Right. It's on the nightstand," she said, retrieving clothes from the dresser. "Plugged into the charger."

Jane laughed. "Oh, Roxie doesn't know what a charger is. It's that long wire, like a string, connecting the wall to the shiny rectangle."

"Aren't you hilarious," Roxie drawled, deadpan.

"Zairn charges her phone," Jane said, rising and smoothing her skirt. "He's like her phone monitor."

"Which is funny if she steals his."

"I don't steal it regularly," Roxie said, leaning on the headboard when she hopped onto the bed to grab the phone. "Besides, it's not stealing, we co-own everything."

"And Roxie technically has like forty phones now. Wait 'til you get to their place in New York. When they all start ringing, it's louder than her alarm clock… which is hilarious because Zairn sets alarms on them too. He hides a bunch so she has to hunt them down one by one."

"They're not alarms, they're alerts. Most of them say, 'Call Casanova.' My guy has serious separation anxiety."

"Aww, he loves you."

"Loves driving me crazy."

Grabbing her clothes, she went into the bathroom to get ready. Hair. Makeup. Everything had to be done right. She didn't want to be drawing attention to herself if the plan was to go sleuthing. Whatever that involved. Roxie was dogged and tenacious. They'd solve the mystery with her spearheading the issue, no doubt about that.

Only thirty minutes later, she came out of the bathroom to a squeal of excitement.

"We found something," Jane said, rushing over to take her hand and lead her across the room. "Roxie's been going through the pictures."

"There are lots of lunch dates." Roxie sat with her

legs crossed in the middle of the bed. "Spa appointments. She's shooting a commercial… not anything more substantial as far as the acting goes. Modeling jobs fill the gaps…"

So far, she wasn't hearing anything useful. "And?"

Roxie held out the phone. "She has an appointment…"

Going over to take the device, she read the enlarged entry. "CComm… Thursday at two. What's CComm?"

"CollCom. The symbol next to it is Julietta's version of their logo."

Maybe if she tilted the phone and squinted. "What's underneath it? What's first strike?"

"We don't know, but it can't be good."

No, it didn't sound good. Striking wasn't often good. Not when it came from someone like Julietta Ines-Kintyre.

"So what's the plan?"

"Only one thing we can do."

Somehow, Roxie's glee increased her dubiousness. "What's that?"

"We have to go to CollCom and find out what she's up to."

"On Thursday?"

"Yep."

That left her… incredulous. "We're going to follow her without being seen?" Wow, okay, the possibilities of what might go wrong were almost endless. "How will we get in there?"

"Roxie edits there, she has credentials."

"Which we won't be using," Roxie said, startling Jane.

"Why not?"

"We won't need them. We have a master key."

"Where did you get a master key?"

Roxie stood to stroke Jane's hair. "Aww, honey, you're our master key."

"I'm your—"

"That's good," she said, inspired by Roxie's confidence. "No one's going to stop Jane, even from entering high levels or restricted areas."

"And they'd stop me," Roxie said. "People always suspect me of being up to no good for some reason." Hmm, wonder why that was. "Even if I got in, someone would tattletale. I think Knox put everyone on alert."

"About?"

"Her and her ways," Jane said. "Knox wouldn't do that. He likes you."

"He likes you," Roxie said, slipping an arm around their golden ticket. "You're going to give birth to the Collier heir one day. The place is basically yours already."

"Thursday we go in?" she asked.

Though Jane may not appear confident, Roxie had enough chutzpah for all of them… and a small army. "Thursday we go in."

TWENTY-SIX

IF ONLY SHE GOT to Thursday without incident. No, it wasn't meant to be. Temptation wasn't done with her yet. She just hadn't known it.

In fact, naively, she'd begun to relax around Eclipse again.

Their breakup was done. Their relationship over. She hadn't seen Zach before their naked meeting, why should she see him given their association was finished?

After dropping off a report with Chester, which was really just an excuse to check the guy was strung right, she called the elevator to go down to the IT department. Again. Her mission? To take another swing at talking them into setting up an additional desktop or two in the boardroom. The Ranby Kearns cohort would get so much more done if they could have several people on the network at the same time. Surely, by now, she had to be wearing the tech guys down.

The elevator descended a couple of floors and stopped. If the technical team didn't help her out soon, there would be no point.

On reflex, when the doors opened, she stepped back to make room for whoever may enter.

And then it happened. Temptation delivered a test.

"…didn't say that we would."

Zach's voice raised her chin. His words stalled, as his form did between the doors. He about-faced almost on the spot, blocking the guy behind him from getting in.

"Full?" Javi asked and stepped backward.

"Full," Zach said and retreated from the doors to let them close.

They were alone. They shouldn't be alone. Alone had to be bad when there were potentially cameras watching. Shit. Did she just look? Who looked for cameras except someone trying to avoid them?

They couldn't talk. Shouldn't. She'd said they wouldn't sneak around but being alone felt exactly like that. Like they were. Oh, if only…

Sex.

Where had that word come from? Why was sex in her head? Why was she thinking of touching him? Of wrapping her arms around him and… Oh, damn, he smelled incredible. Her eyes crossed as they closed. What was that cologne? She needed to find out the name to buy some. Her muscles loosened, becoming more compliant, yielding… Shit, her body was responding to their proximity. Since when was she such a horny—since Zach, that's since when.

The elevator stopped.

The doors opened.

Right. That was her stop, she had to…

He didn't give her an inch of space to get around him. The urge to look him in the eye was almost overpowering. But if she did it, if she peeked up and… She had to go. To move.

Edging around him, she went out, moving slow in contrast to the hammer of her heart. She didn't turn and didn't hear a word. A few paces down the corridor, the elevator doors whooshed shut, and she kept on walking. Forget it. Forget him.

Something snagged her wrist. Not something. Someone.

Yanked to the side into darkness, a door closed.

Disoriented and boosted up to sit on a hard surface, hands grabbed the front of her thighs, driving up under her skirt.

"We can't," she gasped before her eyes had even adjusted enough to identify him.

His fingers clawed their way over her hips to scoop under her ass. "This isn't sneaking," he murmured, the fabric of her skirt pulled tight across his wrists.

She caught his powerful forearms. "It is." Losing herself in him would be easy. The notion was too tempting. "We're in the dark. Alone. In secret." With his hands on her body, him between her thighs. "Oh, God, Zach, this is the definition of sneaking around."

Her head tilted to meet his lips. On one breath, she said no, in the next she was surrendering. In the dark, alone, in secret, there was no other way to describe that moment. When his fingers curled, tugging her butt to the edge of whatever was beneath her, the thick, demanding need in his slacks broke the last thread of her control.

Grabbing his face, she yanked him down, forcing their kiss to deepen. They were there, in their last chance to be together. That could be it, their final opportunity. They had to be safe. She didn't know where they were, what room they were in, or who may be outside listening to the sounds of her want growing, her need demanding. But he did, maybe he did. They were safe because she trusted him. Damnit, they were playing with fire.

His mouth descended, her head went back. Every one of his kisses on her throat meant more than carnal satisfaction. It was a memory of his need imprinted against her. Couldn't they stay there forever, lounging in the tattoo playing across the raw nerve endings speckling beneath her skin?

"Zach," she panted, unbuckling his belt, freeing him with her sure grip around his shaft. "This is wrong."

His kiss found hers with such force, her head thudded against the wall. That hurt, but not as much as saying goodbye to this man or sacrificing the chance to have a thorough farewell.

He mumbled something against her that she didn't understand and snagged her lower lip in his teeth. The steadying force of his forearm behind her hips held her in place as he shoved her underwear aside and plunged into her. The thick, full, pulsing want was almost enough to finish her. Being occupied by him, being filled up, the world existed in him. They were the only people alive.

Without him in her hand, it felt empty, but she'd surrendered him to a deeper part of herself. A more intimate and profound piece of her soul held him. Even as he pounded into her, fast and with such urgency, she couldn't breathe as quick as he moved.

Another mumble came from his lips before he pulled all the way out. Bereft, she yelped. How could he leave her? How could he go when she needed him so much?

His mouth replaced his cock, teasing her most intimate corner. He kissed and licked, pleasuring her with such ferocity that she grabbed his head in both hands. Some instinct had meant to push him away, but she couldn't bring herself to do it. Her fingers tightened into fists, pulling his hair so hard it would hurt his scalp. But it was all need. He growled against her. The sheer overwhelming intensity of the orgasm that ripped through her stole everything she'd ever been. Her whole body clenched, frozen in the moment of satisfaction, of gratification, of hedonistic joy.

She couldn't open her eyes. Couldn't breathe. Couldn't function.

Not until he slammed into her again and her mouth opened in one long wail. His hand clamped over the noise, holding her still and quiet. Her eyes popped open to lock onto his that were narrowed and dark, almost lost in their feral command. He wanted her silence. Wanted to preserve their moment.

He pulled out and pushed in, stimulating her through the aftershocks into another dizzy and disorienting climax. Shattered by his deep surge into her, pushing hard, his hand dropped and his mouth once again landed on her head. She could feel the tightness of his jaw and his gritted teeth against her hairline, and then he stilled. Neither moved.

Did he regret what they'd done?

Or fear they may regret parting too soon?

She'd promised they wouldn't sneak around and yet there they were, screwing in some shadowy non-descript corner of his skyscraper.

"It wasn't wrong," he mumbled, his mouth still against her. "Being with you is not wrong. It's wrong that we're kept apart." He eased back to meet her eye. "This was meant to be more than a rebound. You're not a rebound. You have no idea how that's tormented me since I heard it from your lips."

"It's easier to think of me that way." Her heels slid off the surface she still sat on. "If we think about us as a fling, it saves us facing the truth of what we might have been."

"What we still can be," he said. "Three months is not forever. After that—"

"I don't want you waiting." She caught his shirt in her fists on his abs. "I can't ask you to hold on, and I can't either. Our lives can't exist on pause."

"Three months—"

"I know," she said, cutting him off. "And I told you I'm not saying no, but if someone from your board or a reporter asks, you have to be able to tell the truth. You're not involved with anyone." With gentle pressure, she pushed him away to slide back onto her bare feet. She searched the floor for her shoes and bent to put them on. "If this is Julietta, she expects this. For our hormones to screw us. You shouldn't want to give her the satisfaction."

"This is not about her satisfaction. It's about mine. It's about what's right."

"Will it be less right if we try to pick it up again another time? Who says it has to be here and now? Maybe our timing's just off."

"But you won't make any promises."

"You shouldn't either. Be open to whatever life brings you. If nothing else, this has proved we never know what's right around the corner. What we might stumble into."

"Amour…"

Catching the back of his neck, she eased him down to kiss him one last time as she retreated toward the door, fumbling behind her for the handle. "No more," she whispered. "Be patient."

With that, she opened the door just enough to

swerve around it, go back into the hall and close it behind her. He'd wait a minute. He'd know to wait a minute before coming out, wouldn't he?

She exhaled, trying to be subtle about running her hands through her hair. She was probably a mess, on the outside at least. On the inside, she should be, but the warm, joyful endorphin high that came with the contentment of being with him still flooded her.

It was their farewell. They deserved a farewell. That was it, as she'd said, no more.

TWENTY-SEVEN

"THIS IS INSANE."

Thank God someone said it aloud. Of the three of them, Jane was the most nervous, which was ironic given she'd get in the least trouble if they were caught being sneaky. Not that they were doing anything bad or evil, but it wasn't really honest and upstanding either.

They got a cab a couple of blocks from the hotel. No fancy cars or chauffeurs for their mission. No, they were incognito. From Jane's massive beach bag came two wide brimmed floppy hats that joined the oversized sunglasses both women were already wearing.

She was prompted to hail the cab and read out the address from Jane's phone. Not to CollCom, no, to a medical center she'd never heard of. Going direct would be too obvious, and they wanted to be inconspicuous.

Roxie and Jane were recognizable. But it wasn't until that cab ride that she truly appreciated they were in the epicenter of their notoriety. People in that town knew Knox, they knew Zairn and Zach too. For the time being, or at least until Julietta got her way, she was anonymous. She'd never been more grateful for that.

Her friends didn't want anyone to know they were sneaking into the studio on their secret mission. Neither did she.

After paying the cab driver in cash, they made their way to a coffeehouse stuck between a liquor store and a fast-food joint. A prime position to stake out the parking lot entrance waiting for Julietta's arrival.

"How will we know it's her?" she asked, watching cars pass on the wide street and disappear off in different directions.

"Julietta and Kesley are using the same car company," Roxie said, eyes trained on the view. "It just so happens that Zairn is paying for Kesley's car service. For insurance purposes, Astrid, one of Zairn's assistants, had to call and confirm the license plate numbers for all vehicles they were sending in and out of Kintyre's."

"Julietta's."

"Right."

Jane showed her the three license plate numbers on her phone's notes app.

"And they just gave you that?"

"She knows the password and passed security," Roxie said. Okay, maybe what they were doing was a little more than dishonest. "For what we're paying them, that call should've come with a happy ending."

"It's crazy," Jane said from next to her. "The amount they pay for things. The car bill would cover our Chicago rent for a year."

"And then some," Roxie said.

Car services were par for the course. While her family weren't CollCom, or probably Zairn Lomond, rich, she was used to the finer things in life, the convenience that came without having to worry about money.

For more than an hour, they sat there observing the vehicles filtering into CollCom. Thankfully, Roxie forewent the binoculars, they might be a little conspicuous.

At two minutes after two Julietta's car pulled up to the security box, paused until the barrier rose, and sailed onto the lot.

"Come on, let's go," Roxie said, already halfway out the door.

Skidding to a halt, Roxie lurched backward to snag

Jane's hand to yank their friend out onto the street.

"Oh, don't—"

"No time to waste!"

Roxie raised her free arm and ran across the street, avoiding this car and that. There weren't many near misses, but it wasn't as discreet as the disguises suggested they wanted to be. She stuck close, trying her best not to slow them down or cause an obstruction.

"Can we walk in the parking lot?" she asked as they returned to a normal pace on the sidewalk.

No one walked anywhere in LA. Especially not people entering a studio lot like CollCom. There may well be a side entrance for pedestrians for those who didn't or couldn't afford a vehicle. Everything was expensive in LA.

"Can we just walk in?" Roxie scoffed and put an arm around Jane's waist to thrust her forward. "Lead the effort, honey."

"Me?"

Despite her visible anxiety, there was no time for Jane to back out. Poor woman was in the spotlight whether she wanted to be or not.

The security guy stuck his head out of the box as they approached. "Can I help you, ladies?"

"No, we're fine," Roxie chirped from behind Jane. "My boss doesn't need to explain herself."

Jane whipped around. "Your…"

"I'm sorry, ma'am. I know you don't like to explain yourself." Roxie peeked at the security guard. "She doesn't like to explain herself."

Containing her smile was impossible. The demure, kowtowed, subservient Roxie was an incredible act she'd never known her friend could carry off. A woman of many talents, Roxie could carry anything off. Imagine if Zairn were there to see his fiancée deferring as though afraid of her friend. In the performance, she guessed, they weren't friends, they were boss and employee.

"I'm sorry, I don't—" Roxie cut the guy off by reaching around to lower Jane's glasses to the end of her nose until recognition crossed his face. "Wait, you're—"

"That's right, she is. She doesn't like to be delayed

and Mr. Collier isn't a fan of men who waylay his fiancée."

"Waylay—oh, God, yes. Anything you need, ma'am? You want me to call a cart?"

"No, we're fine," Roxie said, slipping an arm around Jane to guide her on while nodding at her to follow. "And we'd prefer if you didn't mention this to anyone... It's a surprise visit."

The guy likely wouldn't have a direct line to Knox's office... if he had an office, but Roxie was thorough, no taking that away from her.

"Now what do we do?" she asked, matching the hurried pace of her friends who were speeding along.

"We find out where that car went."

"Did it park?" Jane asked.

"Cars like that don't park in regular spots and then let people out. You know that, honey. People who use cars like that are VIPs. There's only one place VIPs go on this campus."

She'd say that Roxie moving with such purpose was encouraging, but Roxie always moved with purpose. Even when she didn't have one. It was part of that confident charisma she oozed like she belonged absolutely everywhere she was... even when she didn't.

Did she have that before Zairn or was that what came with security? Financial security. Material security. Sexual and emotional security. From what she'd seen, the couple had it all.

Most couples she had experience with had some sort of power imbalance or power war going on. One was more dominant than the other or they fought against each other, butting heads, desperately trying to come out on top. She didn't get that sense from Roxie and Zairn.

They had somehow cracked what so many strove their whole lives for. The couple had actually found a healthy, fulfilling, equal relationship. Were Jane and Knox the same? She hadn't quite figured them out yet.

"Why don't you wear your engagement ring?" she asked Jane as they trekked on in Roxie's wake toward an open area with a prominent building at the center.

A gleaming car remained at the bottom of the stairs

to that building. What was it waiting for?

Jane glanced at her own left hand. "I don't have one."

"Knox doesn't believe in giving a ring?"

"He hasn't yet," Roxie said, still half a step ahead. "Although…" she tilted sideways and lowered her volume, "I have heard the first of the Collier boys to get engaged gets Mimi's ring. Cha-ching! You think mine's slick? Mimi wears the Hope Diamond."

"It's not the Hope Diamond," Jane said.

"Have you met her?"

"No. Have you?"

"Okay, I'll give you that. Zairn's seen it and he said it was the Hope Diamond. You can see pictures of it on the internet."

"I don't know why we're talking about this," Jane said. "We're not engaged. We're not getting engaged."

"Of course you are. He just has to figure out how to do it right. Out of every woman we know, there's no one who's spent more time thinking about her forever guy popping the question than you. The guy must have performance anxiety. He has to get this right. He almost lost you once and doesn't want to go through that again."

"How do you feel about a hand-me-down ring?"

Surprise colored Roxie until she caught on to her teasing smirk. "That's true. Good question, Lilya. How lazy is that? Giving you a ring that's already in his family. He doesn't even have to go to the store. Mimi can just FedEx it to you. He doesn't have to be there; he knows what it looks like."

"Stop it," Jane said. "I'd be ecstatic to get a ring from Knox—or whoever I end up marrying. Maybe we won't get engaged. Maybe we'll never be engaged. Maybe we won't go the distance."

"Oh, who are you kidding?" Roxie scoffed. "The man is nuts about you. He has enough money and influence that even if you try to get away, you won't be able to. He'll hunt you down and ruin any man who tries to take his place."

"He's not as ruthless as you think. You always butt heads. You're catty with each other. They're so alike," Jane explained to her.

"I can see that. I can see how you'd fall in love with a man like your best friend."

"Knox is not like me. It's not like she's sleeping with the male version of me. I'm much funnier and definitely hotter, though…" her chin angled, "not by much."

"The man is ridiculously handsome," she said.

Roxie nodded. "His brother, Cam, is too."

"Is their mom a knockout?"

"Don't even get me started on Thena," Roxie said as they swerved away from their trajectory to steal around the side of the building. "Until we've finished our mission."

TWENTY-EIGHT

THE FIRST DOOR they tried didn't open. The next one had a security lock that required a fingerprint.

Roxie and Jane looked at each other.

"Mine won't work." Lilya glanced back and forth at them. "Roxie, you must be authorized. Remember Zairn's phone? Everything was green."

"Yeah, but if we use our fingerprints, there's a log of our entry. Knox probably has an alarm setup to go off whenever I open a CollCom door. He's learned his lesson. I only got one under the radar moment and I used it already."

"May—"

Just at that, another door, ten yards away, opened. A guy came out, cigarette packet in hand.

Roxie scampered over and grabbed the door before it could swing shut. "Thank you," she chirped like the guy had intended to let them in. He just stood there flabbergasted as they snuck in and the door clicked shut. "Who smokes anymore? Dirty, nasty habit."

A stairwell. Okay.

"Worked out for us, didn't it?"

Roxie led them up one side and took them directly out into a corridor, pointing left. "Front door's up that way."

"Do we want to go the other way? How will we find

out where she is?"

"Why was the car still outside?"

"Maybe she was waiting."

"For who? Why?"

"Does she have to sign in?" The three of them loitering there, without purpose, would get conspicuous fast. "Let's go see if she—"

"Wonderful to have you here," a male voice boomed from the direction of the front door. "Every time I see you, you're more beautiful, Ms. Ines-Kintyre."

A guy came into view at the mouth of the hallway. Jane squealed, Roxie grabbed both of them and ran across the corridor, through an open doorway, kicking the stopper from beneath it to let the door swing shut.

"Okay, well, we know where she is," Roxie said when it clicked into place.

"Who was that with her?"

"I don't know. Security. Some guy in charge, obviously."

"We can't hide in here all day."

Through the small round window in the door, movement showed Julietta and her people passing by. All three of them vied for a view through the tiny glass pane.

"I'll be damned," she said. "That's definitely Julietta." With a man she didn't know. The third person? She and Roxie made eye contact. "Reeve Crosby."

"Reeve Crosby," Roxie agreed. "The worm. The guy's been sniffing around a while. Maybe he's up to something. Someone's feeding the beast. First strike," as it had said in the diary, "what does that mean? Suddenly it feels sinister. The first of how many?"

"Could she hit him in the press?" Lilya asked. "Is that what this is about?"

"Maybe there was a reason she didn't out the 'who' at the same time she was leaking information about Zach's love life."

"That's possible," Jane agreed.

"There's only one way to find out who he is."

"We need to go after them," Roxie said, pushing down the door handle.

"Wait!" Jane grabbed her friend's wrist. "They'll see."

"Maybe," Roxie said, grabbing off their hats to stuff them into the beach bag and delve in deeper. "That's why we brought these."

Next to appear were two platinum blonde wigs. It was impossible not to laugh.

"You can't be serious," Jane said.

"Flip it," Roxie said. "Flip over." Jane muttered to herself but flipped her hair to help don the wig before helping Roxie with hers. "I always wanted to know what we looked like shiny blonde." A pair of glasses came from the bag next. "Everyone in LA is blonde. We won't be out of place; we'll blend right in."

"You guys are so much fun," she said, still laughing.

"I'm always up for a caper," Roxie said, sliding on her own cat-eye glasses and opening the door to slip out into the corridor.

They had the advantage of speed. Julietta moved slow, forcing anyone who was with her to do the same. They ran along the corridor as quickly as they could without flat out sprinting. The elevator doors closed as they reached the end. She just caught a quick glimpse of Julietta's red dress.

"Where is it going? Which floor?"

Something else appeared from Jane's bag. Walkie-talkies.

Roxie thrust one into Jane's hands and another into hers. "Tell me where it stops."

Their friend dashed through a door into what had to be another stairwell. Jane was staring at her walkie-talkie.

Lilya turned both on and stepped back to watch the numbers above the elevator doors illuminate. "How does she come up with this stuff?" she asked Jane. "The wigs? The walkie-talkies?"

"Roxie's resourceful. People might write her off, especially now she's with Zairn, but she's savvy, switched on, more aware than she gives herself credit for."

Six. The elevator stopped on six.

She raised the walkie-talkie to her lips, but Roxie's voice came out before she could press the button. "Red Leader to Daphne and Velma. Come in Daphne and Velma."

A whisper of a laugh came from Jane. "Trust her to use cartoon characters."

"Who's who?" she asked. "You're smarter and prettier than me."

"Daphne and Velma come in," Roxie hissed.

She pressed the button to talk. "We're here, Red Leader. Six is the answer."

"Six, roger wilco."

"Your friend is hilarious," she said, opening the stairwell door for Jane. "Fun and a little nutty."

"She'd tell you that's the perfect combination," Jane said, pausing in the doorway to show a quick smile. "And I hate to tell you, but she's your friend too."

Yes, she was. And one she valued already.

They hurried up the stairs as quickly and quietly as possible. If they were caught, Jane would be the least likely to get in trouble, but Roxie would be the most capable of talking herself out of a jam.

"This is crazy," Jane said when they got to Roxie peeking through the stairwell door.

"They're in there," Roxie said, pointing toward an open door further down the corridor.

And it closed.

"They're in there?" she asked. "What's in there?"

"I don't know, but we have to find out."

Yeah, they did. "Julietta's up to something."

Like they weren't. "It can't be anything good. We have to get closer."

Was it adrenaline or fear that sped her pulse? Whichever, this clandestine sneaking around was exciting… wasn't that what she'd done with Zach?

Biting her lip, she checked her new friends, eager in their pursuit.

"Shit," Roxie said and leaped aside, pushing Jane as she went.

"What?" she asked, peeking through the glass only to see what Roxie did: Knox coming down the corridor with two others.

"You've gotta take one for the team," Roxie said, yanking down Jane's top to reveal more cleavage.

"Me? What are you…?"

"Find out if he's going up or down," Roxie said, yanking off Jane's wig too. "Give us a signal."

"A signal?"

"Behind your back, is he going up or down? We'll do the opposite—"

"But what if he—"

"Just tell him you're here to visit," Roxie said, jerking open the door to shove her friend around it.

"Oh, this is bad. So bad."

"She'll be fine."

Keeping low, they snuck a look out just as Knox noticed Jane and his lips moved.

"Hey, Blossom, what are you doing here?" Roxie said in her best Knox impersonation. "If he's showing those guys in, his office is up the stairs. If he's showing them out, it's down."

The group stopped when Jane reached them. Immediately, Knox put an arm around her.

"I like how he is with her. How he doesn't shy from claiming her."

"Like Zach can't do with you?" Roxie asked. "I'm sorry this is all happening around you."

"I'm sorry Zach is going through this. This is hardest on him."

"Was that a signal?" Roxie jolted. "She pointed up."

"Does that mean we go up or he's going up?"

"Him," Roxie said, grabbing her to push her down the stairs quickly.

The door they'd been at opened a heartbeat later.

"You know your way up. I'll join you in a second," Knox said. Footsteps sounded above them. When the sound faded and another door closed, he spoke again. "What's wrong?"

"Nothing," Jane said.

"You never just show up, you always call. Why didn't you call?"

"I'm sorry, I didn't realize I'd be interrupting."

"You're not interrupting. You're never interrupting, Blossom. Everything else in my life interrupts being with you.

Everything else should be apologizing. I'm worried."

"You don't have to worry."

"No? But you—"

His words stopped so quickly that both she and Roxie leaned out to peep up at the couple, locked in a passionate kiss. As the amorous twosome parted, both friends leaped back out of view.

"Okay, now I'm even happier to see you," Knox said, his voice low, gruff… horny.

"I've never made out with the boss."

"That'll be the opener. Ever have sex with the boss on his desk?"

"We can't do that! Knox, oh my God, what will people think?"

"Have you?"

"No! I have never had sex on the boss's desk, no."

With Jane, and the way she was, it was impossible to tell if the innocent, coy thing was an act or if that was genuinely her honest reaction to the proposition. Knowing Jane, the latter was more likely.

"Something we'll remedy today," Knox said.

"Oh, no, I… You have your meeting. I couldn't—"

"You can sit in," he said. "Come on."

Their footsteps overhead signaled the couple's departure.

"Woman down," Roxie said. "Gone, but not forgotten… Now it's just you and me."

And how would they find out who Julietta was meeting with? That was the key to finding out what they may be facing.

"How are we going to—"

"The old-fashioned way," Roxie said and snatched her hand to sweep out of the stairwell.

The door had a window in it, just like all the others. Walking past could be risky, but Roxie stopped just before the window and pointed up at the nameplate above.

Beverley Woo.

They looked at each other.

Who the hell was Beverley Woo?

TWENTY-NINE

"SHE'S AN AGENT. And a producer," Roxie said. "Woo has dabbled in a bunch of roles. I don't know that she works exclusively for CollCom."

"She's an outside contractor," Lilya added, stabbing the last couple of pieces of pasta on her plate.

Thursday's adventure at CollCom was basically an extended lunch break. Because she'd run back to Eclipse as soon as their sleuthing was over, the trio had agreed to meet for a late dinner the next night in Roxie and Jane's hotel suite.

Roxie, as always, was an exceptional hostess, mixing drinks, selecting music. The social air in the dining room was a perfect cover for their plotting.

"Does that mean Beverley Woo is a dead end?" Jane asked. "We went through all that—"

"Went through all what?" Roxie asked, smirking. "You got to do it on the boss's desk, didn't you?" The blush on Jane's cheeks said it all. "We need more information. We have to go back."

"Go back where?"

"To the house. We need another look at that diary. We didn't go far back or forward enough."

"So we still don't know who the father is."

"She must have marked her due date," Jane said.

"We should've looked."

"That was a rookie mistake," Roxie agreed.

"Okay, so when?" she asked.

"Tomorrow. According to the information we do have, she's out tomorrow night."

"Where?"

Roxie shrugged. "I don't know, it just says 'appointment.'"

Curious. And strange.

"She's right," she said, picking up her purse to fish out her phone.

After a couple of swipes, noise carried from the living room, suggesting they were no longer alone.

She tensed, Jane did too. "Who's that?"

"Likely your boyfriend or mine," Roxie said, rising from her seat.

"I thought you said they were at the club," Jane hissed.

A moment later, Zairn appeared in the arch to the dining room.

"You're supposed to be working," Roxie said to him, topping off their wineglasses.

"We came to invite you to join us," he said, stepping aside to reveal Knox… and Zach.

Right there in front of her was the man she'd feared running into at work. Again. Somehow, she'd convinced herself they would never cross paths in a private hotel suite. Why was that important? That it was private or that no one would ever know if they—

"We're having dinner." Roxie put the wine bottle down. "Sweetie."

"Looks to me like you're finished."

"Barely. And what about dessert? Do you see dessert? I love dessert."

"Want me to serve that up in private?"

"That wouldn't be very kind to our guests, would it? And maybe we don't want to go out painting the town crimson every night of the week."

"It's okay." Lilya tucked her phone back into her purse while pushing her chair back. "I should get going anyway."

Roxie's focus went to Jane. "If we're going to the club, we need something to wear. Let's go find something." Scampering around the table, her friend wasn't discreet about walking right up to Zairn, against him, using her body to pressure him backwards. "We're about to get naked and try on lots of dresses. You should come be a part of it."

"The naked part is fine," Knox said.

Jane went to link her fingers with his. "I want your opinion."

"Subtle," she said as the foursome departed, leaving her and Zach alone. "We don't have to be awkward, do we?"

"I'm not awkward. Except the minute you saw me, you tried to run out of here like the place was on fire."

"It's not because I don't want to see you," she said. "It's because I do."

"And you don't trust yourself? You don't trust me?"

"That and..." she trailed off.

Sure, she didn't trust herself not to take advantage of being alone with him, near him...

"That what?"

On a sigh, she rose to her feet. "It hurts." That was the stark truth. "I miss you. It's not your fault, it's nobody's fault, but that doesn't mean I don't wish..."

Without hesitating, he closed the space between them. "Don't wish, what?"

"It's too difficult," she said, closing her eyes. "It's too complicated. I'm the one who keeps telling you this has to stop, that we have to be honest when we say we're not involved. Yet, when I look at you... in person, like this... it's not easy to... When I look at you, all I want is..."

"To be involved," he finished for her.

There was no other way to put it. That was exactly what she wanted. Knowing he did too only boosted the ache.

Resigned, she forced a smile to her lips. "It's always been this way. I've never been able to keep my hands to myself around you."

"You did the night we met."

And now all she wanted was him naked. "That was different," she said on a whisper of a laugh. "There's not keeping my hands to myself and then there's flat out assault."

He laughed. "I wouldn't have minded."

"Javi might have."

"I did think about it."

"Think about what?"

"Would've been great cover if you'd got naked with us too."

"Oh, so I'd play Julietta?"

"Because you thought we were together." His smile faded. "What do you think now?"

"That it's insane you could go from a woman like her to a woman like me. We're so completely different."

"I'd say I was young, dumb, and full of—"

"You don't have to explain yourself to me. That's not what I meant."

"I wasn't that young, and I wasn't that dumb. Everyone warned me. I wanted to believe the best of her. Everyone deserves a chance. So many people are misunderstood, especially women with ambition."

"There's ambitious and then there's mercenary. Without a doubt, she's the latter. But we've all made mistakes in the past. Been with people we'd rather forget."

"Nathan... or me?"

"Neither." They weren't the only men in her past. "We all present the best versions of ourselves in the new stages of any relationship. You were hardly together before you got married. You didn't know each other."

Was she talking about Julietta or herself?

The back of his fingers grazed her jaw. "Amour..."

"Don't." She ducked away from the caress. "We know where that leads."

"We're both single. Why shouldn't it lead there?"

"Because you're doing it again," she said, taking a more deliberate step back. "You're idealizing this. Me. Us. Life isn't a fairytale, it's not always right to do the grand, romantic thing. We'd be together if we could be, but we can't. I'm not going to stand by and watch you give up half of your company for the sake of my pussy."

"You think that's all it is?"

"Zach," she said on an almost whimper. "Please."

"Okay." He retreated a few yards. "You said you were leaving. I shouldn't have got in the way. I apologize. Go."

Looping her purse strap over her shoulder, she was decisive in her march to the threshold of the room. Right there, she stopped dead. It shouldn't be like that. What if that was the last moment she ever spent with him?

As she spun around, he was closing the space between them. Ducking down, he caught her head and joined their mouths. That kiss should be their opening salvo, not their final goodbye.

Tears escaped her closed eyes, trickling down to meet his hands and his kiss. It couldn't go further. They couldn't do more.

Pushing his chest once, twice, she slipped out of his hands embrace. "I'm sorry," she whispered, rushing away.

She didn't open her eyes until he was behind her. Swiping the tears from her face, she hurried out of the suite to stab the elevator button at least a dozen times.

Why did it hurt?

They'd only been together for a month. Losing him shouldn't be tearing her apart. Every time she saw him was pain. And then he put it on her to be the sensible one. Shouldn't he want to protect his company? To keep it out of his ex-wife's clutches. Avoiding each other was the only way to go, but that night proved even with the best of intentions they could still come across each other.

Life wasn't fair or easy. Did it have to be so cruel too?

THIRTY

"ARE WE SURE Julietta's not in the house?" Jane asked. "Like sure, sure, sure? Positive sure? Doing this again feels like tempting fate."

"We're sure," Roxie said, as light and assured as ever. "She has that appointment."

"And Kesley?"

Huddled in another of Knox's cars that Saturday night, Roxie was putting on a pair of black leather gloves. "She's out too."

They'd parked twenty feet from the intersection on a street perpendicular to Julietta's. They couldn't see inside the Kintyre home. The broad gates were open, but the driveway curved, so they couldn't see the house itself. No light shone in the looming darkness beyond the driveway, but they couldn't know for certain that no one was home.

Someone being home would be better than someone happening upon Roxie when she was in there. In the former scenario, Roxie would think on her feet and make up a reason for the random visit. And Julietta had just swanned into Knox's house, so she could announce it as tit for tat.

If Roxie got caught in the woman's bedroom, taking pictures, yeah, that would be a harder sell.

"How can you be sure Kesley's out? It's not the Queen Dinner."

They didn't have the safety net of the event beneath them that night. Jane was right, it was riskier. They'd got away with their intrusion the first time, would they get away with pulling the same stunt twice?

Roxie smiled. "No, she's got better than that tonight."

Was there such a thing? "Better than the Queen Dinner?" she asked. "I thought she was Zairn obsessed."

How could Roxie be so relaxed? "She is. It's him she's meeting."

That startled her and Jane. "Zairn? She's meeting Zairn? Your fiancé? What for?"

"Dinner."

"Wow, how did you convince him to do that? I thought we were keeping the guys out of this. Did you tell him what we're doing?"

"We really should've talked before—"

"I didn't tell him," Roxie said, cutting Jane off. "I texted Kesley from his phone inviting her to dinner… then deleted the message and blocked her number so he won't get any follow up texts from her."

"I had no idea you were so devious," Jane said, semi-impressed. "What will she do when he doesn't show up? Won't she just come back home?"

"Oh, he will show up because I told him to meet me for dinner."

"So Zairn thinks he's meeting you? Kesley thinks she's meeting him? When?"

"Right about now. Shame my phone is out of juice and my Casanova won't be able to reach me… I only need ten, twenty minutes. I'll go in, take the pictures." She produced a digital camera from a pocket on the thigh of her pants. "And then I slip out. That's it."

"Does it have to be just you?"

It sort of felt like they were feeding their friend to the wolves. She didn't want to abandon Roxie. The woman would never put anyone else in the firing line. Still, was it cowardice not to force herself into the situation or smart to let Roxie go alone? One would be quicker and stealthier.

Roxie was the one with security clearance. It really had to be her. Unfortunately.

"This will be fast and easy. Trust me, I can do this. I'll be right back."

Roxie jumped out of the car. She and Jane looked at each other. If real life was anything like the movies, Roxie had just jinxed her fate.

"She'll be okay," Jane said, turning to watch their friend hurry to the end of the street and creep across into the open gates of the Kintyre marital home.

Once Roxie was out of sight, all they could do was wait. Without her phone, they had no way to reach her to check in. If Zairn was going to be on the warpath, no line of communication wasn't necessarily a bad thing.

Roxie had tricked her own fiancé. That was another clash Roxie would have to deal with. Zairn wouldn't get mad… would he? Would he actually sit and eat with Kesley or cancel? If it was the latter, the actress could be back any minute.

She held onto hope her friend would triumph. Two minutes. Five minutes… Okay, come on Roxie, time to get out of there. Taking pictures of the daybook's pages was the point of the mission. How long did that take? Would Roxie push it? Yes, of course she would, this was Roxie.

They got to ten minutes. Roxie had to be nearly done. Were they getting away with this? Were they actually going to triumph? The prospect of success burned bright on the horizon… until a car appeared, slowed, and turned into the driveway.

She and Jane locked eyes. "What do we do?"

"Nothing we can do. What can we do?"

"Shit."

"Yeah, this is going to be bad."

***

BAD DIDN'T BEGIN to describe it.

When the cops showed up, things got serious fast.

Not long later, the cop car came out again, this time with Roxie in the back seat.

At a respectable distance, they'd followed her to the police precinct and parked on the opposite block. A lone photographer by the side door got a picture of Roxie being led inside.

"What do we do?" she asked, turning when Jane didn't immediately answer. "What do we do?"

"This is out of our league," Jane said, scrolling through her phone to dial a contact.

Only a couple of rings later, the line connected.

"What did she do now?" Zairn's voice came from the handset between them. "Other than set me up on a date with my ex-girlfriend?"

"Just remember how much you love her," Jane said, bracing in a wince.

"Jane..."

"It's possible she needs a lawyer."

"She got arrested? Again?" he asked and exhaled. "What is it with my woman and LA?"

Somehow, this felt like her fault. "There's a photographer at the precinct."

"One of Knox's?"

"I don't know," Jane said. "Want me to call him?"

"Yeah, I'll be busy posting bail," Zairn said. "Does he know what the three of you have going on?"

"No."

"No," Zairn said. "Because it would just be dumb to clue the guy with the most sway in this town into your game. Stay where you are. Do nothing. Someone will be along to bring you back to the hotel... With or without my girl."

"Z—"

"Stay put."

The line disconnected.

For a second or two, they said nothing.

"I've never heard Zairn so..."

"Me either," she said, though her experience with him was more limited.

"Should I call Toria? I'll do that after."

"After you call Knox? This is kind of getting away

from us, isn't it?"

More than a little, there was no "*kind of*" about it.

Jane was dialing again and this time took the phone to her ear. "Yeah, more than a little," she said and started. "Remember that I love you… No, it's not…" They made eye contact. "There's a photographer… We need your help."

THIRTY-ONE

EXHAUSTED, THEY SAID little on the way back to the hotel. The adrenaline had ebbed, leaving her kind of numb. They got into the elevator and Roxie selected the floor for the suite.

She reached for the buttons. "I'm on—"

"No," Roxie intercepted her hand before it could make contact. "We didn't finish. After what went down, we should stick together tonight. Just in case."

Did that mean sleeping in Roxie and Jane's suite or going back to her room later? Maybe they just needed to have a drink and talk about what happened.

Roxie beeped through the suite door, and they traipsed down the marble foyer. Backup emergency adrenaline reserves kicked in when someone stepped into their view in the living room beyond.

Zairn.

"Here goes," Roxie mumbled and pasted on a wide smile. "Casanova!" The seductive lilt to her voice was definitely an angle. "Have you missed me?"

A stern brow wasn't typical for Zairn Lomond. The guy was one of the easiest going she'd ever met. Especially when it came to his fiancée's antics.

"It wasn't her fault," she said as Roxie spoke too.

Jane was quick to add her own culpability. Still talking over each other, the three of them came to a stop in front of him. He probably couldn't decipher what they were saying, but she couldn't stop herself. Roxie couldn't take the fall. Shouldn't. That's what she'd done through every stage. She'd taken the blame and all the hits while the rest of them stood safe on the sidelines.

"Enough!" Zairn called, raising a hand. "All of you sit." He stepped back and pointed to a couch. "Now."

They shuffled past him and another couch to sit down where he'd indicated. Rather than sit with them and perhaps reduce some of their apprehension, he chose to stand on the other side of the coffee table.

"This is a really good couch," Roxie said, bouncing in the middle seat. "Want to watch movies tonight, baby? Lola Bunny is around somewhere."

Zairn crooked an unimpressed brow. "What is it with you and LA? You know the history here. You know how Ackley feels. Why would you take the risk of getting yourself in trouble like this?"

"It was important," Roxie said and shrugged. "You trust me."

"I trust Ackley to do whatever it takes to attack me. That means attacking you. Hurting you. Why would you make it so damn easy for him? I know you like to ham it up, but you're smarter than this."

"This was not me hamming it up," Roxie said, surging to her feet. When Zairn raised his hand again to show her a palm, she plonked back down between them. "You've already made up your mind. You think this was a game and we're ridiculous immature brats taking advantage of the privilege you afford us."

Roxie wasn't looking at him. Her tone was so matter of fact. It wasn't like their friend to be resigned to any fate.

"You want to know why I'm mad? Why I'm reacting to this different than your other games? Cops carry guns, Lola. And Ackley controls the men with the gavels. Was it worth it? Whatever you were doing there, whatever your purpose, you took it on without telling me. That's not what we do, Lo." Slowly, Roxie's chin rose until her eyes found his.

"That's not what we do."

"We were protecting you," Roxie said, yielding to his hurt. "You, Knox, and Zach."

"From what were you protecting us?" Zairn asked. "Because from where I'm standing, you were the one who needed protecting tonight."

"You know who the father is," Roxie said. Zairn's expression shifted. "Don't you?"

"We have a good idea. You never asked wh—"

"Because we don't want to hear it from you. Any of you could get into trouble for revealing the truth."

"It's not about getting in trouble, Lo. Eclipse is at stake."

"Yeah, and that's why we weren't going to put you in a precarious position. We need to know why the secret is so important… and if there's any way to leak it."

"You think if you leak it, Zach's off the hook?" He looked at her. "That you can be together again?"

"He's important to me," she said, ready to take ownership of her decisions. "Whether we can be in a relationship doesn't matter. He's important to me."

"And he's important to you. We were trying to do what you couldn't," Roxie said. "We wanted to help. To do it without compromising any of you. If we could do it and help someone important to you, why wouldn't we? What if it was Toria or Astrid? Wouldn't you want to help me? Help my friend?"

"Yes, but we—"

"That's all we were doing."

"By breaking and entering?"

"I didn't break anything. My print is authorized on the system."

"Which is the only reason they let you go with a warning," Zairn said. "This could've been a press bonanza. Knox is still at CollCom trying to put this in a box. You think a cover up helps Zach?"

"I think you're being a hard ass for no reason," Roxie said, finding her temper as she shot to her feet. "I think you're pissed at me about the Kesley thing—"

"You made me complicit. I'm an accessory to

whatever the hell you were up to tonight. What the hell did you think you were going to find in her house? You think she'd just leave evidence lying around?"

"I knew exactly what I'd find in her house," Roxie said without shame. "'Cause it's not the first time I've been in there."

Zairn ran a hand through his hair. "Please tell me you're kidding."

"Got away with it, didn't we?"

"If we need something, you come to me," he said, resolute, his hand falling back to his side. "I fix shit like this. You stay the hell out of it."

"Oh, yeah, right, like I've ever been the run to my guy, damsel in distress type girlfriend. You have Kesley for that."

"Please don't fight," Jane said, standing up. "Please don't let this hurt your happy ever after."

Poor Jane really sounded scared.

Roxie took her hand. "We scream at each other all the time."

"Because she's infuriating," Zairn said.

Roxie blinked at her fiancé. "And you believe you can fix everything. Not everything is broken."

"You want to know who the father is?"

"I don't want to know from you," Roxie said. "You keep your secrets. We're going to figure this out ourselves. You'd be surprised just how wily we've been."

"Do I want to know?"

"Probably not," Roxie said. "You should just trust me."

"I trust you," he said, accepting their truce. "Doesn't mean I don't worry about you too." He opened a hand to her and Roxie went around the table. "At least Toria wasn't here."

Putting an arm around him, Roxie peeked at them across the table. "If Toria was here, we'd have been in Beverley Woo's house."

That was funny, but she wasn't quite ready to laugh. Jane either, if the way she slumped down to the couch again was an indicator.

"Beverley Woo?" Zairn said. "Why would you be in

her house? What's she got to do with it?"

"We're still trying to figure that out."

Zairn wasn't just curious; there was something knowing about the way his eyes tapered.

"Does the name mean something to you?" she asked.

"Anyone who knows what goes on behind the scenes hears Beverley Woo's name and immediately thinks Karryn Keller."

"Karryn—who's—the talk show woman?"

"Oh, God." Jane gasped. "Karryn Keller's done some of the most hard-hitting interviews in media history. She's interviewed queens and dictators."

"What has she got to do with this?" Zairn asked.

"Julietta was meeting her," Roxie said. "Beverley Woo, with Reeve Crosby, and some other guy at CollCom."

"At CollCom? And you didn't tell Knox?"

"We didn't know it was… You think Julietta's doing an interview?"

"I think we should find out," Zairn said, his arm dropping from Roxie's shoulders to take her hand instead. "And I think we should talk to a lawyer."

"I already talked to Dunlap tonight."

"Not that lawyer," Zairn said. "Come on."

"Do I have to?" Roxie asked, dragging her feet.

"I'm not letting you out of my sight until I'm confident you remember what city you're in." He pointed at Jane. "You stay here. Knox will be back as soon as he can be."

No instructions for her.

The suite door closed, signaling their departure.

Roxie and Zairn would be okay. Their relationship was strong enough to survive hiccups like that night.

Beverley Woo. Karryn Keller.

If Julietta was going on TV, if she was doing an interview, what was it she planned to say?

Her stomach lurched.

Nope, that wasn't just anxiety, it was actual nausea.

Leaping from the couch, she ran through the suite to the restroom. Her stomach had never been weak. Maybe it was nerves. Maybe it was stress. She heaved and then followed through, emptying her stomach into the toilet she reached just in time.

Every part of her ached with the effort. It cleared and she breathed, taking a second before flushing and closing her eyes.

Sweat beaded on her brow as she dropped back onto her butt. Life had never been so strained. When she and Nathan broke up, everything seemed different and out of place. More so because she moved state than left him behind.

Still, she wasn't weak or high-strung, not enough that anxiety alone should make her sick.

"The doctor's on his way up."

Twisting toward Jane's voice in the doorway, she dropped back to lean on the wall. "I don't need a doctor."

"You were sick last week too. If you're ill, you can't neglect your health. He works here in the hotel; they have a doctor on call all the time."

"And you want him up here? Tonight? Knox is still trying to put out one fire."

"Your health is more important than… Why is it a scandal that you're ill?"

"It's a scandal I'm in the suite at all," she said. "Why would I be here? In a suite occupied by you, Roxie, Zairn, and Knox Collier? I'm fine. I don't need a doctor."

"You wouldn't be puking if you were fine," Jane said.

"And if they try to pair me with Zairn or Knox… or Zach?"

Jane rested a shoulder on the door frame. "It would cause a scandal."

"Right."

"But your health…" She came closer. "What are your symptoms? I'll tell the doctor."

"There are no symptoms. I'm just tired and puke randomly. It's all the stress. All this Julietta stuff."

"Any allergies? Underlying health conditions? Regular medications?"

"No. Honestly, Jane—"

"You need to look after yourself. I'll do it. I'll tell the doctor the symptoms. Maybe he can give you something to settle your stomach. If he thinks we need a blood test, I'll tell him I want my own doctor to do it and then we'll take you somewhere."

"You have a doctor?"

"No, but he doesn't know that," Jane said, grabbing a washcloth to run it under cold water. A chime came as she wrung it out. "Here…" Her friend folded it and handed it over. "Put this on your head and stay here. I'll be back in a minute."

And when she did come back ten minutes later, Jane was ashen.

"What?" she asked, scrambling to her feet. "What's wrong? What did he say?"

"He doesn't want blood." Jane's hand came from behind her back to show the plastic tub with a screw-on lid. "He wants pee."

"But why would he want…" Her heart sank. "Oh, shit."

THIRTY-TWO

JANE WOULDN'T TELL anyone. She wouldn't. She'd promised not to. Even Roxie was out of the loop; she tended to tell her fiancé things and they couldn't ask Zairn to lie to his best friend.

Pregnant.

What a fucking idiot.

Pregnant.

Okay, so she hadn't been alone when it happened, but could the timing have been any worse?

She'd peed in the cup and the doctor confirmed it.

Pregnant.

Six days had passed, and she still couldn't get her head around it. She was expecting a child. Creating life… and she wasn't remotely qualified to nurture or guide it.

Some would argue being a woman was qualification enough, but it didn't feel right. It felt like she should be doing something, working or preparing for growing a child in her belly, but there was nothing to do. Nothing. She just had to… accept it was happening.

Another human was growing inside her… and it enjoyed making her nauseous.

"You're spacing out again," Jane said, laying out things from her basket on the blanket on the floor.

Being the only other one who knew the truth, Jane was her whole support network. Meeting for lunch in her hotel room had become a regular date. Privacy was important and everyone else was busy in the day, so they could get away with being secretive.

"I'm sorry."

"It's been almost a week."

"I know."

"You haven't even told Zach yet, have you?"

She hadn't told anyone. How could she talk about it sanely when it seemed so abstract?

"No. Have you told Roxie?"

Jane shook her head. "You told me not to. Every single time we see each other, you ask me that question. Every single time I tell you I haven't. I won't. This is between you and Zach."

And Jane, apparently. God, she needed the woman's counsel. Needed the support. But it wasn't fair to ask her to keep secrets. What else could she do?

"I have to have this baby. I've thought of the alternatives and I just can't bring myself to do it, or to really think seriously about doing it."

Her friend's smile crept higher until her lips pulled back to a grin. "You're going to be mommy to a little tiny, cute baby," she squeed.

A whisper of a laugh left her lips. "If there was a right person to have on the inside of this, I suppose it was you."

"You're so lucky! Zach will be thrilled."

"Will he? We're not even together. I don't know how this happened. I mean, I know how it happened, but… Jesus, I don't want to ruin the guy's life."

"I don't think he'll see it that way."

"I know, he's Mr. Stand-Up-And-Take-Responsibility, but this is the last thing he needs right now with Julietta still looming in his life."

"Julietta's the past and you are the future. You and the baby are his future. Where will you live?"

"I don't know."

"Roxie and I will be back in New York at some

point. You'll have a support network there if you need it. You and the baby will be looked after. Rox and I will help. Toria too. I know you haven't met her yet, but she's really protective of her girls."

Was she one of their girls now? After all she, Jane, and Roxie had been through, it was hard to make an argument against.

"I'll have to tell my family," she said. "I'll have to tell my ex."

"It will be in the papers," Jane said. "When it comes out. Maybe it won't be front page news, but it will be common knowledge." Something she'd been trying not to focus on. "This baby was meant to be."

Sitting on the floor on the blanket Jane had brought, there were sandwiches and fruit laid out with tiny little cupcakes that Jane had iced herself. Her friend wanted to cheer her up. To support her. It was nice of her to go to the effort to make it seem like they weren't skulking in the shadows. They were meeting in the light. Of her private hotel room. Picnicking outside was impossible if they wanted to avoid questions... and the media spotlight.

"Have you and Knox talked about kids?"

"Not in any detail," Jane said. "It's one of those things that will happen eventually."

"You know each other, you have the foundation of your relationship. Zach and I were only finding our way when we had to say goodbye."

"It wasn't a forever goodbye."

"Wasn't it? It feels a little like—"

Banging on the door interrupted. They hadn't ordered anything or called downstairs.

After exchanging a curious glance, she stood and went over to check the peephole.

Knox.

Funny. Speak of the devil.

She raised her brows at Jane and opened the door.

He came barreling in, passing her without acknowledgement, holding his phone up.

"You're pregnant?" he barked as the door clicked back into its frame. She froze. Jane's eyes darted back and forth between them. "Why in the fuck wouldn't you—"

"Me?" Jane asked, shaking her head. "How could I be pregnant?" His head tilted and if she wasn't so in shock, she might have laughed. The how was pretty damn obvious with such an amorous couple. "No, I mean, how could you think that?" Jane shifted onto her knees. "Why would you think I was pregnant and didn't tell you?" He handed his girlfriend the phone and she unlocked the screen to read. "A bill. You got a bill for…"

"A medical consultation, including a pregnancy test and a prescription for prenatal vitamins. Ask me again how I can think this? Why in the fuck would you—"

"Stop swearing," Jane said, getting to her feet. "It doesn't change anything. No matter how loud you yell at me, the facts don't change. Why would you be mad at me for being pregnant?" She gasped. "Do you think it traps you? That I'd do it on purpose to corner you?"

"No," he said without faltering. "I'm pissed that you did it yourself. I'm pissed I wasn't there. I'm pissed you felt you had to go behind my back and—"

"She didn't go behind your back," she said, going over to join the couple. The truth would out, it was inevitable. "Well, she did, but she did it for me."

"Lilya, you don't have to—"

"It's okay," she said, smiling at her friend before looking Knox in the eye. "It's mine. The consultation, the test, the prescription." Now he faltered. Surprise came in a blink. "Jane was worried because I'd been sick. I didn't think for a second…"

"You getting rid of it?"

"No!" Jane exclaimed, hitting his arm with the back of her hand. "Don't say that. Why would you want her to get rid of a tiny, innocent baby?"

"Can't think of any other reason Zach wouldn't tell us."

"He doesn't know," she said, swallowing though her throat was dry. "No one but me and Jane know."

"And the doctor," Jane said and gasped again, grabbing Knox's arm. "Will your family think—"

"I took care of it," he said, glaring at her. "This

consult was a week ago."

"I know."

"Everyone thinks Julietta's baby is Zach's," Jane said. "And the contract means they can't be together. What is Lilya supposed to do?" He said nothing and Jane got closer. "I'm actually asking you, babe, we need your support."

"Hmm," he said, shaking his head. "This is not my shit to deal with."

"Knox," Jane whined and slid an arm around his waist. "We've been dealing with this alone. We need a man's perspective."

"You saw how pissed I was when I thought you were dealing with this without me, Blossom. You do need a man's perspective, Lilya, but not this man. It has to be Zach's. It can only come from him."

And she wasn't even mad or scared, just resigned. "You're right. I have to tell him."

Her friend relaxed against her guy as he put an arm around her shoulders. "How will you do it?"

"No time like the present." She went to retrieve her purse then came back to kiss Jane's cheek. "Thank you. For everything."

"Don't say that like I'll never see you again."

She glanced at each of them. "I'll tell him, but I have to give him time to process. I'll keep my distance until he has a chance to come to terms with this."

"No, come to the suite tonight. I want to know how it goes," Jane said. "And you deserve our support too. One thing me and Rox always promise, we won't let our relationship issues fracture our friendship. We're your friends whether Zach wants to be a part of this child's life or not."

Such a sweetheart. "Thank you, I appreciate that. I appreciate everything you've done. But if Zach asks me to stay away, I will. I've had your support this week. He'll need the support of his friends, need them to get him through this."

"It's not a death sentence," Jane said. "He's going to be a father."

"For a guy like Kintyre, that's no little thing," Knox said. "Break it to him gently."

Was there any other way than just to say it? She was pregnant. That was it. Fact. And now it was time to share that truth with the man fifty percent responsible for the predicament. Strength was what she needed… and a good dose of luck.

THIRTY-THREE

ECLIPSE.

Somehow it seemed different as she ascended the stairs to the executive mezzanine floor. No one should look twice; she flitted around all over the building in the course of her work.

Going up there wasn't business. No, this time it was different. No one but her knew just how different.

Zach's door was open. He was in there, with a young blonde, one of the assistants.

At the threshold, she leaned into the room. "Knock, knock." Both Zach and the assistant looked up. "Do you have a minute, Mr. Kintyre?"

Using his last name like that was a smokescreen. Maybe the assistant would just accept her professional demeanor at face value. No one suspected their relationship, did they?

"Yeah," he said and nodded at the assistant.

The blonde scurried past to depart, closing the door, trapping her inside.

"I have something to tell you."

"Shoot," he said, moseying around his desk.

Seeing him so loose, so relaxed, it felt wrong to shatter his peace. Except that was the whole reason for her visit. She could chicken out, back away without revealing the truth… But Knox knew. If she didn't tell Zach, Knox would. He'd have to. Knox had no loyalty to her. Then Zach would wonder why she hadn't been the one to confess. They needed trust. Failing the first test wouldn't set a good precedent.

"I, uh…"

"Whatever it is, I'm here for you… Is this Ranby Kearns business? Did you find something in the audit?"

Of course he'd think it was professional. Their personal relationship hadn't seeped into his office. It had been a safe, business-only space. Another sanctuary she'd sully and shatter.

"No," she said. "It's not Ranby Kearns news."

His frown formed. "Is it Julietta? Did she do something? Were you approached by a reporter?"

"No," she said. Making him guess was unfair. "It's nothing bad."

Or was it? Her own world had been shaking on its foundations since she found out. His would likely do the same. Though he had recently gone through this, with Julietta, maybe that was like a soft reveal, setting him up for this, the big one.

"It's personal… isn't it?"

If it was business, she'd have spat it out, or sent someone else to do it in her stead.

"It's not a big deal." Damn, her stomach was doing somersaults. This was not the time to get sick. Was the baby or anxiety behind it? "It is a big deal. But I don't want you to think it's a big deal."

He laughed. "Tough to do when you won't tell me."

"Okay, so here it is," she said and swallowed the saliva pooling in her mouth. "I'm pregnant."

His ease faded as his brow lowered. "You're what?"

"I'm pregnant. I'm knocked up. It's just the way it is. I'm pregnant."

A moment passed before his throat bobbed. "And the only reason you'd be telling me is…" He paled and sank down into the chair thankfully there to catch him. "It's mine." Her lips were dry while her mouth was swamped, so she just nodded. "You're having my baby."

"Surprise," she said, feeble in her lack of enthusiasm. "I'm sorry, Zach. I really am. I wanted to tell you because I figure it's the right thing to do. I've thought about it and have decided to do this. I'm keeping it."

"You're keeping it," he muttered, unblinking in his daze.

"Yes. But I won't put you on the birth certificate. You'll keep your company and won't ever be required to pay child support. I know you can afford it, but that's not the point. This is my decision. I won't dragoon you into it. No drama. No press. No one but us knows." She started to go but looked back at him one last time. "I didn't mean for this to happen, but I'm not sorry it did."

Leaving the office, her pulse pounded, yet she felt better. He knew. What more could she do? Her child would never feel like an accident, like it was unwanted. She'd support the baby herself. Nothing would get in the way of that.

THIRTY-FOUR

THAT NIGHT WHEN she reached the top floor, the suite door was an inch ajar, which saved her from knocking or waiting. Except she didn't see a soul when she went inside. Where were her friends? They weren't waiting for her in the living room. Maybe in the dining room.

"We need to talk."

His voice whirled her around.

Zach.

Maybe she should've seen it coming, that he'd ambush her like this. Shouldn't he need more time to adjust? She'd only told him a few hours ago. Had he thought the situation through? His thoughts should be in order, his sense aligned, before they talked. Was this him doing what he thought was the right thing out of obligation?

"We shouldn't do this," she said. "Not yet."

"We have to talk about this. It's not going away. We have to face it together."

"Not yet," she said again. "Eclipse—"

"We're going to be parents. That's marginally more important than a pile of bricks encasing strands of figures."

"No, it's not more important in your life. That's where your focus has to be."

"You don't have to worry. Our child will never want

for anything. Whether we have half of Eclipse or all of it. Hell, we'll give her the whole damn thing and watch it disintegrate under her leadership. I started at the bottom once, I can do it again. I have a fuckload more support now than I did when I was eighteen."

"You shouldn't be thinking this way. I didn't tell you so you would trash your life, throw everything away. Eclipse is important, and it should be important. For the next ten, eleven weeks, it should be the most important thing in your life."

"Our child is the most important thing in my life. Now and in the future. For every week from now on. This one and any others we might have."

Her head shook. "Don't say things like that."

"I think we're beyond having plausible deniability about our relationship. If someone asks who the baby's father is, what will you say?"

"That it's none of their business."

"You'll say that to your family?"

"Yes, and I'm going back there soon to do exactly that."

"You're moving back to Boston?"

"Not immediately. I'll finish my contract here and complete the next one at RCI in New York. Beyond that, I'll take some maternity leave. I'll have to find a new apartment. My savings will cover the necessary expenses."

Medical bills, nursery décor, clothes, diapers, what else did a baby need?

"You don't have to worry about that," he said.

"I know you're in the category of super-rich, but I don't live on the street or dumpster dive. I can support this child. I have my own portfolio, my own priorities."

"What is your priority?"

"Leaving this conversation."

Something she should've done before it started.

Stalking across the room, she had to round the couch. That was where he intercepted her, blocking her path, getting right up close, right against her.

"Why are you being defensive?" he asked, his voice a low murmur. "We created this child together. We'll raise it together too. Whether you want to be with me is irrelevant. I'm this baby's father."

Fighting it was impossible. She had to look him in the eye, even knowing it would be a mistake.

Gazing into him, she couldn't stop the honesty spilling out. "I don't know how to do this," she whispered. "How to separate what I feel about us from what's right for our child."

"Us can be right for our child," he said, touching her hair. "Stay here with me, in LA. We have the space. Knox will sign the house over to us or we'll get our own. We'll get married—"

"No, this is exactly what I didn't want. I don't want you to feel obligated to do the right thing." She leaped back a step, restraining herself from putting those last few words in air quotes. "I'm attracted to you, yes. I know you're attracted to me, and we had a great time together, but that's not a sound foundation for a marriage. Didn't you learn anything from your relationship with Julietta? I don't want your company, your money, your home. And I'm not interested in being a trophy wife."

"You're being defensive again. Somehow, you've made me the bad guy, so you feel you have to push back. Have you forgotten what being together was like? I didn't bully you or have any interest in issuing commands. I'm telling you we can figure this out together, equally, as partners."

"That's not very romantic either."

"Screw romance, you don't give a damn about it. You don't think if I believed that shit would bring you back to me, I wouldn't have filled your hotel room and office with flowers every day? You're level-headed, Lilya. Sometimes too much. Pragmatic. Maybe I have to be the romantic in this relationship. Maybe I have to see its potential because all you see are obstacles. You think the worst, assume the worst, and I let you put that barrier up between us to save Eclipse, just like you told me to. You were right. At the time, it would've been lunacy to sacrifice Eclipse and have Julietta in our lives indefinitely rather than just run out the clock and then be together. Let's not be under any illusions, that's exactly what

I expected would happen. This was always on the horizon. Being with you was always what I wanted."

"We can't get married for the sake of a child."

"If you don't want to get married, we won't get married. You don't want to do it this year? We'll do it next year or in ten years. Marriage is less important to me than creating a solid family, as embracing this gift."

"We weren't given a gift, we were careless."

"Why are you having this child if you believe it was an accident? That it wasn't meant to be?"

"It's not the child's fault," she said. "It's not our baby's fault that its parents got too caught up in the moment to care about protection."

A condom had broken the first night they were together. They hadn't used them at Eclipse at all, any of the times they did it there. She was on the pill; they should've been safe. Apparently, fate had a screwy sense of humor.

"When do you think it happened?" he asked.

"Early. Like in our first few days. The dates work out and in case you were wondering, there was no one between you and Nathan. I broke up with him six months before I came to LA."

"I don't doubt you. I don't doubt the paternity of this child. I'm asking you for a chance to be its father… with you."

With her. Together. It wasn't marriage, but it was tempting. Mr. Always-Do-The-Right-Thing would marry her if she said she needed that piece of paper. She didn't.

"There's something I've been wondering about, worried about."

"Tell me."

"Whatever we choose to do, if you want to be a part of this child's life—"

"I do."

She laid a hand on him, calming his urgency. "I won't stop you. When this child is born, you will be its father, if that's what you want. But like I said in the office, I don't need anything from you. I don't expect or require anything. If you choose not to be a part of this child's life, that's okay too. Don't feel obligated. Please don't think this is your duty, that you have no choice."

"What's worrying you?"

"If you choose to claim paternity, someone will do the math."

"They'll figure out we were together before the contract was up." His lips thinned as she nodded. "I know what you're saying, and I know you want me to be smart and sensible about this, but I can't. This child is more important than Eclipse, it just is."

"Our child is the most important thing in the world. And if prioritizing him means sacrificing each other—"

"Amour," he said, moving right up against her. "I've wanted you since the moment I laid eyes on you. Losing you to the Julietta shit was punishment for rushing into that relationship. I learned my lesson. I learned how to distinguish real from fantasy. In my head, I made her into something she wasn't, saw what I projected onto her. With you, there was never anything more real. I didn't have to turn you into a fantasy because you were authentic in every way. I was always going to come for you. Whether here, in New York, or Boston. I wanted to honor your wishes, but as soon as the deadline passed, I was going to find a way to make you mine."

"Before you knew about the baby?"

He smiled. "Yes, Amour. I didn't know it until I lost you... until I hung up that phone the night we hit the press..." The night of the Queen Dinner. "I didn't admit it, even to myself, but..."

"But...?"

"I love you, Amour." The calm acceptance that washed over him was like a magic spell, he just looked lighter. "I can't be without you. Whatever happens, whatever you decide, I'm in love with you."

And that was what she feared facing herself. Love. If they'd found it, if she'd found it, the person she was supposed to be with, then the baby had forced them both to address it. She could've walked away, would've at the end of the contract. If he'd come for her then, would she have given in to what she felt for him? There was no way to play out that game of what if. What was for sure? She believed him. The certainty burning from within him was pure and honest.

"If we were to be together," she said, curling all but her index finger into a fist against his chest. "If, and that's a big *if*…"

"If?" he prompted with the twist of a smile not far from his lips.

"Your life would be a nightmare."

Instantly, he frowned. "Why?"

"Because I'm not the type of woman to bite my tongue and I'll bet Julietta isn't either. To have both of us in your life at the same time, with her calling the shots in Eclipse, you'll get grief night and day. I may have no stake in Eclipse, but it's as much my baby's birthright as hers."

His frown deepened. "Eclipse is not her child's birthright. I am not the father of her child."

"The world doesn't know that. The baby doesn't know that. Maybe it's my pregnancy, but it's got me looking at hers in a different way. She's going to give birth to a child that the world thinks is yours."

"And the world means less than the child itself."

"Her child will grow up believing you're its father. You can't embrace our child and ignore hers. The little one will have no reason to believe it's any different from ours. If she was carrying your child, I would expect you to treat it the same way that you would treat ours. Like I said, it's not the child's fault that it was conceived."

"The difference being, I wasn't there when Julietta's child was conceived."

"Now who's getting defensive?"

"The child you're carrying is ours." His tension was palpable. "The child she's carrying is nothing to me."

"That's not the child's fault. There has to be a plan for extricating yourself from the Julietta situation. If her baby's born and the world still thinks you're its father, that's it, you have to be its father."

"For the rest of its life?"

"Yes," she said despite his incredulity. "Whether it knows the truth, whatever the headlines read around the time of his or her birth will be recorded for posterity. Those words will be there, and this child will have questions. Are you its father? Are you not? Did you plan to raise it and then our child stole you away? It will want to know why it was punished, disowned by—"

"Hey now," he said, his knuckles resting on her cheekbone. "Don't let it upset you."

But it was upsetting her. Right or wrong, smart or stupid, maybe she was just hormonal.

"We have time, Zach. You want to talk about being given a gift, maybe that's it: time. We have the time to do this right. Our child is yours no matter what. It's not a problem or a dilemma or anything we have to navigate, it's just fact. The first three months of a pregnancy are the most dangerous, everyone knows that. We have time. Until we get past twelve weeks, we shouldn't tell anyone anyway."

"Jane knows. Knox, Roxie, Zairn—"

"I know, but we can trust them."

"I told Javi."

"I don't want to tempt fate. We declare this, start making plans for this, and something goes wrong… I'll be devastated."

"We'll be devastated."

"Let's just let my body do what it was designed for. I'll do everything I can to keep our baby safe and minimize risk factors."

"So we concentrate on Julietta? It doesn't seem right."

"If you want me to think about us having a future, I want to be the only two people in this relationship. One of three in this family. I don't want Julietta calling the shots, or her child growing up resenting ours."

"I hear you. As always, you're right." Except if that was true, they wouldn't be in their predicament. His fingers curled around the back of her neck. "It's complicated and might be difficult. It sure won't be easy. But I'm excited."

"You're going to be a father," she said, letting loose her smile. "It's kind of hot."

His smile became a grin. "Finally, she gets it." And when he stooped, angling her face upward, she didn't resist his kiss. His lips retreated a millimeter from hers. "I'm staying here tonight."

That startled her. "You're staying here? In the suite?"

"There's a third bedroom. The house echoes until I leave the front gates. There's always a photographer or two waiting, trying to catch me in a lie."

They hadn't lied, but they had kept secrets. By association, their friends had done the same. They never asked for an apology or guilted them for it. What did it say about them as human beings that they'd roped people they cared about into their complex plot?

"My room's downstairs," she said, her eyes on his. "I should say goodnight."

"Maybe you should." Zach's fingers combed into her hair at her temple. "But I don't want you to, Amour. I want you here, with me, both of you."

When his fingertips touched her stomach, refusing wasn't an option.

"Zach," she breathed as he came lower to unite their mouths again.

For all the talk about smart and sensible, some things were just instinct. Others may argue it was hormones. Maybe it was. This man was the father of her child. She owed it to their offspring to give him a chance, providing they didn't let it go so far that they couldn't stand to look at each other.

Laying her hands on his chest, she pressured him away a little. "We have to agree," she said as his lips sought hers again. She swallowed through the panting of her shallow breath. "If we try this, if we do this, we always put our child first. I don't want us to grow to hate each other or resent each other. We always have to be united."

"That's an easy promise," he said and given how much of a stand-up guy he was, she couldn't see him ever being the type to demonize the mother of his child.

If anyone deserved to be demonized, it was Julietta. With the resources he had at his disposal, he could tear the actress's world apart, but he didn't. He was too decent for that.

"Zach…"

As she threw her arms around him, he held back.

"And I'll make you another. I'll dedicate myself to this family. Put it before everything else. Whether it means giving up the company and the money, and moving to a hut in the wilderness, I will do what's best for this family."

As if the guy hadn't already sunk her enough. She tightened her hold, and he stooped lower, kissing her jaw before picking her up to carry her through the suite to a bedroom. He kicked the door shut and she shook her shoes from her feet.

"Are we alone?" she asked as he laid her down and stood up to tug off his jacket. "In the suite?"

"Amour, I don't give a damn."

Excitement came with liberation. Until that moment, being alone seemed like no big deal. Raising a child by herself was a commitment she'd accepted and sub-consciously started to prepare for. She wasn't alone anymore.

His hands, his fingers, his kiss and caress, she'd missed it, dampened down the cravings that screamed at her to go to him. The nights she'd lay awake wishing he was next to her again clashed together in an endorphin crescendo, obliterating that sorrow in a second.

"Zach."

She couldn't stop saying his name, like she had to convince herself this was a reality, not a fantasy.

Their lives were entwined now, together or not, they'd created a life, one that gave them new purpose and direction.

Their clothes disappeared and their mouths found their harmony in a kiss so deep and devouring that her existence became about this man, that moment, the acceptance. It was a promise compounding a promise. A need steeped in a desire so passionate, it wasn't possible to resist the addiction.

She trusted him. That's what it was. As ridiculous as it may seem from the outside, her body had picked the best possible father for her offspring. There wasn't a cruel or selfish bone in his body.

"Zach," she said again.

His tongue circled her nipple. "I'm with you,

Amour."

And that was it, he was hers. They'd face every challenge in the future together. It wouldn't be adversarial or dramatic. There was nothing truer than their love. Nothing but their child.

THIRTY-FIVE

THE NEXT DAY brought new life and new perspective. It was easy to get caught up in feelings and wish for the best. They couldn't afford to live in a bubble with all that was going on, but hormones weren't the only force at work between them.

Being in his arms was safe. She couldn't remember such contentment. With most men, the relationship was driven by the pressure of what they wanted, be it sex or attention. Usually, the former.

With Zach, she didn't feel that. There was no urgency. It seemed they had all the time in the world and could enjoy each other forever.

Such a powerful man would no doubt be constantly busy. Getting him on the phone would probably be impossible, let alone trying to set up a date or get any sort of face time. She knew better, or should know better, having dated wealthy men in the past. It wasn't like she had a proclivity for them. Life put them in her path.

Long ago, she'd vowed never to be a girlfriend to voicemail again. Zach wasn't that guy. Wouldn't be that guy. If something made her unhappy or there were barriers between them, he'd stick by his word and prioritize their family. He would.

After making love in the morning and showering together, they entered the suite's dining room. The other two couples were already enjoying breakfast.

"Good morning," Roxie said without hiding her mischievous grin.

"You two made up," Jane said, almost as elated, but not in such an impish way.

"From what I heard, they made up three, maybe even four times last night."

"Rox," she whispered on a snicker, sitting after Zach pulled out her chair and pushed it back in under her.

"Don't be ashamed of it. Own it."

"Making up's the easy part," Knox said, less impressed by their reunion. "Do you have a plan?"

Zach sat next to her and picked up the French press to pour coffee. "We plan to raise the baby together."

When he picked up another cup, she put her hand on his. "Not for me."

He paused like he didn't get it. Confusion only lasted a flicker of a second. "You want decaf?"

"I'll have to get used to life without it."

"This is why we can never have kids," Roxie said. "A life without coffee isn't one worth living. It's cruel and unusual punishment. We almost ordered decaf but weren't sure you'd make it out of the bedroom today."

And if the press got wind of decaf making its way to the top floor suite, they could have a whole new problem with media speculation.

Impatience shimmered around Knox. "This is a strategy meeting."

"Funny, I thought it was a breakfast."

Roxie's quip didn't go down well.

"Knox is right," Zairn agreed. "There has to be a plan to handle this."

No one was looking at her. The gravity of the development, of her pregnancy, struck her in a new way. Maybe this was how Julietta felt when she found out she was with child. It hadn't been done on purpose, by design or coincidence, yet the child was an inevitability. She had to handle it somehow. Putting it on Zach was the safest course for Julietta. For her, the last thing she could do was to admit the paternity of her baby.

"No one has to know," she said. "For now, it stays between us."

"That you're pregnant or that he's the father?"

"I'm proud of our child," Zach said before she could answer. "I won't—"

"We talked about this. Remember? The gift of time?"

"The sex probably fuzzied things up for him," Roxie said. "Men get fuzzied by sex. It's how you get them to buy you shoes."

"I have never in my life bought you a pair of shoes, Lola."

Roxie scoffed and slanted Jane's way. "But he's sure paid for them."

"You're two months pregnant," Knox said, bringing them back to the point. Jane must've filled in the details. "That gives us seven to get this right."

"Uh, people will start to notice before then."

"And I'll have to tell my family too," she agreed with Roxie. "The news doesn't have to include outing the father."

Zach hadn't gotten over his offense. "I want to celebrate this, to embrace it, not hide from it."

"I know," she said wondering if he'd forgotten everything they discussed the previous night. "We'll get there. The first thing we have to do is find a way to get you out of being the father to Julietta's child. Are you sure that's what you want? If you want to accept—"

"That's what I want."

"Next we consult a lawyer," she said, fixing on Zairn. "Someone you trust without connections to Julietta."

"I'll do you one better," Zairn said. "Someone we can trust without any interest in Julietta's agenda succeeding. Someone who takes loyalty to Zach and the truth as seriously as he does anything."

"Javi," Zach said, attracting everyone's attention.

"Exactly."

"Javi's a lawyer?" she asked. "I thought he was your VP."

"He's both."

"Did he advise you to sign the contract with Julietta?"

"No, he advised the opposite, but that was more about being my friend than anything related to the law. After I gave him the broad strokes, he refused to even look at the contract. If that was the gist, he couldn't see any advantage in signing it."

"But you did anyway."

"I wanted it to be done," he said. "At that time, I wasn't interested in rushing into another relationship."

"Is that what we're doing? Rushing into this?" She didn't let him answer. "Javi needs to look at the contract now, as my lawyer."

"Yours?"

"Yes, because if he's my official counsel, we have attorney-client privilege, which means he doesn't have to discuss anything we discuss, even if subpoenas are one day involved."

"I like her way of thinking."

Loosening up Knox didn't seem like an easy task, but she'd managed it.

"Admitting you're not the father of Julietta's child is easy, or it would be. You could go on the news and do that; it'll be the truth."

"Except that corners her," Knox said. "We announce he's not the father and she'll announce your relationship."

"Our relationship gives her the leverage she wants. One whisper to the media about the paternity of her child and half of Eclipse is hers. And given we're going to be parents, there's no denying it. Even if we tried, we'd be proven wrong eventually."

Because their baby was the proof. A DNA test could absolve Zach of his responsibility to Julietta's child. But one with theirs would be the same as signing Eclipse away.

Zach inhaled. "Whether or not it's Julietta, like you said, at some point, someone will do the math and figure out we were together before the deadline. We need to check for landmines that could come back to bite us."

"Is it retroactive?" Zairn asked. "Does it include former relationships?"

"I don't remember. I'll find it and give it to Javi."

"I'll give it to Javi," she said. "You're staying out of this. The further away from it you are, the less question there can be as to whether you did anything wrong. I didn't sign the contract, I'm not bound by it, but I also don't want to see you lose half your company or have our family held hostage by your ex-wife's whims."

"A breakfast and a strategy meeting," Roxie said and clapped, then threw out her arms. "Decaf for everyone!"

THIRTY-SIX

"WHAT DO YOU THINK?"

Three days went by before she saw the contract. Of course, Zach didn't hand it over blatantly. She'd mentioned it might be a good idea to leave it lying around somewhere for her to pick up. He had.

After handing it off to Javi at work, she waited another three days for him to set their meeting. Did it really take three days to review the thing? God, she needed Zach's stability. Keeping a lid on her anxiety was easier when he was around. With him, more interesting things always came up. But she was doing this for him, for their family. The sooner they had a plan, the better.

Since coming together again, they'd spent every night in the suite. But to keep a clear divide, she'd asked Javi to meet her in her hotel room. The one paid for by Ranby Kearns. Although the meeting wasn't hidden from Zach, she didn't want him present. If they did all end up in court one day, a clear separation worked in their favor.

"We should've done this over dinner," Javi said.

Frustration curled her fingers. "Please. You read it?"

"Cover to cover."

"Do we have any hope?"

"Actually…" he said, one corner of his mouth slid

upward. "We have more than that."

"More?"

"Potentially."

"You said Julietta was meeting with Beverley Woo?"

"Yes."

"Beverley Woo who's directly connected to Karryn Keller?"

"So?"

"So everyone suspects a tell-all interview."

"Uh huh." This was taking far too long for her liking. She gestured for him to speed up. "Keep going."

"The contract," he said, planting a straight forefinger on the papers stacked between them on the table. "Prevents Zach from having a public relationship with anyone in the specified twelve-month period."

"I know that. I hope I'm not paying you for this."

He laughed. "This is good. It's good news. I wish I'd read the fucking thing a year ago."

"Why?"

"'Cause it would've taken the pressure off. Turns out Zach's divorce lawyer wasn't completely inept. Zach can't have a public relationship, but she can't be the one to out him."

In surprise, she blinked. "Julietta?"

"Can't be instrumental in its exposure."

"Oh my God."

"Yeah," he agreed.

"So if it was her who told the press, or anyone who's connected to her—"

"The contract's automatically void. If she plans to do a tell-all interview with Karryn Keller…"

"Oh my God." She struggled with the implications. "She could've screwed herself already."

"Potentially."

He opened his hand above the contract. "We need proof. Something that would hold up in court if she takes it that far. It can't just be what you, or anyone, thinks. Someone would have to testify that she categorically told them about Zach's relationship with you. Not even just that he was in a relationship, but specifically with you."

"You think we'll struggle to get that?"

"You and me?" he asked, pointing back and forth between them. "Yes. We can't just stroll up to her father and ask if he made the call."

"He was meeting with Reeve Crosby," she said, recalling the night she met Zach. "Why was he doing that? Reeve Crosby was there at the meeting with Beverley Woo too."

"He may be your weak link, but he won't snap for us."

Her gaze settled on him. "Knox."

"Right."

"For him, it takes one phone call."

"The problem is…"

She gritted her teeth. "Knox isn't supposed to know about the contract."

"They listed Knox as a confidante. He hasn't signed the contract, but Zach was living with him. It was necessary for him to be in the loop." Right, yeah, she knew that. "Knox knows about the contract. That's a given. We don't have to worry about that."

"So what's the problem?"

"Asking Reeve Crosby about the relationship confirms it." Javi's finger relaxed until his palm was flat on the contract. "The media are all about the speculation right now. They have not announced any categoric, irrefutable proof that Zach is in a relationship or that you're connected to him."

"Does Reeve know about the contract?" she asked. "Does he know Julietta's playing him?"

"Unless someone asks him, we have no way of knowing what he knows."

"Except asking him reveals the existence of the relationship we are trying to conceal." With a huff, she slumped against the back of the dining chair. No one could just ask, or they'd be doing Julietta's work for her. "When Zach said complicated, he wasn't messing around. What do we do?"

"I know about the contract because I am a confidante."

"But you're also my lawyer."

"Another complication. A smart one though."

"Okay, but how does that—"

"The meeting took place at CollCom. If Knox or someone close to him were to mention the meeting with Beverley Woo or even that Reeve Crosby was on the premises…"

Hope. Oh, she perked up. "He might ask questions about that. About the purpose of the meeting. About what they discussed."

"And someone might tell him about the tell-all interview."

"We have to talk to Knox."

"Hold up, there's another step. Someone might relay to Knox that the tell-all interview is happening, but that's not enough. Beverley Woo has to reveal what the meeting was about. The substance of it. Not just that the interview will take place. Planning an interview is not a breach of the contract."

"Telling Beverley Woo or Reeve Crosby about the relationship is."

"Yes. Beverley has to explicitly tell Knox about the relationship and, ideally, reveal your name. The information has to have come from Julietta or her father. Knox must learn about your and Zach's relationship directly from Julietta's source."

That was the breach. Julietta giving out information about the relationship was her being instrumental in it becoming public knowledge. If they could get confirmation Julietta had told someone, anyone, about the relationship, the contract would become irrelevant. They'd be free to be together.

Processing what was required, decisions came fast. "I need a phone number."

"Knox's?" he asked, fishing his phone from his inside pocket. "I'd do it myself, but if we're relying on attorney-client privilege…"

"No," she said, shaking her head. "Zairn. I need to talk to Zairn."

Though Javi squinted, he didn't question her. He

scrolled to the number on his phone to send her the contact.

She wasted no time calling and raising the phone to her ear.

"Zairn Lomond," came the reply, but it didn't sound like him.

"Zairn?"

"Tibbs, his assistant. What do you need? Where did you get this number?"

"From my lawyer," she said. "Is it possible for me to talk to him?"

"I don't know. Who are you?"

Right, of course. "Lilya Kearns."

There was a pause. "One moment."

The line went completely silent. Mute. She held her breath, hoping the assistant would get her through.

A second later, Zairn's voice rose on the line. "Lil? What's wrong? Where's Roxie?"

"I don't know. She's fine... as far as I know. This isn't about her. I need to talk to Knox about something, but I'm not sure he'll hear me."

"Him and Rox rub each other the wrong way sometimes, but he's a good guy."

"I don't doubt that, but I don't want to put pressure on Jane. If he doesn't want to help, he doesn't have to. If she asks, he'll do it and if it goes wrong..."

"This is for Zach."

"There's a technicality, a kind of loophole, in the contract that might help us out."

"What is it?"

"I don't want to go into too much detail. Let's just say it would be really helpful if, somehow, Knox could find out, legitimately, that Julietta visited Beverly Woo at CollCom."

"Okay, that's doable."

"Would he be able to talk to her about that? Is that something Knox would do? Approach her direct?"

"If it involved his close friend's ex-wife? Yes." That was a relief. It had to seem natural, not choreographed. "And what would he want to talk to her about?"

"Whether there's an interview. More specifically, if

Ms. Woo was to mention what tidbits Julietta might have offered. For example, if her ex-husband was seeing someone, who that someone may be."

"If Julietta said it."

"It doesn't have to be Beverly Woo. Her or Reeve Crosby. Anyone. Whoever is easier to approach. We need someone to state Julietta told them about the relationship."

"I'm with you," he said.

"There has to be a chain of events…"

"That would stand up in court," he said. "I get it. This conversation never happened."

"And Knox can't—"

"Reveal the relationship himself," Zairn said. "We're on the same page. Leave it with me."

"Thank you. I apologize for roping you in, approaching you with this, but—"

"You're not in this alone. We all want Zach free of Julietta. It's on all of us. Fixing it will be a team effort."

She smiled. "You want me to find out where Roxie is?"

"No," he said quickly, a smile in his tone. "When trouble finds her, someone will be in touch. They always are."

"She adores you."

"And I her. We'll get through this. We have a future together, all of us. Take it easy."

He hung up and she exhaled. *A future together.* That sounded nice. She'd thought about her future with the baby and even with Zach. Zairn's point altered her perspective. Zach's friends and their partners would be in her life too. That wasn't a bad future to look forward to.

"What did he say?" Javi asked.

She sighed. "Now we wait."

THIRTY-SEVEN

HER MIND WAS STILL racing when she got back to the suite that night. Everyone was already there, movement and conversation from elsewhere carried to the living room, but she didn't seek anyone out. Slipping off her shoes, she lay on the couch, her hands flat on her belly.

She was pregnant.

Somehow it was just mind-boggling. She was going to be a mother.

"Hey, honey!" Roxie stood at the end of the couch. "You okay?"

"Yeah," she said and inhaled as she sat up. "Are there dinner plans?"

"We're going on a double date."

Except there were three couples.

Jane came from the direction of the bedrooms, male voices not far behind. "How are you doing, Lilya?"

Why was everyone talking to her like she was dying?

"I'm fine. You're going out?"

It wasn't possible for her and Zach to go out together in public. They'd be left… Oh, they'd be left alone. She smiled.

"And she's just figured out why we're going out," Roxie said and came over to sit and give her a hug.

Beyond Jane, Knox and Zairn were talking with Zach. Were they talking about that day? About their phone conversation. She hoped not. It wasn't that she wanted anything hidden from Zach, and she didn't want anyone to lie to him, but the whole point was to insulate him.

Zairn's eyes met hers. Despite itching to know how the conversation went or if Knox had been receptive, she didn't ask. She wouldn't mention it at all. Like he'd said on the phone, their conversation never happened. As far as the rest of the world was concerned anyway.

"Ready, Lola?"

Roxie jumped up and went to grab her fiancé's hand. "Ready."

As Jane came over, she stood up to accept the woman's hug. "Call us if you need anything."

But she had Zach, what else could she need?

The foursome traipsed toward the door.

"Don't wait up," Roxie called back, and then they were gone.

One day they'd be able to go out on a triple date. Providing the mess was done with before she gave birth. Afterwards, there may not be much time for dating.

"You hungry?"

"I am hungry," she said, strolling to her man, exhaling satisfaction when he kissed her. "Will you order something while I get changed?"

"What are you in the mood for?"

"Hmm," she purred, twining her arms around him.

"Dessert is guaranteed, Amour," he said and kissed her again. "But we have to keep that baby fed."

"Something light, chicken or fish. He chooses his moments to make me sick, usually the most inconvenient ones."

But Zach smiled. "I still can't believe it." His open hand slid onto her belly. "That our child is in there."

"We haven't had much time to talk about the parenting stuff."

"We have time tonight. Alone time." He kissed her head. "Go get changed. I'll order food."

If the hotel knew the other couples had gone out, it

might be suspicious to order two meals. Maybe she was overthinking. Slinking to their bedroom, she took a quick shower and slipped into a simple, comfortable dress. No need for makeup and fancy hair or flashy clothes. In the not-too-distant future, Zach would watch her push a human out of her body. If he could see her at her worst and still love her, they wouldn't have to worry about illusions in their relationship.

When she returned, he was in the living room, food laid out across the coffee table buffet style.

"I thought something less formal tonight," he said, sitting on the couch.

Barefoot and in jeans, he reminded her of their first date.

"That's a good idea." She went to join him, her hand sliding down his leg as she sat. He kissed her. Just a quick, simple kiss, yet it put a smile on her lips. "I like that you do that."

He started to build a plate. "Do what?"

"Kiss me," she said, stroking his leg, increasing her pressure. "Whenever we've been apart, you kiss me." Sometimes more passionately than others. "You're affectionate, I like that."

Because what was wrong with being honest?

He offered her the plate. "When we've dealt with the problems, you'll have to get used to me doing it in public too."

"I might like that," she said, pushing back into the corner of the couch, picking up her legs to cross them in front of her. "Is it an LA thing?"

He laughed as she bit into some chicken. "Maybe it is, I don't know. I just like kissing you."

And there was nothing wrong with that. "I like that you do."

Their eye contact lingered. "You sorry Roxie and Jane went out?"

"I was, for a second, but we don't get much time alone. And we'll go out with them sometime later. We have time."

"Yeah. We do." He drew in a breath and went back

to putting another plate together. "Though not forever."

"Not forever?"

"This little one will be here before we know it."

"You want to make plans? Can we do that?"

"We can do whatever we want." No, they couldn't. "In our conversations. We're alone. Everything we say here is us, just us."

The set of his brow hardened. His head moved as his attention went toward the window, but she read a shift in him.

"Stop being angry," she soothed.

"How can I not be angry?" he snapped. "It's my damn fault we're in this mess."

Shaking her head, she put her plate aside to crawl closer. "We're going to be parents, Zach."

"Which should be a happy thing. We should be able to celebrate it. It shouldn't be a secret."

"It's a secret now because that's what's best for our family. I told you I want to get to twelve weeks before we tell the world. We still have three weeks to wait. Stop focusing on your ex-wife and embrace the choice of your family." Picking up his hand, she put it on her stomach. "We need this little guy to cook for three more weeks. I'm not taking any chances on tempting fate."

He relaxed a little, his thumb moving in a caress. "I want to protect him and you."

"I know," she said, her hand moving in sync with his. "Be happy with us too. Please."

"I'm happy with you. That's why I get frustrated. I'm so damn proud of you, thrilled about our family, and I can't tell a soul."

"We don't need the universe's approval to make this real. We're real."

He nodded. "We are."

Widening her smile, she took his plate to set it aside. "No drama tonight," she said. "Have you thought about names?"

"Baby names?" he asked and laughed. "I have actually."

"Me too. What do you like?"

"Nothing too out there. It's an LA thing to give kids crazy names. I'd prefer something more traditional."

"Any names important to you? Would you want to name him or her after anyone?"

"I don't think so. I've never thought about whether I'd want my son to be Zach Kintyre the second. I want him to forge his own path, but maybe he'd be proud of our family. I don't know."

That didn't seem to be the moment to talk about a hyphenate. "Is it a boy you want?"

"I don't know. It's cliché, but I guess so long as they're healthy, it doesn't matter. Do you have a preference?"

She shook her head. "I want to know before though. If we can get a scan and they can tell us, I think it just makes sense to know. Is that okay? I can find out and not tell you. If you want it to be a surprise—"

"It's a surprise whenever we find out," he said. "Whether it's during a scan or after the birth, isn't it always a surprise?"

Yes, and she liked that his thinking aligned with hers. Being on the same frequency would be so important, especially in parenting.

"I like Jasper and Harrison for boys. If they're not too out there. I wouldn't mind if he was a Zach, though I don't know how I'd feel about calling out my son's name in bed. I say your name a lot when we're having sex."

"Okay, and that settles it," he said with mock authority. "No Zach the second."

"Girl names are more difficult." She stole a spring roll from his plate because it was closest. "Do you have any thoughts?"

"I think before we pick names, we have to decide where we want to live."

She swallowed what was in her mouth and put the other half back on the plate. "I've been thinking about that too." She grabbed one of the linen napkins to wipe her fingers. "I want to see out the RCI contract, but that will take us right up to January."

"You're due in January."

"Yeah."

"You want to give birth in New York?"

"I have some time off for the holidays, we can spend them wherever you want, but after…"

"After you want to be in New York to finish at RCI?"

"I don't know," she said and sighed. "There will be so much to plan, so much to do. I want to work as long as I can, but I want what's best for the baby too."

"We'll spend the holidays together, then we'll stay in New York until you deliver."

"We?"

He nodded, easing her against the back of the couch, resting there with her. "I will never bully you, Lil. I hope you know that."

"I do," she said, stroking his arm.

"I meant what I said about us being partners. This is equal. All the way. If the RCI contract is important to you, then I want you to see it through. I'll spend as much time in New York as I can while you're there. I don't want to miss the pregnancy."

"I'll take weekends whenever I can, come back here to you."

"Our friends are in New York as well, don't forget. Would you consider staying there?"

"There?"

"Rouge HQ," he said. "Zairn has a building by the park. Knox and Jane have talked about staying there, temporarily anyway. If they're there with Roxie and Zairn, I'll know you have people around."

"It might not be so easy to watch your child disappear to some random city."

"No, or its mother, but New York comes with a support system."

"But you'll be here all by yourself."

He was quick to smile. "There are some Colliers still here. Rourke and Dyce live just a few hours' drive north, less than that in a chopper. I'm okay in California. But, if you want, I can talk to Knox about staying—"

"I don't want people disrupting their lives for us."

"What about after the baby's born? You want to live in New York full time?"

"I always planned to take some time off. I never decided how much. But there's no reason we can't spend it here in LA. After that, I have no idea where contracts will take me. I don't like the idea of either of us being away from our child for long."

"We'll talk about that later," he said, brushing his finger down her jaw. "We have to get through the birth first."

"We?" she asked, amused. "You plan on pushing this baby out?"

"I'll be your coach. I'm an amazing coach. It's all about that positive attitude, baby."

She laughed. "If you try that while I'm in pain, I'm likely to hurt you."

"Are you worried about it?"

"Right now it feels like this remote thing. It's abstract. I can't picture it. I'm sure that will change as he gets bigger and we take classes."

Something they wouldn't be able to do together until the world knew.

"You want a water birth, a home birth, anything like that?"

"I want a quick and painless birth," she said. "I'm not interested in being a trooper or a martyr. If there are drugs and I need 'em, I want 'em."

He laughed and pulled her head to his lips for a kiss. "Okay, baby, you got it. Whatever you want will be yours."

Whatever she wanted. She wanted him and the child inside her. Neither had been in her plans, but now that she had them, she never wanted to let them go.

THIRTY-EIGHT

A WEEK HAD PASSED since her contract meeting with Javi and phone conversation with Zairn. No one had brought it up again. No one.

She didn't want to doubt Zach's friends but was nervous. Did the men have it under control? Was she assuming too much? The longer the situation went on unchecked, the closer they'd get to the crescendo of Julietta's plot. Maybe they'd got it wrong, maybe the divorcée was wilier than they believed. Waiting wasn't easy, it wasn't fun.

"Lil!" Roxie called.

She'd just finished drying her hair. When she popped out of the closet, her friend was in the bedroom doorway.

"Are you okay?"

"Yeah. Zairn just called to say they're on their way back."

Later than usual that Saturday night. Typically, their men tried to be home between eight and nine, and it was already after ten. Home… Could a hotel suite be "home"?

"Okay."

She, Roxie, and Jane had already eaten dinner together and had a couple of drinks. Virgin for her, of course. Non-alcoholic wine wasn't actually that bad, she was becoming accustomed to it.

"He said we should turn on the TV," Roxie said, equally confused. "Jane's cuing it up."

"Turn on the TV? Why?"

Roxie went out; she followed in her wake. "I don't know. He didn't tell me and just said he didn't want us to miss it."

When they got to the living room, Jane was crouched by the TV, mouth open. Karryn Keller filled the screen.

"What's going—"

"Oh my God," Jane said. "Roxie…" The woman's wide eyes landed on them. "Oh my God!"

Was this the interview? Was it happening? Julietta wouldn't be so careless, would she? To announce the relationship on air, to broadcast it to the world? The contract would go down in flames and Zach would have all the power. What was Julietta's game?

Roxie grabbed her hand and pulled her over to sit on the couch, both tense and expectant.

"It can't be easy sharing these things," Karryn said. "You're here tonight to set the record straight."

"Because it's the right thing to do," a female said.

The picture changed.

Not to Julietta.

Karryn wasn't interviewing Zach's ex-wife at all. She was interviewing Zairn's ex-girlfriend: Kesley Walsh. What the hell was going on?

"Oh my God," she said, mirroring Jane's sentiment.

"Julietta and I have been through a lot together," Kesley said. "But I don't think it's right that she tear down a man she once loved simply to gain sympathy and improve her chances of snagging high profile, coveted roles."

"And you know this? You know she was—there was a plot, an undertaking to slander Zachary Kintyre?"

"I can tell you the marriage ended because of infidelity. Hers, not his. Coming to the settlement in the divorce was difficult. Zach had no desire to hurt the woman who'd cheated on him. He just wanted to be out of the relationship."

Those were practically his exact words.

"I'll be damned," Roxie said. "I knew there was a reason I liked her."

"Oh my God," she whispered.

Kesley went on to lay out how the relationship ended, the contract, even that Julietta was the one to leak Zach's relationship, which would screw the actress up royally.

Twenty minutes in, the guys arrived back.

"Is there anything that woman won't do for you?" Roxie asked Zairn as he sat down next to her and kissed her cheek.

"What she was doing was wrong."

"If you ask Kesley, she'd probably say you dumping her was wrong."

"We've never gone out of our ways to hurt each other," Zairn said. "She's a decent person. Just…"

"Needy," Roxie finished for him, flashing Zairn a grin. "That's fine by me."

Roxie grabbed her fiancé's face and pulled his mouth to hers for a kiss.

Zach just stood there in the space between couches fixated on the television.

"Zach isn't the father of Julietta's child?" Karryn asked.

Kesley didn't hesitate. "No, it's a physical impossibility. Julietta herself told me she and Zach haven't been intimate since before he filed for divorce."

"Why would Julietta put it on him? Why call him the father of her child?"

"Because the true father of her child is married and has his own profile to worry about."

The interviewer probed deeper. "Do you know who the father of her child is?"

"Yes."

"And will you—"

"Not here today, no."

"Because…" Karryn prompted.

"Because he's a liar and a cheat, but he's also rich and influential. He could cause problems for someone. Tie them up in a legal mess. I don't want to be that someone."

She went to Zach. "Are you okay?"

He didn't speak, just stared at the TV.

"I won't apologize," Knox said.

Zairn backed him up. "I was in on it too."

Though that much was obvious given the identity of the interviewee.

"Julietta's interview was setup for next week," Knox said. "We let her keep on thinking it was going to happen and slipped Kes in under the radar."

"Kesley learned about your relationship from Julietta," Zairn said. "This is all truth."

"It came from me," she said, curling her fingers around Zach's forearm.

Knox and Zairn had gone much further than she ever could've imagined. Having someone confess that Julietta had given them knowledge of the relationship voided the contract. Kesley was announcing the truth to the world, freeing them from their chains.

They owed a debt that she'd try her best to repay.

"Lilya didn't know we were going to do this," Knox said, trying to protect her.

In the same way that she, Roxie, and Jane had tried to protect their men.

But she wasn't going to give up that easy. "I take full responsibility. And it wasn't hormones. I found out that the contract would be void if Julietta was instrumental in exposing any relationship you may have. If she outed you, it didn't count. And she did. Kesley knows it."

It was an avenue she hadn't even considered given the women were close friends. But Kesley had traveled the world with Zairn, been intimate with him, they had a relationship, a history. Maybe Kesley was just doing what was right. Maybe she was trying to win the affection of a man she still craved. Or maybe she wanted to hurt and ruin her best friend. Motivation was really irrelevant when it served them so well.

That sounded callous, but she didn't mean it like that. Just as her reasons for wanting it to happen were her own, so were Kesley's, and it wasn't necessarily her place to probe. The woman was doing them a service, giving them a gift so much bigger than she could ever know.

"Say something," she said, gripping him tighter. "Scream if you want. Yell at me."

"It's over."

Not a great way to start. Over…?

"Jules will take this to her lawyers."

"Good thing ours are better than hers," Zairn said to Knox.

"You know it."

Zach didn't mean it was over like they were over. Did he?

His static expression was impossible to interpret.

"She'll tie us up in court," Zairn said. "No doubt about it, but Eclipse is safe."

"And she won't win much public sympathy," Roxie added. "People like Kesley and they like Zairn more. Seeing Kesley doing this, the world knows it's Zairn sanctioned, and me sanctioned too. I'm quite happy to talk about this on my stream."

"It's whatever Zach wants," Jane said, the gentlest of them.

"I should call Jules," Zach muttered.

"No, you shouldn't," Knox and Zairn said together, standing in sync.

"This is nothing to do with you," Knox stated. "You didn't instigate this. You didn't encourage it. You're not responsible for it."

"Call her now and all you'll get is abuse," Zairn said, "and four thousand questions in the witness box about the conversation."

"Any and all communication with, and relating to, Julietta goes through lawyers from here on out. That goes for all of us." Knox made eye contact with everyone but settled on Roxie. "RK. That goes for you too."

"People will ask," Roxie said. "I do Q and As online all the time."

"If people ask, tell them the truth. While there's the potential for further action, you're not allowed to talk about it. Hell, just go with 'I'm not allowed to talk about it.'"

"I don't know if people will believe I'd follow the

instructions of anyone who tried to dictate to me, but…" Roxie shrugged and settled back on the couch. "It's for the greater good. I'll do it for my godchild." Zairn rolled his eyes. "Getting in there early, Casanova."

"Do you think anyone wants you to be responsible for teaching a kid right from wrong?"

"I'll teach your kid right from wrong."

"You will run our household from day dot. You do now and will then. Our child will know that. We're just lucky you take us along for the ride."

A distant sound caught her attention. "That's my phone. I left it in the closet."

She took a step before Zach grabbed her arm. "Leave it."

He was looking at her. Thank God he was looking at her and wasn't just gawping at the screen.

"Are you mad?"

"It's no less complicated," he said, cradling her cheek. "You took a risk doing this, all of you did, and I can't express my gratitude. It leaves me indebted to all of you."

"You're indebted to no one," Knox said. "This is what family do for each other."

The men made brief eye contact, though hers never left his until it came back to her.

"It will be safer to stay here at the hotel for a while. There are multiple ways in and out. It's easier to conceal our arrival and departure in a place that has so many people going in and out. You might want to take a few days off work."

"It's the weekend."

"A few days after that."

"Shit," she said. "I should call Frank."

No doubt that was who'd been blowing up her phone.

"Later," Zach said, guiding her onto the couch. "Let's see what else Kesley has to say."

If they were going to answer questions on the charges laid at their door, it would be best to know what those charges were. Otherwise, they could admit something that wasn't already out there.

The "smart" wasn't on her mind when Zach put an arm around her and settled her body against his. His embrace brought relief for both of them.

The Julietta problem may not be entirely resolved, but at least they didn't have to hide their connection anymore.

THIRTY-NINE

WATCHING TURNED OUT to be a good idea. So far, Kesley had confirmed Zach's relationship based on what Julietta had told her. But she hadn't named Zach's other half or revealed the existence of their child. It was possible she didn't know the latter, but she doubted Kesley was in the dark as to her identity.

What would happen if Kesley didn't name her? For the relationship to be truly revealed and the contract definitely voided, they needed Julietta to have spilled more than something that could be shrugged off as benign rumor.

But it wasn't over yet.

"You've done an amazing thing," Karryn said to Kesley on the TV. "Setting the record straight. Showing support for your best friend's ex."

"It's not about supporting Zach."

Karryn smiled. "Zairn Lomond then, the men are close."

"I've seen this unravel from both sides. I'm not sure there are any winners, I'm just conveying the facts, as I know them."

The interviewer inhaled. "I suppose there's only one more question to ask." She paused. For dramatic effect. "Did Julietta Ines-Kintyre tell you who Zachary Kintyre was in this new relationship with?"

Kesley licked her lips. "Yes."

"And who is it? Anyone we know?"

Oh God, was she going to say it? Wasn't she? They kind of needed her to, yet her heart pounded, fueled by adrenaline. Everyone seemed to draw closer to the screen as Kesley's furtive eyes rose.

"Lilya Kearns, of Ranby Kearns."

"Good girl," Zairn muttered, sharing a quick smile with Knox. "That was a good question. Direct. Gives us what we need."

"You fed them it in advance?"

"No way I'd let them fuck this up," Knox said. "And she was instructed to ask at the end, limits the time for further questions."

Smart. Maybe this guy did know what he was doing.

Karryn wasn't done. "Have you seen them together?"

"No."

"Have you spoken to either of them?"

"The first and last time I met Lilya Kearns was the night of the Queen Dinner."

"What was your impression of her?"

"Oh, I think I'm the last person who should be judging other people's characters," Kesley said with a polite laugh. "Apparently, I'm not such a great judge of character."

After a subdued laugh, Karryn Keller began to wind down the show.

The sound of her cellphone carried to them again. Now that her name was out there, it became so much more ominous. All she'd done was sit there, yet she was exhausted. Still, it couldn't be delayed forever.

She kissed Zach's jaw and stood up. "I have to talk to him sometime. Kesley has done the hard part. This shouldn't take long."

She hoped.

It was no surprise to see her uncle's name on the screen when she reached the device in the closet. Taking a second to steel herself, she slid to answer.

"Uncle Frank," she said, fighting to relax her jaw.

"Have you lost your mind?"

Of course that was the first question. The whole damn planet thought she'd lost her mind. One way or another, their relationship was going to come out at some point. Zairn and Knox had fixed it so Zach wouldn't lose half of Eclipse in the process. The fallout of an affronted relative was nothing compared to that threat. She'd take it. She'd take all the grief Frank could throw at her.

"Maybe I have lost my mind."

"You couldn't have told me before Kesley Walsh was up there declaring it to the world?"

"There are reasons for things happening the way they did," she said, wandering into the bedroom. "But it's out now."

"And you're not denying it?"

"I'm in a relationship with Zachary Kintyre."

As if saying those words made it real, a sense of fortitude came with relief.

"This happened on the contract. He seduced you?"

"It could be argued I seduced him," she said, knowing her uncle wouldn't appreciate her being glib. "Does it matter how it happened?"

"No, it doesn't." The sense of bluster behind his voice was equally resigned. "You need to come home."

"Why? I have work here."

"Not with Eclipse. Do you have any idea how you've jeopardized the operation? We have built our reputation over generations. We're tough. Impartial. Fair. Objective. Neutral. No one would believe you've maintained your objectivity while sleeping with the man at the top."

"Is that what this is about? Zach doesn't ask me about my work at all. We don't talk about it. I made it clear from the beginning that being together wouldn't sway my opinions, and he's never asked for special treatment or dispensation."

"Regardless, we'll send someone to take over in your place."

"Frank—"

"It doesn't matter," he said, something strained yet gentle in his tone. "I can trust you. Everyone at Ranby Kearns can trust you. Kintyre and Eclipse can trust you. But in the war of public opinion—"

"Since when are we subject to public opinion?"

"Since you started sleeping with the ex-husband of one of the world's most famous and beloved actresses."

"That's what it all comes down to? Julietta?"

"We have to cover our asses. If you're with him and it's real, he'll understand."

"But you want me to come home?"

"To show face here? Yes."

"It's not my responsibility to calm the troops, that's on you."

"Get your ass back here. Grab the reins of your department. Show your mother she raised you right."

Her mother was less than fifty percent responsible for her upbringing. Frank was the one who took care of most of it. Losing her father had taken a lot from her mother. People liked to tell her that the woman was a shadow of her former self, but having little memory of her mother before, she couldn't comment on whether it was true.

"Does Nathan know?" Frank asked.

She closed her eyes. "It's not my responsibility to fill him in on my life choices anymore. We're broken up and have been for a while. He doesn't care."

"He has to show his face in this building too." No surprise her uncle was still at work. "No man wants to be made a fool of."

"I moved to New York. Away from Boston and Ranby Kearns. So I could live my life without all this bullshit. Without what should be right and shouldn't. How things *look* or *appear*."

"You don't think we know it's bullshit?" he asked. "We do. But this is the way the world works."

"What about RCI?"

"You can kiss that contract goodbye too. I doubt Matteo Reid or Kinloch Gramercy-Peake wants the girlfriend of a competitor examining their books."

Was that the time to tell him both men were Zach's close friends and had known about the relationship since practically the beginning? No. That information could wait.

"Do I have a future at Ranby Kearns? If I'm never

going to be trusted to do my job—"

"You don't get to quit and take the easy road out. I expect you to be in my office within twenty-four hours."

The line went dead.

"What did he say?"

Zach's voice brought her around.

"That I'm a screw up. Seems all I do these days is disappoint people and bring more stress and aggravation to their lives."

"You haven't disappointed me."

She exhaled a laugh, her tired chin dropping as her phone hand fell to her side. "Didn't expect me to get pregnant though, did you?"

"Neither did you," he said. "And I don't want us talking about that as if it's a negative. Yeah, it was a surprise, but I'm already grateful to this child."

"Grateful?" she asked, her attention rising to his. "Why?"

His slow smile matched the pace of his progression to her. "You were ready to run out on me. Ready to call it quits. And this little one said 'you're not abandoning my daddy.'"

He put his arms around her and hers rested on his chest. "You know I don't know a thing about parenting?"

"We'll learn."

"It's possible I'm going to be out of a job. What kind of mother does that make me? I'm wrecking his chances of a decent future already."

"You've met my circle of friends," he said. "Not a single one of them would hesitate to employ you. Neither would I."

"Is it still called nepotism if there's sex involved?"

Though wasn't her job at Ranby Kearns achieved through the same ends? She'd trained and worked hard since before she was old enough to be paid. She'd earned that job.

"Frank can't fire you for getting pregnant. You told me yourself that you didn't have to declare relationships to those at the top."

"I've never had a relationship with anyone at your level in an organization I'm auditing before. Never really had a relationship like this, to be honest. Maybe I should've declared it."

"Would it have played out any differently if you'd told Frank?"

"He'd have told me to dump you sooner. Maybe we wouldn't have—"

"It wouldn't have mattered. By your math, you got pregnant our first weekend together. We'd always have ended up here."

"Maybe he was right."

Leaving his embrace, she tossed her phone to the bed and went back into the closet. How much should she pack? Her things were spread between that suite, her room downstairs, and whatever she'd left at Zach's. Was she going home for the weekend or indefinitely?

She grabbed the gym bag she'd brought her clothes upstairs in and tossed in a couple of toiletries. One way or another, her friends wouldn't steal or abandon her stuff. Her collection of things still in Frank's house would suffice. Better that than hauling heavy luggage all over the place.

Over time, her life got spread thinner and thinner. After riding this storm, it wouldn't be a bad idea to think about regrouping. But she'd worked all over the world and was used to picking up and leaving at a moment's notice, traveling light.

Zach joined her. "Going somewhere?"

"Apparently," she said, putting on her necklace and bracelet. "I can't really give you more than that until I've seen him."

"Him?"

"Frank."

"He wants you back in New York?"

"Boston," she said, picking up a few other pieces for the bag. "That's where he is."

"For how long?"

"I don't know."

"I don't like the idea of you tiptoeing home with your tail between your legs like we've done something shameful," he said. "Javi can handle things here. Zairn and Knox are around if he needs counsel he can trust."

"You don't trust your board?"

"To look out for their own interests?" he said. "I do. The circle of people I trust with the wheel totally and completely is small."

"What a surprise," she said without sincerity and showed him a smile. "It's okay." She scooped her hair up into a ponytail. "You don't have to come. You can stay here."

"I want to come. You didn't make this baby by yourself."

"Frank doesn't know about the baby yet."

"Are you going to tell him?"

"I'll judge his mood," she said on a shrug. "We're not at twelve weeks. You know I was waiting for that watershed before telling everyone."

"Do you plan to have dinner?"

She squinted at him. "Tonight? I've eaten."

"With Frank. In his house. Out with friends or family. Do you plan to socialize?"

"I don't know. It depends how long I stay."

"Will he notice you're not drinking alcohol or coffee?"

She smiled, catching up to his thinking. "Frank spends more time at the office than you, Knox, and Zairn combined. I can't imagine he's changed much since I lived there. Would he notice? Maybe. If we were in that situation."

"You'll raise his suspicions at least."

And maybe he'd think their love was about a child rather than each other? "People can suspect all they like. I don't owe them any explanation. There are only two people who I owe anything to right now." She went to take his hand and laid it on her stomach. "That's my baby and his or her father."

"Our little one hasn't put up any fight yet," he said. "He or she trusts their mother. I do too. But you don't have to go through any of this alone. You're not alone."

"So pick up the phone if I call. Let me vent or give me advice. I don't know what Frank wants and I don't want to go in too heavy-handed until I've got a lay of the land. Showing up together might put him on the defensive. I know how to handle Frank; I've been doing it all my life."

"Okay, but do you have to go tonight?"

"He wants me in his office within twenty-four hours."

"It's a five, six hour flight."

"I might have to wait on standby and that can take—"

"You have a plethora of jets to choose from," he said. "I hope you fly Eclipse. There's no need to hide it, everyone knows we're together now. If you get on what Jane calls the 'Zee-Jet' tongues will start wagging. And I have it on good authority, Zairn and Roxie have had sex all over that plane. I don't know that I'd want to touch anything."

"I'm already pregnant," she said, looping her arms around his neck. "What's the worst that can happen?"

"Prefer Z's plane to mine?"

"Prefer your bed to anyone else's."

"Stay the night. Leave in the morning."

He didn't need to give her the hard sell. She wanted to be with Zach, to sleep with him next to her. She'd never get used to it, waking up and seeing him there by her side. Something always clenched within her. More than desire or even security, she felt whole next to him, in his arms, in his life.

And now it was official. They were a couple. The universe knew. Finally, she could embrace being his.

FORTY

SHE CONSIDERED MAKING a stop at the house after touching down in Boston. But when she got into the car waiting for her at the airport, keyed up, she wanted the initial meeting out of the way.

Zach's phone went to voicemail. Damnit.

No safety net. No one to talk her out of it. To confirm if launching herself into a confrontation was a good idea or a recipe for disaster.

She was on her own.

She and the baby anyway.

Ignoring the prying eyes and whispering gossips, she strode into Ranby Kearns HQ with complete confidence. Maintaining a brisk pace to build her heart rate, adrenaline was good cover for any insecurities that might creep in.

Not so long ago, she'd been an executive in one of the top floor offices directing their employees. Was it anyone's place to judge her? Just because her life had become more public than she'd like didn't mean they owed anyone anything.

Except Kesley.

People might think she'd be angry with Kesley for outing the relationship. Those who didn't know about the contract anyway.

This had been the only way it could ever have gone down. Within the confines of the contract.

She owed the woman a debt.

Having the truth broadcast gave them cover. The evidence was plain enough to stand up in any court. It wasn't whispered maybes, a game of Telephone, Kesley told it like it was. It just so happened Julietta had done the wrong thing.

Zach hadn't called back.

They'd spoken not long after her plane took off. He'd been on his way into the office and ended the call by asking her to keep in touch. Maybe he was in a meeting.

No turning back.

At least the Ranby Kearns elevator accepted her security clearance. A sign her uncle wasn't quite ready to toss her out on her ass. Going up, she shook her hands at her sides. The adrenaline had to keep going. It couldn't wane. She'd walk in there, look Frank in the eye and tell him he had no right to stifle her career based on her choice of life partner.

Frank was a reasonable man. A patient man. Typically.

The reason Ranby Kearns had a reputation for being so fair was him. Often, he was the only sane voice in an argument. The one playing mediator and calming everyone down.

When the doors opened, she kept her eyes locked onto the path ahead, leveled her chin and strode on out. Frank's office was in her sights. The place he'd told her to be within twenty-four hours. She intended to deliver and threw open the door to go in, but… there was no one there.

Damnit. The momentum was lost.

She didn't fear her uncle and doubted she'd become a blubbering mess. Though God only knew what hormones would do to her.

He wasn't there. Where could he be? Anywhere given it was a workday. Every day was a workday.

She tugged her phone from her purse, dialed his number, and waited for him to answer.

"I'm here. Where are you?" she asked before he even had a chance to speak.

"This is Mr. Kearns' assistant. He's in a meeting right now. Where are you?"

"In his office."

"Stay there. He'll be back soon."

"Soon?"

What was soon?

The moment the assistant hung up, she called Zach. Again, he didn't answer. And she'd thought he wasn't the type to dodge his girlfriend's calls. What else had she been wrong about?

Javi? No, if Zach was busy, chances were his lawyer was too. Roxie would only inflame her outrage.

Jane was the best bet.

"He's not here," she said when the line connected to her friend. "He demands I come all the way here and then doesn't even show up for the meeting!"

"Where are you?"

"In his office. Where he told me to be. Where he should be, but he's not."

"I'm sure he'll be there soon," Jane said, ever calm and gentle. "He didn't know exactly when you would show up. He's probably eager to have the conversation too. He's a busy man——"

"I'm busy!" Or she had been until her uncle pulled her off the Eclipse contract. She went to sit in his chair. "I don't know what he wants from me." Her pent-up need to vent was depressurizing. "He demanded I come here to explain myself. What is there to explain? I fell in love with a man and the relationship is complicated, but it's really no one's business."

Especially now they were free of the Julietta problem. Semi-free anyway. And that woman's deeds were under serious scrutiny from the press. The legalities were stacked in their favor, but Zach's ex wouldn't go quietly.

"No, but the world doesn't work that way," Jane said.

"And Zach isn't picking up."

"Did you call Roxie?"

"No," she said on an exhale. "I thought about it, but figured we'd end up in some kind of spoof SEAL movie skit, crawling on our bellies through dirt all night."

Jane laughed. "Sounds like Roxie. You should've let Zach join you."

"I don't want his and Frank's relationship to start with hostility. Frank's important, he's always been there for me. Yes, he oversteps, but almost everyone I know does."

Because they were all type-A personalities. Strong. Driven. Ambitious. That was life at the top. Everyone except Jane anyway. She seemed like the only level-headed one among them most of the time.

"Don't focus on the bad," Jane said. "Your uncle cares about you. He wants to know that this relationship is real. That you won't get hurt or be used. You should see this as a positive. It's always better to have people care about you than not care at all." She smiled. That was the reason she'd called Jane. Just like that, her stress level dropped. "And you have the baby to think about now. All this tension and upset can't be good for the little one. Zach loves you. The baby loves you. All of your friends love you. No matter what your uncle says, you have a home here, security here."

"It doesn't seem right to be completely dependent on Zach."

"I agree," her friend said. "Knox offered me my pick of work with CollCom. I should choose to work there. One day our children will work there. I'd rather be involved in the process than on the sidelines wondering if my children were being treated right."

"So you think I should work for Eclipse?"

"Either that or we go out on our own," Jane said. "I haven't settled on anywhere and don't want to be completely dependent on my man either. But he tells me anything I want to know, so for now, I feel like I'm on the inside."

Going into business with Jane didn't sound like a bad idea, though the beauty didn't exactly have the killer instinct required to climb to the top.

"Maybe something in charity," she said. "A non-profit."

"We'd certainly have plenty of donors."

Fundraising would be fun. Because with Zach, Knox, and Zairn in the mix, as well as their network of friends, they were connected enough to have access to all kinds of resources and services.

"Now if only I could get hold of my man," she said.

"I'm sure he has his reasons for being unreachable."

"I'll go try him again. Thank you, Jane."

"Any time," she said, and the line disconnected.

Trying Zach's number again was fruitless. Voicemail.

"You know…" she said into her phone, pushing back in Frank's chair. "One day, in the not-too-distant future, I'll be calling to tell you that your child is trying to make its way into the world. That I'm in labor. You know what would be really great in that scenario? What would make me really happy? If you actually picked up the goddamn phone. No need to panic, Jane calmed me down. But what would make me feel better? Hearing your voice." Yeah, it was embarrassing to admit, which would be why her gaze dropped, but it was the truth. "I miss you. It's been less than a day and I miss you. Thank God I'm having your—" The office door opened and in came Frank… with Nate. Her ex. Crap. "Call me later." She hung up, rising from the chair. "Did you need reinforcements?"

"I need to know what the hell is going on," Frank said. "I thought I could trust you."

"You can and you do. This isn't about trust. You're pissed because of the way you found out. Not to get into too much detail, but I actually didn't know last night was going to happen before last night."

Okay, so there had been a loose plan, but she hadn't known about the interview or Kesley's involvement.

"Zachary Kintyre? How on earth—"

"The *how* doesn't matter."

And it was a fun story or would be a fun story to tell friends. Her uncle wouldn't appreciate it.

"Did he pressure you?" Nathan asked. "Harass you? Corner you?"

"You know me better than that, Nate. If any man tried to pressure me into anything, I'd shove my six-inch heel so far up his—"

"Okay, so it was consensual."

"It's more than consensual. We plan to have a future together."

"Don't you find the timing convenient? That he just happens to fall for you at the same time he needs a favorable outcome from the company you work for?"

"Zachary may want to win, but he wants to win fair. He's not interested in screwing over RCI or Gramercy. You want to pull me off the Eclipse job? Do that. But there's no reason I can't work the RCI contract."

"Matteo Reid might have something to say about that."

"Maybe. Do you want me to get him on the phone? Have him sign a disclaimer that he understands and accepts my intimate relationship with Zach and is happy for me to proceed? We can get one from Kinloch Gramercy-Peake too."

"And Jamison Dawes?"

Okay. He was the third potential buyer.

"Possibly," she said. "My connection to him is vaguer."

"Oh, but you have a connection to Kinloch Gramercy-Peake and Matteo Reid?"

"You said you plan a future," Frank said. "Does that mean marriage?"

"Please don't get Zach started on marriage. He'd marry me tomorrow. It's not something I need."

"As I know all too well," Nathan muttered.

"If you have something to say to me, say it."

"Less than a year ago, you weren't interested in marriage and a future, now suddenly you are?"

And just like that, she decided to keep the baby news to herself. For the time being anyway. If she told them, they'd reduce her relationship with Zach to obligation and necessity.

"Does he love you?" her uncle asked.

"Yes."

"Do you love him?"

"I do."

A petite brunette with glasses poked her head around the door. "Sir, your next meeting is—"

"Yes, thank you, Mieux."

The brunette departed.

"Mew?" she asked. "Is that what you called her?"

"It's her name," her uncle blustered, gesturing as though to shoo her question away, "it's French. We have things to discuss. Important things. We'll do it at dinner tonight."

"You're coming home for dinner?"

"Eight o'clock," he said, already stalking to the door to disappear out.

The silence between her and Nate wasn't awkward, but there was a sense of expectation.

"Anything you left at mine is at Frank's now," he said.

"Thank you."

"Do you need a car or—"

"I'm good. I guess there's someone working in my office," she said as Nate strolled toward the exit.

"No, actually." He opened the door a couple of inches. "Frank was always hoping you'd come back to Boston eventually. He won't take this well. LA's a helluva lot further than New York."

Was that why Frank was angry? It hadn't been her intention to leave Ranby Kearns, though if it became too difficult, she'd have no choice. Would she choose her job over Zach? No. No job was worth turning her back on the father of her child.

But Frank was the closest thing she had to a father. He had such high hopes for her taking over in his stead while she was with Nathan. They'd spoken about them being a power couple. She dashed all hopes of that future when she ended her relationship with Nate.

Now she'd taken up with Zach, who lived thousands of miles away.

What was her uncle feeling? He'd held onto her office. She almost couldn't believe it. That it was unoccupied gave her an out too, a chance to submerge herself in what she knew: work. If her contract with Eclipse was over, someone would have to take her place. Compiling a report would aid a smooth transition for her replacement. She'd be on the outside looking in. Perspectives were changing every day.

FORTY-ONE

SHE GOT OUT of her chauffeur-driven car when it stopped at the stone stairs to her uncle's house.

Huh, curious. There was another car in the driveway, at the edge of the gravel, farther from the house, facing the route out.

Her vehicle drove away, around the house to the garages no doubt.

That other car was odd, but not her business. Her uncle's guests—

The back door opened. Someone was in there. Intrigue rooted her to the spot. Who could be loitering?

Zach.

She gasped and rushed to him. He slipped his phone into an inside pocket, freeing his hands to scoop around her face as he stooped to join their mouths.

What was he doing there? Shit. Well, at least his not answering calls made a little more sense.

She pulled back, her head still in his hands cradling embrace.

"What are you doing here?" she asked, kissing him again and once more. "Why did you come all the way here?"

"Sorry to see me?" His thumb moved on the apple of her cheek, smudging the moisture that must've escaped her eye. "We're a family, Lilya. You don't leave your backup on the other side of the continent. We're together. We're doing this together."

As her eyes sank shut, tears streaked her face.

Stepping in against him, she breathed in his scent. "I missed you."

"I got your message," he said, kissing the top of her head.

"My message? Is that why you got on a plane? I didn't mean—"

"My flight left an hour after yours," he said. "I knew sending you alone was a mistake before you even took off."

Curling her fingers around his, she took a reluctant step back. "Frank will be home for dinner soon."

He nodded. "I spoke to the staff."

"They didn't let you in?" she asked, leading him toward the stone stairs up to the front door. "I can't believe they left you in the driveway."

"They invited me inside."

She stopped to look back at him. "But you stayed outside? Are you protesting?"

"We're doing this together," he said. "But this is your family. We play it your way."

So he'd waited for her to invite him in. This guy was constantly surprising her. Going inside, they went upstairs and along the hallway to her bedroom that looked out across the walled garden at the back of the house.

It was only when he closed the bedroom door that she let go of his hand to head across into the closet.

"I need to have a shower," she said, stepping out of her shoes. "I'll be quick."

"A shower alone?"

He came in close to her back, coiling his arms around her. It was impossible not to purr in delight and slide her hands down his embracing arms.

"Dinner is at eight," she said, her eyes closing. "If you join me in the shower, we'll never make it in time. You want to make a good first impression on your new in-law?"

"Frank and I have met before."

Her eyes opened. "Oh my God, you've met before."

"Yep."

"Of course you have," she said, wriggling around to face him while remaining in his hold. "Did you get along?"

"We met in professional circles. I respect the man."

Her brow bobbed as her attention drifted. "We wouldn't be working for Eclipse if he didn't feel the same."

"Technically, he's working for Gramercy," he said. "Ranby Kearns' contract is with them."

"Yes, but he'd have told Mr. Gramercy-Peake straight out if he didn't think Eclipse was a worthy bidder."

"Kinloch knows my weak spots better than I do," he said on a snicker that stole her focus back. "He's been doing his due diligence on me since we were kids."

"I forget all the time that you know him. I've heard things about him, you know?"

"What things?" he asked, his lips thin in their amusement. "People talk too much."

"I bet there are things people say about you. About Zairn and Knox too."

"Oh, yeah," he said, nodding before he kissed her head and let her go. "We're used to people telling us things about each other all the time."

"I didn't know you were close. I've never seen all of you together... anywhere."

"We don't advertise our history. The friendship is authentic, we don't need to broadcast it. We're there for each other. Brothers. It's not about show, it's—"

"Real. I get it." Tracing her fingertips down his arm to his hand, they tracked their way back up. "Frank's the closest thing I have to a father."

"I know." His knuckles grazed her jaw. "And I'm a reasonable man."

"I don't want you to argue and—"

"Hey now, you can trust me. I didn't come here to blow this up. Frank and I are family now too, we have to be respectful of each other, to compromise."

"What does that mean?" she asked, suspicious of the confidence in his smile. "Compromise?"

Taking her shoulders, he turned her around to boost her toward the bathroom. "Trust me. Go shower. We don't want to be late for dinner."

FORTY-TWO

DINNER WASN'T EXACTLY a formal affair. When she'd lived with her uncle, they often only saw each other in passing at mealtimes. That was why walking into the dining room, complete with fully set table, provoked her foreboding.

"Oh, God," she whispered. "This won't end well."

"It will," Zach said, holding her shoulder. "Trust me, Amour."

Trust him? What did that mean? And why did he keep saying it with such mischief? What did he have to do with how the dinner was going to play out?

He steered her to the table and helped with her chair before sitting next to her. Though there was wine on offer, he picked up the water pitcher to fill their glasses. For the first time, she yearned for wine. Maybe alcohol would make the whole process smoother.

Her hand rose to her stomach. "Be good, little one," she whispered.

Zach paused. "You okay?"

"I don't know if the nausea is him or anxiety."

He put down the water to slide his hand over hers. "If you're not strong enough for this today, we'll—"

"I'm strong enough," she said, guiding his hand to her face. "We're strong enough." She didn't consider herself weak but couldn't deny having him there gave her more stability. "Are you strong enough?"

He didn't get beyond smiling when her uncle came marching in.

"Kintyre," her uncle barked.

Zach stood. "Mr. Kearns."

"Is this a game?" her uncle asked, coming up close. "You think you can play with my family?"

"Your family is my family, sir." Zach didn't flinch. "No one's playing. This is real."

"What are you hiding?" Frank asked, rocking on his heels. "This the level you'll stoop to?"

"Stoop to for what?" Zach asked.

"To win the bid."

"I understand you're dubious. Tonight will alleviate your concerns. Trust me."

There it was again.

"How are you going to do that?" Frank asked. "I don't see how it's possible without all the players in the room. Ranby Kearns have a responsibility to level the playing field. To deliver the facts and figures to the appropriate people. These things have a process for a reason. Kinloch Gramercy-Peake—"

"Cares about his company, I know. He won't undertake the sale lightly and it's not all about money. He's narrowed the field not to those who offer the biggest numbers, but to those who can take care of his people. His legacy. Such as it presently is."

"Such as it presently is?"

"He isn't dead yet, is he? Who knows what else he might achieve?"

"No one knows exactly why he's chosen to sell. It was a shock across the business world. When the Gramercy and Peake families were joined by his parents—"

"His lineage is undeniable. I suppose you assumed your legacy would follow the same path," Zach said. "Joining your niece with a Ranby."

Something that wouldn't happen. Nathan wasn't there, thank goodness, but the idea lingered in the air.

The only one still in her seat, she used the position

to deescalate. "Can we sit down, please?" she asked, reaching for Zach's hand. "We don't want to get off on the wrong foot. We don't want to be fighting."

"We don't," he said, breathing out while bowing to kiss her hand.

Someone else entered, the housekeeper, but she stopped by the door. "Mr. Kintyre? Your guests are here."

"Your guests?" she asked just as her uncle seemed to notice there were other places set at the table.

When the housekeeper stepped back and three men came in, shock raised her from her seat.

Matteo Reid. Kinloch Gramercy-Peake. Jamison Dawes. All the players in the room. Goddamn, her guy was good.

"How did you…?" her uncle murmured, though he probably hadn't meant to.

"I'm seeing too much of you these days," Reid said when Zach went to shake his hand.

"Last time, I swear," her guy joked. "This won't take long and it's only Boston. I promised Merci I'd have you back to her before bed."

Zach switched to shake Kinloch's hand. It was a wonder she recognized the guy with the beard and the unkempt hair. Maybe the man was selling because he was falling apart; he didn't look like the reputed meticulous man usually gracing the business pages.

"I wouldn't be here for anything less," Kinloch said as Zach rested a hand on his arm.

The guy was tall. Seriously tall. Taller than she'd known. Zach was over six feet, but Kinloch still towered over him.

"Appreciate you rejoining civilization, K2," Zach said.

"Begrudgingly," Gramercy-Peake muttered as her guy progressed to Jamison Dawes.

By that point, Matteo Reid was upon her. "Lilya."

He was polite enough to kiss her cheek, which startled her so much she froze. He didn't notice and went to her uncle. Then Gramercy-Peake blocked the light. All light. He was so damn big.

"Lilya," he said in a bassy note that tightened her shoulders.

How did he say her two-syllable name in a single beat like that? His gaze dropped to her stomach. Panic brought bile to the back of her throat; he knew about the baby. Oh, God, he knew. But did he know not to say anything about it? Did he know it was a secret?

"Mr. Gramercy-Peake."

"We're family now, Lilya," he said and plucked her hand from her side to kiss the back of it. "It's a pleasure."

What the hell was going on?

When Dawes appeared in front of her, she wasn't sure what to expect. Zach was there to put an arm around her.

"Your guy's too decent," Dawes said. "You need to toughen him up."

He sauntered off to sit down on the other side of the table. Everyone else was sitting too and there she was with Zach, still agog.

The heat of his mouth fogged her hair. "Trust me, Amour."

Trust was one thing. Whatever this was, she couldn't even hazard a guess how it would play out.

"Mr. Gramercy-Peake is selling his company," she stated aloud, more to herself than anyone else. "His extremely successful multibillion-dollar business. The process is moving toward the final stages."

"Have to pick a winner first," Dawes said, frowning at her. "That why we're here?"

"Everyone saw the Keller interview," Zach said, once again slotting her onto her seat.

A server came in with appetizers, but no one looked at the food. Zach was the center of attention.

"Your ex-wife's a piece of work, Kintyre," Dawes said.

"No argument here," Zach said. "We're here because we need the key players in the same room. Lil and I are together, and given Ranby Kearns role—"

"Before we get to that..." Reid said, leaving the thought open.

Before they got to what? There was more than what they already had on the table? Matteo Reid didn't usually say much. And from the look he and Zach exchanged, he didn't plan to be the voice of whatever else was going on.

"Yes," Zach said, linking his fingers in front of his plate. "A better place to start… Given the breadth of Gramercy, it was always going to be difficult to fold into any single network. Reid and I are serious about our interest and our regard for the corporation. So serious that we don't want to take the risk of being singularly responsible for—"

"You're going into partnership," Dawes said, sinking back in his seat.

"We've decided it's the best way forward," Zach said, turning his attention to Gramercy-Peake. "The amended proposal is already on its way to you. Without the Massey IP, Reid's bid was weakened, though not enough to be taken out of the running completely. I believe he and I are stronger as a unit. Together, we offer a transcontinental appeal that will allow holistic management. Gramercy will not be neglected. It will have more support than ever."

"You set this up to screw me over?" Dawes asked. "It's nothing to do with what's best for Gramercy."

"You compete more with Venture on the global market than either of us," Zach said. "Reid and I are not suggesting you're removed from the running. The contract still has to be won fair and square. It will stand up to severe scrutiny."

"And you do this at your girlfriend's dinner table?"

"Because she still has to do her job. She and I started our relationship while she was working with Eclipse. Her professionalism has never wavered, and it won't."

"No, sure, 'cause she'll advertise any dirty dealings she finds because that won't impact her bottom line at all."

"Lilya is not financially dependent on me and never will be. I put it to all of you that Lilya be allowed to continue her work. That she sees out all the contracts she was already involved in."

"She was in my books before she was in yours," Dawes said. "And I never got the perks you did."

Her hand shot over to Zach's, hopefully calming

him before he could respond to the provocation. "My work is above board. All of it," she said. "My relationship with Zach hasn't altered that."

"RCI is last on her list." Dawes poured wine into his glass. "You need a go from all of us before she'll be allowed to work that contract. Ranby Kearns short of employees?"

"It's not about Ranby Kearns being short of anything."

"Lilya didn't know I called you here tonight, any of you. This is me asking you. Man to man. If there's hesitation, we don't want there to be any possibility Ranby Kearns findings or reputation can be called into question."

"I have no problem with it," Reid said.

"I trust Ranby Kearns," Gramercy-Peake said.

"So I'm the only one with a problem," Dawes said. "You can't honestly expect me to grant your wish. The deal's incestuous enough as it is. Makes you wonder if anyone outside the circle had a shot. I know there were plenty other bidders scared off."

"That's not what we're trying to do, Dawes."

"Then explain it to me. What does it matter if she sees this contract through or not? She has the perfect reason not to. You got together, good for you, but there are consequences." Something she knew too well. "She can't do her job. It's as simple as that. Not on this deal. And I'm surprised no one else has said it to you."

They may well have said it. Or they would've if anyone had a chance to weigh in. Between their relationship becoming public on television the previous night and them running off to Boston, there hadn't been much time to caucus. Not that she was aware of anyway.

Zach's hand turned under hers to twine their fingers together. "Lilya's done nothing wrong."

"I'm not accusing her of doing anything wrong," Dawes said with surprising neutrality. "But you have to see that she's become the weak spot of this deal. Whether I grant my approval or win the bid, it doesn't matter. There will always be the question. Doubt. Ranby Kearns may work with other people, but they can't deal with anyone connected to you, not anymore, not so long as she works there."

Was he right? Maybe instead of stamping her feet and demanding her position, she had to see that Zach's life had changed too. Ranby Kearns life was different.

"I disagree," Zach said.

Of course he did, he was defending her.

"Why does this contract matter?" Dawes asked. "Why not just fly her off to somewhere else? Put her in Europe or Asia, anywhere else, while this dies down. The only reason to be so adamant with this deal is if there is something to cover up. Something you don't want someone else to find."

"It's nothing to do with that. It's about professional integrity. Would you let someone you care about be bundled off and hidden out of sight, even when they've done nothing wrong? Lilya doesn't deserve to be—"

"I'm pregnant." The simple words had a profound effect on the room. Everyone froze. Dawes' glass stopped on its way to his lips. Even Zach took a few seconds to look at her. She shrugged. "It's going to come out eventually, right?"

"You're pregnant?" her uncle asked from the head of the table, his eyes wide.

"Mr. Dawes, it's not so simple to just fly off to some other corner of the world. I want to finish what I started. And I want to give birth in this country. In LA, I can be with Zach. If I see through the RCI contract, I'll be in New York, where I'm based anyway. I'll get consistent care from familiar doctors. I've never done this before, had a child, and it's daunting. I don't expect you to understand. It's impossible for anyone who doesn't have children to understand. Zach and I aren't just a couple having some fun, we're starting our family. We're putting down roots for our child. There's nothing more important than our family. And if that means I have to resign, I will."

Dawes put his glass down and paused before clearing his throat. "We'll withdraw our bid," he said, standing up. "You'll have the paperwork tomorrow."

And that was it. Jamison Dawes strode from the room and was just… gone.

"Why would he…?"

"That's… interesting," Zach said, wrapping his

fingers around hers. "If I'd known the way to scare off the competition was to get you pregnant, I'd have done it years ago."

"Ha, ha," she drawled.

Her uncle wasn't as amused. "You're pregnant? You're… pregnant?"

"That's not why Zach and I are together," she said, intercepting his objection before he could jump to the wrong conclusions. "Other factors complicated our relationship, but I knew I loved him before I found out about the baby."

"I was never going to let Lilya walk away. Complicated or not, she's the woman I love, the only one I want to be with. The only woman I want to mother my children."

"Did you say the same thing to your wife when you got her pregnant?" Frank asked.

Zach turned to her. Telling the truth about her pregnancy wouldn't grant them any reprieve or gain understanding. Kesley may have claimed Zach wasn't the father of Julietta's baby, but without naming names, who would believe her one hundred percent? As far as the world was concerned, he'd impregnated two women. With that came a lot of judgment.

Julietta still loomed large in their life.

FORTY-THREE

"I'M GOING TO RESIGN," she said, tracing a line up and down his sternum.

"Don't make decisions like that now."

They hadn't had sex. But just lying there with him, in a bed that had once been hers, home was the man, not the building.

"I have to."

"No, you don't. Reid is fine with you being part of the audit team at RCI."

"It's pantomime. Is there any chance you won't win Gramercy now? Your friend will not throw his company into the open market again. Your partnership guarantees success."

"Everything has to be done right. For the partnership and the takeover."

"Do you think Matteo Reid can't back up his promises? You think he'd dupe you?"

"No," he said. "But we want everything concrete. No accusations of any special treatment or nepotism. All's fair in love and business."

"You told me something was going to change. Weeks ago, you said it. You and Reid have been talking about uniting for the Gramercy takeover for a while."

"Yeah. He blew part of his plan to sweeten the deal

when he got with Merci. His position was weakened, but not to the point his offer was an insult. It was competitive, maybe too competitive."

She shifted the angle of her head. "He chose Merci over RCI? A woman over what was best for the company?"

"Something wrong with a man valuing his woman more than his business?" he asked, a smile in his voice.

"No," she said, resting her cheek against him. "It's just hard to picture him as the type. What's Merci like? Roxie likes her."

"Roxie likes everyone. And everyone likes Zairn."

He laughed, but the implication wasn't funny. "Roxie is a good person. She went way above and beyond for me, for us, she got arrested for us."

"Z told me about that. A caper doesn't seem enough. You took some risks."

"For you."

"We weren't together."

"Doesn't mean I didn't care about you. I don't want Julietta to have sway over your life. No one should be able to manipulate anyone like that. She wanted our relationship to come out, so she could get her hands on your company. If she had control at Eclipse—"

"She would have leverage to keep me quiet about her affair."

"What comes next?" she asked. "I was in such a hurry to come here and calm things with Frank that I… Frank will never understand, not until he knows the truth. Right now you're just the asshole who got two women pregnant, one after another. Have you heard from Julietta?"

"The rules stand. None of us are to have direct contact with her. There's a meeting tomorrow. With the lawyers."

"You and her?"

"Supposed to be, but if you need me here—"

"There's nothing here for us now, is there? Frank knows, he'll tell Nate, and until the truth comes out about Julietta's baby, we can't make them understand this is real."

"Why did you tell them? Why announce it like that?"

"It just felt… necessary. This is something we can

be honest about. I trust Frank to keep it quiet. Reid and Gramercy-Peake already knew. If you try to say otherwise, I won't believe you."

"They know about our baby."

"What did they say? Your friends? Do they think you're crazy?"

"Crazy for what?"

"Getting with a woman dumb enough to get herself pregnant."

"You are not dumb. My friends can see that I'm happy. They know me. They trust me."

"They trusted you with Julietta and look how that turned out."

He laughed. "Actually, all of them warned me against marrying her, just like we warned Reid against marrying Madelyn."

"You didn't listen. Will you listen to what they tell you about me? To take your time in this relationship, that there's no rush?"

She hoped to God that was his friends' advice.

"I told them you wouldn't marry me," he said. "That's all the guarantee you're not crazy that they needed." That wasn't happy or a joke. No, something else gave those words weight. Something inside him. He laid his hand on hers. "I want to get married, Lil. It's just who I am. I want to be married to the mother of my children."

She sighed. "Okay," she said, opening her fingers under his.

His stilled. "Okay? Is that a yes? You'll marry me? Shit, baby, did you have to say yes to the least romantic proposal I ever made?"

Licking her lips, she turned her head to rest her smile against him. "You said it yourself, I'm not romantic, I'm pragmatic. You're right. I didn't want you to marry me out of obligation, but you loved me before the baby. You meant that, didn't you?"

"This is the most right I've ever felt with a woman. With Julietta, there was excitement, but it always felt like some part of her *needed* me. You don't need me, Lil, but I need you."

"Being married makes sense on a practical level, especially with the baby. We need to make medical decisions, property and asset choices. We'll need a prenup."

"Oh, and she gets down to it."

"The money doesn't matter. If you don't want a prenup for that, we won't have one. But we need to discuss custody and visitation, set boundaries and expectations, in case it all falls apart. And we need to update our wills, to assign godparents. Who do we want to look after the baby if something happens to us?"

"Roxie asked first."

Most of the friends she'd had in Boston had drifted away when she moved to New York. And she hadn't been in Manhattan long enough to develop any deep connections.

"Frank is the only family I have, but he's older now, and wouldn't know what to do with an infant. I can't put that on him. I love Roxie, but Jane's a more natural mother."

"I don't think you have to worry about Jane and motherhood. When that train leaves the station, it's going to make a lot of stops. Mimi loves babies."

"So you think Jane and Knox will have plenty of their own? Does Zairn want kids? We have to think of this as a serious proposition. Anything could happen. This is the most important decision we can make for our child."

At least until after it was born.

"You've seen how Zairn looks after Roxie," Zach said. "The press portrays him as a playboy, but that's image misdirection. He's never been frivolous."

And he'd been the one she called when she needed help. Jane called him without hesitation when Roxie was in trouble. Zairn took everything in stride and was more astute and responsible than the media gave him credit for.

"You'd trust him to raise your child?"

"Yes."

No hesitation. Only certainty. "Well, that was easy," she said on a tired exhale and closed her eyes. "I created a transition report for whoever takes over from me at Eclipse. There's two months left on the Ranby Kearns contract. Providing they don't send someone to go over my work. If they do, that contract will have to be extended."

"I won't let anyone doubt you."

"It doesn't matter. We have battles to fight on other fronts. More important battles."

Like with Julietta and her lawyer. Just because the world knew didn't mean they were off the hook regarding legalities.

"She'll claim Kesley is lying."

"Yes," she agreed. "That she didn't say anything. If they can prove Zairn told her or Roxie…"

"It won't come to that. We won't be dragged through the courts."

"How can you be sure?"

"Because we still have an ace card. We still have the identity of the true father. If Julietta wants to play dirty, we'll play dirty."

"She brought up Teagan to Jane and me at the Queen Dinner."

"Zairn told me."

"Does Knox know?"

"If Knox knew Julietta had threatened his brother, she'd be picking up cans in some shithole city out in the back of beyond. No one messes with a Collier. And with Cam, Knox is extra protective."

"Because?"

"Cam gave it up, the lifestyle, the perks, and the challenges. Cam is mellow, he's calm, reflective, considered… which aren't qualities the other Collier boys possess. Cam won't fight for himself. He won't come out swinging anyway. Knox sees that as his responsibility. They're close. There's a lot of history there."

"Will Julietta cause trouble for them… with Teagan?"

"No," he said. "Julietta might be spurned, but she's no fool. Taking on the Colliers would be career suicide. Even with the Baker backing her up. If she opens her mouth about Teagan, she'll deserve everything they throw at her. Not they, we, everything we throw at her."

Because he'd always stand with the people he cared about. "You're like an honorary Collier."

"Yes."

"And Zairn, does he have family?"

"Roxie's it. Roxie and Ballard, I guess."

"I am honored to be a part of your life," she said, brushing her cheek back and forth on his pec. "To be a part of your family."

"Always," he said and kissed her head. "Always, Amour."

FORTY-FOUR

THANK GOD for private jets.

Yeah, okay, so she'd had the privilege before, but it was a different thing being a mile from the earth and all alone with the man she loved.

And there was no waiting.

They landed in California, went back to the hotel to pack her things, and still had time for food and a nap before the afternoon meeting.

Julietta was tall, so she picked her highest heels and was fastening an earring when Zach's reflection appeared in the vanity mirror next to hers.

"Car's here," he said, skimming a hand down her spine.

"I'm ready."

His hand stopped on its route back up. "You're coming?"

"Yes, I'm coming." Her arms dropped. "Why wouldn't I be coming?"

"I didn't think that…" He blinked, apparently considering it for the first time. "I want you to come."

"Good, because I am coming." Snagging his hand, she grabbed her purse and dragged him to the elevator. "Where's the car? Out front or—"

"Out front," he said, selecting a floor then gathering her against him. "You're coming with me."

"I can't believe you thought I wouldn't."

"We didn't discuss it."

"Would you have just left me sleeping? What if I hadn't woken up in time?" She smoothed his lapels. "What happened to you don't leave your backup behind? If you're mine, I'm yours. It's as simple as that."

"You're mine and I'm yours." The feral satisfaction in those words sent a primal chill through her. "Until death do us part."

"That's the idea."

"If I'd known you were coming, I'd have had your ring waiting for us when we got off the plane." Letting her go, he stepped back. "Wait…" He dipped his hand into his pocket to produce a leather box. "Oh, wow, what's this?"

"You did not."

But he was already sinking down onto one knee. "Lilya Kearns…" Okay. Her sinuses tingled as her hand rose to pinch her nose and cover her mouth. Why did this feel so epic? Her blood rushed faster, hotter, excitement wet her eyes. "Will you make me the happiest man alive and…" The doors opened. "Marry me?"

She couldn't take her eyes away from his. From that smile. From her future. "Yes," she said, a grin splitting her face. "Oh, God, baby, you know I'll marry you."

He slipped the solitaire onto her finger as he rose, capturing her face to join their mouths. That was when the applause rose.

Breaking the kiss, the open elevator doors showcased the hotel lobby. And the group of guests behind a stunned Reeve Crosby.

"Guess you got your scoop, Reeve," Zach said, holding her to his side. "If you'll excuse us."

Guiding her out of the elevator and through all the congratulations, there was no way everyone in the lobby knew the significance of that proposal. No way that they could—she stepped outside and the shouting started. Did everyone know her? Were all the people there for them? What was happening?

LA was used to security guards and chauffeur-driven cars, but she'd never had people, strangers, screaming at her like that. The noise. The shuffle of movement and shouts. It was as disorienting as it was engulfing. One voice became ten until no individual was decipherable.

It was by Zach's grace that she got in the car at all, she'd never have found it alone. Her pulse was still racing after the first three blocks.

"Are you okay?" Zach asked, opening his hand under hers to slip his digits between them. Her ring. She was staring down at the ring he'd put on her finger. "Second thoughts?"

That couldn't be further from the case. "I guess this squares your debt to me."

"My debt?"

Tipping her chin up, she met his eye. "I told you there wasn't anything I needed that you could buy."

Understanding relaxed his brow. "In the boardroom, the day after we met."

"When you were trying to quid pro quo me into staying quiet."

"You were right," he said. "Most things worth having can't be bought."

"No, they can't, but I was wrong too. Turns out you can make all my dreams come true."

"You are the dream, Amour. This. Us. Everything. It's all I've ever wanted."

The commitment wasn't daunting, it exhilarated her. "I'm not going to hyphenate. Julietta hyphenated; did you ask her to hyphenate?"

"No," he said with a head shake. "With her career…"

"Right, of course. Ines was what people knew. Do you want me to hyphenate?"

His lips curled. "That's your decision. I'd be honored if you were a Kintyre."

"Me and the baby." She pulled his hand to her belly. "This feels sort of… overwhelming."

He massaged her through her dress. "In a bad way?"

"No, it feels like…"

"Exciting?"

"Right, but more than that, it's… There's so much possibility right now. It feels like we can do anything we want."

"We can. Do you want to get married before the baby's born?"

"I don't know."

"Do you want to do it here or in Boston? New York?"

"I don't know," she said and laughed. "This just…" Resting her arms on his chest, she got closer. "This feels right, doesn't it? You're a good man and I love you. You'll be an amazing father to our child. I want us to be together."

"We are together." His caress moved to her hip. "We're going to be together."

"Did it feel like this with Julietta? Maybe it feels right now, but later on—"

"This is nothing like what I had with Julietta. You have to stop comparing the two. It's apples and oranges. You're nothing alike. Our relationships are nothing alike. Every part of this is new to me, just like it's new to you. We'll figure it out. Together. We'll take every step together."

"I don't know about the wedding. The when, where, how, it will happen. But there is one thing I'd like to state upfront."

"Okay," he said.

The seriousness of his expression was such a delight. "I want to go on a honeymoon." His concern ebbed to a smile. "Somewhere warm. No work or lawyers or family dramas, just us and our little one."

"What if we get married after he's born?"

"You wouldn't want him with us?" she asked. "I don't think of parenting as a chore, it's a privilege. What we have, we can't take for granted. Every parent deserves a break, of course, but he's a part of this. He's the one who made this happen. He stepped up for us when everything was trying to tear us apart."

"Okay, he can come," he said, sweeping his hand into her hair. "You sure you're up for this today?"

"I was up for it until you…" Glancing at her ring again, it was almost impossible to believe. "How did you size it perfectly?"

"Roxie's ring fit you when you were engaged to Zairn for the evening." As she laughed, he kissed her cheek. "Rox and I forgive you both."

"My one indiscretion," she said, tucking her head under his chin as he put an arm around her. "If it's any consolation, he was a terrible fiancé. He only showed up for a few minutes then left with another woman."

"Didn't set the bar too high, did he?"

"You're already a better fiancé," she said, leaning back to show him a smile. "He never kissed me."

"That's an honor I'll never neglect."

Drawing her chin up, he lowered his mouth to hers. It was just a kiss. A joining of mouths and tongues and need that bred stability. This was it. The last man she'd ever kiss. Somehow, it was inevitable. Being with him. Entwining their lives. This was the path her life was supposed to take.

Her awareness of everything else disappeared. All she wanted to do was be there with Zach, kissing him until the end of time.

Unfortunately, that wasn't possible.

Something she forgot until the car lurched to a halt.

Zach broke the union. "I can do this alone," he panted under his breath. "If you want to wait down here. You don't have to come in."

"I want to come in," she said, linking their fingers again. Would she be an aggravating factor? Maybe. But Zach was the person she cared about. "Unless you don't want me to come in with you."

His smile grew, and he kissed the back of her hand. "Come on."

They ascended in a glass elevator with a security agent. She wasn't sure if the guy was with them or part of the firm they were visiting, but his presence at least gave them the chance to refocus their minds. A proposal. A make-out session. It had been a busy day that started on the other side of the country.

An assistant ushered them into a boardroom with a long oval table and various stacked bookcases. Less than a minute later, a suited man came to join them.

"Mr. Kintyre," the guy said, frowning at her as Zach got up to shake his hand.

"Crispin, this is Lilya Kearns."

Although she got to her feet, they didn't shake hands.

The frown on his face came with some eye movement. "I know who she is," Crispin said. "The whole world knows who she is. Do you think it's wise to have her here?"

"Why shouldn't she be here?"

"Julietta's temper is—"

"Not my problem anymore, Crispin. And after today, it won't be yours."

Before anything else could be said, the door opened again. Julietta came in with two men in suits. Maybe one of them was the Baker. Or maybe she needed two lawyers.

"What is she doing here?" Julietta asked, stopping near the head of the table. "Why is she here? I won't do this with her in the room."

"Do what exactly?" Zach asked. "You wanted this meeting."

"No, I wanted to talk to you, but none of your stupid people would let me. And there's a problem with security at Knox's house."

"No problem," Zach said. "We solved the problem by taking you off the authorized list. Is that what you came here for? I already signed the paperwork. The house, what *was* our house, is yours. Nothing else binds us to each other. Your alimony will continue, according to our divorce agreement."

"Except you breached the divorce agreement," Julietta said, looking her up and down like she was scum. "By running around with your little slut."

"Lilya is my fiancée." That startled more than just Julietta, but Zach remained steadfast. "Thanks to you."

"To me?"

"If you hadn't run your mouth to Kesley, I would've been bound by the contract. But seeing as you were instrumental in the relationship being revealed, you voided the contract."

"That's not what that means."

"That's exactly what it means. My lawyer checked. Lilya's lawyer checked. Hell, Lilya's lawyer's lawyer checked. You voided the contract when you told Kesley."

"She told the world. That was her choice. I didn't tell her to do that. I didn't know—"

"It doesn't matter. We've promised Reeve Crosby an exclusive, so he won't be telling your side of the story either. Did you really think it was smart to wake up the Colliers?"

"This was your friends. You put them up to this."

"No, I didn't."

"The Colliers don't scare me."

"Yes, they do. And you're welcome, Jules, Lilya didn't convey the threat you made against the Colliers to them. But I might."

"You won't do anything," Julietta said, regaining some composure as her lips curled in perverse delight. "Because my lawyers are going to make sure I get half of your precious Eclipse. So long as I have power there—"

"There are two problems with that. First, you voided the contract, so they have no grounds to enact that clause."

"And second?" one guy with Julietta asked because the woman was too busy fuming.

"I no longer own shares in the company." Another surprise. "I sold my controlling interest last week."

"To… to who?" Julietta stuttered.

"A third party."

"Who?"

"None of your damn business, Julietta."

"You can't do this."

"I can," he said, cool, calm, and collected. "Nothing in the contract between us prevents it. Eclipse, according to our prenup and divorce agreement, is mine. I don't need your permission to sell. You can sue me for half what I got for the sale. One dollar. Cash okay, or would you prefer a check?"

"In court, I'll—"

"Take this to court and you better be willing to go all the way, Jules. For everything to come out. Everything." He drew out that last word, conveying a deeper meaning.

"I'm done pulling my punches and putting up with your bullshit."

Julietta's ire snapped to her. "This was you. You did this. You changed him. You stole him away! I'll sue you! I'll sue both of you! Half of Eclipse belongs to my child!" The talented actress hugged her stomach at just the right moment. "It's his birthright!"

"Okay, if you want to get dirty..." Zach said, sucking in a breath. "I want a paternity test." Julietta just blinked. "That's right. If you want to pursue this, if you insist the contract has to be upheld and expect me to support your child, I want a paternity test."

"There's nothing in the contract about that."

"No, there's not, but it's not much to ask. And if you push this, a court will order it. What will happen then? Wasn't the aim of the contract to maintain your carefully crafted façade? That's why you put paternity on me. No one thinks to judge the woman who got pregnant by her ex-husband. And maybe you thought we'd pretend to reconcile for a while, and you could have the best of both worlds. But I belong to Lilya now, as she belongs to me, and we prefer a more traditional setup. We're happy with a marriage of two people. Husband and wife."

"You're not married to her yet."

"I will be. Will you be marrying the true father of your child?" Zach asked, his tone growing deeper. "He'd have to divorce his wife first, wouldn't he?"

Julietta glared. "Are you threatening me?"

"Take one step," Zach said, cold, slow, devious, not his usual demeanor at all. "That's all it will take, Jules. One single step. A hint of a step and the Colliers snap their fingers. CollCom beat WMC any day, honey. Want to find out if I'm right?"

Though the beauty glanced at his lawyer and to her own, no one had any words of hope.

On an exhale, the woman softened. "Zee-Bee—"

"I have nothing to lose, and I have no interest in enabling your lies. No more. It's over, Julietta. Step off the stage gracefully, don't wait for the hook." Julietta's nostrils flared as her shoulders went back and she stormed over to yank the door open. "Oh, and Jules…" The former couple made eye contact. "I want my name back too. You are not now, nor will you ever be, a part of the Kintyre family."

As his arm came around her shoulders, she smiled. Julietta huffed and went out with the suits she'd brought.

Zach's was quick to depart to. He'd charge for the hour but hadn't done a thing.

Then she and Zach were in the car again, heading for home.

"You haven't said anything," he said, picking up her hand. "Are you okay?"

"That was really hot," she said on an exhale that became a laugh. "I had no idea you were so… Mmm…"

He laughed. "I'm not always Mr. Nice Guy."

"No, I see that. You got to the top somehow," she said. "You could've told me we were starting over before I agreed to marry you. Why didn't you tell me you sold Eclipse?"

"Didn't you ask me to sell it on our first night together?" he asked, leaning in to murmur against her. "Think of all the time we'll have for sex."

"Who cares if the world comes tumbling down."

And right then, she meant it.

"It's a temporary measure," he said, kissing her knuckles. "I'm not sure it would've held up in court, but I did it to make a point."

"Julietta's greedy little fingers don't get to play with what's yours."

"No, they do not," he said, opening her hand to press it against him. "Or what's yours."

"And you said WMC, that's…" He nodded just once. "You don't mean…" Another single nod. "Wow," she exhaled in awe. "I would never have guessed that."

"All in the past. We don't care about them. So long as Julietta leaves us alone, we'll keep her secret."

But it was a huge one. If that truth got out…

"I feel bad for the baby," she said. "The innocent didn't pick their parents. What a mess to be born into."

"Something ours won't have to worry about."

"That depends," she said, switching into the present.

"His daddy might be working twenty hours a day building his new business from the ground up. If we don't own Eclipse, what legacy will our offspring have to continue?"

"Zairn will sell Eclipse back to me if I hold the godparent thing over his head."

"Dangle that carrot and Roxie will make him," she said, her cheeks sore from the width of her grin. "I love you, Zee-Bee."

His smile fell. "No. Nope. Just no."

She laughed. "Amour."

"Much better," he murmured. "Forever, Amour."

Read more from the Roxiverse in
Nothing to Gain...

Thank you for reading this tale!
If you can, please take the time to review.

~

Ask your local library for more Scarlett Finn
novels!

~

For all things Scarlett Finn
check out:

www.scarlettfinn.com

Next in the
Roxiverse: